The Mother-Daughter Book Club

The Mother-Daughter Book Club

SUSAN PATTERSON
AND JAMES PATTERSON

CENTURY

UK | USA | Canada | Ireland | Australia
India | New Zealand | South Africa

Century is part of the Penguin Random House group of companies
whose addresses can be found at global.penguinrandomhouse.com

Penguin Random House UK,
One Embassy Gardens, 8 Viaduct Gardens, London SW11 7BW

penguin.co.uk

First published 2026
002

Copyright © James Patterson, 2026

The moral right of the authors has been asserted

Penguin Random House values and supports copyright.
Copyright fuels creativity, encourages diverse voices, promotes freedom
of expression and supports a vibrant culture. Thank you for purchasing
an authorised edition of this book and for respecting intellectual property
laws by not reproducing, scanning or distributing any part of it by any
means without permission. You are supporting authors and enabling
Penguin Random House to continue to publish books for everyone.
No part of this book may be used or reproduced in any manner for the
purpose of training artificial intelligence technologies or systems. In accordance
with Article 4(3) of the DSM Directive 2019/790, Penguin Random House
expressly reserves this work from the text and data mining exception.

Printed and bound in Great Britain by Clays Ltd, Elcograf S.p.A.

The authorised representative in the EEA is Penguin Random House Ireland,
Morrison Chambers, 32 Nassau Street, Dublin D02 YH68

A CIP catalogue record for this book is available from the British Library

ISBN: 978–1–529–94483–9 (hardback)
ISBN: 978–1–529–94484–6 (trade paperback)

Penguin Random House is committed to a sustainable future
for our business, our readers and our planet. This book is made from
Forest Stewardship Council® certified paper.

For our moms, Lorraine & Isabelle
And their daughters

DRAMATIS PERSONAE

THE MOTHERS

Elin Mackenzie the LAWYER
A successful but overworked corporate lawyer living in Chicago
Relationship status: married, semi-happily
Favorite authors: Anita Brookner, Toni Morrison, Hilary Mantel, Jhumpa Lahiri, Jane Austen

Mariella Marciano the DIVA
A charismatic, flamboyant opera singer with residences in San Francisco and Lake Como, Italy
Relationship status: happily married to money
Favorite authors: Ann Patchett, Taylor Jenkins Reid, Elin Hilderbrand, Elena Ferrante

Grace Townsend the MINISTER
A dedicated, empathetic do-gooder who still lives in her hometown of Bridgeport, Connecticut
Relationship status: eternally single
Favorite authors: Virginia Woolf, Graham Greene, Zadie Smith, Kristin Hannah

DRAMATIS PERSONAE

Jamie Price the HOMEMAKER
A former nanny, now fitness instructor, living near Lake Geneva, Wisconsin
Relationship status: married, but it's complicated
Favorite authors: Diana Gabaldon, Nora Roberts, Elizabeth Strout, Ann Napolitano

THE DAUGHTERS

Brigid Mackenzie the DOCTOR
Elin's serious, hardworking daughter; a neurologist at Mass General in Boston
Relationship status: single, because who has time?
Favorite authors: Siddhartha Mukherjee, Oliver Sacks, Flannery O'Connor, Edward P. Jones

Zoey Marciano the INFLUENCER
Mariella's daughter; a social media influencer living in Brooklyn
Relationship status: has a girlfriend
Favorite authors: Donna Tartt, Judy Blume, Emily Henry, Rebecca Yarros

DRAMATIS PERSONAE

Meredith "Merry" Townsend **the SOCIAL WORKER**
Grace's daughter; a dedicated social worker in Bridgeport, where she grew up
Relationship status: recently single
Favorite authors: Rebecca Makkai, Tayari Jones, Barbara Kingsolver, Kate Atkinson, N. K. Jemisin

Kathleen Price **the LAW STUDENT**
One of Jamie's twin daughters (ten minutes older than her sister); a law student in Chicago
Relationship status: dating half-heartedly
Favorite authors: Sue Grafton, Scott Turow, Megan Abbott

Meg Price **the ASPIRING WRITER**
Jamie's slightly younger twin daughter; a wannabe writer and restaurant hostess in Chicago
Relationship status: Tinder girl
Favorite authors: J. D. Salinger, F. Scott Fitzgerald, former *Chicago Tribune* food critic Phil Vettel

Prologue

Lake Geneva, Wisconsin

June

1

Elin,
mother of Brigid

I don't want to jinx anything, but I don't know how I got this lucky. That's the thought running through my mind as I sit here in the gracious lake house I rented for the weekend, pleasantly full from dinner and just a bit sleepy from two and a half glasses of wine. It's been a long and lovely day. A soft summer rain patters against the windows. With me in the large but cozy living room are my three best friends in the world. And in the kitchen, giggling like little girls, are our beautiful daughters.

To whatever higher power assigned Mariella Marciano, Grace Townsend, and me to the same University of Wisconsin-Madison freshman dorm corridor way back when (a fourth-floor walk-up in Adams Hall): *Thank you, I owe you. Big-time.* We three have been like sisters ever since, and we tease Jamie Price about being our new young friend—because we've known her for only twenty years, and she's only in her forties. I hired Jamie to be Brigid's nanny (and my Girl Friday) back when Brigid was in elementary school. We bonded immediately, and within a year, Jamie was the fourth member of our gang.

We all call and text each other regularly. We always send cards on birthdays. Some years we take trips together—to Florida beaches or New York City museums. We've bonded over our careers and *Christmas on Nantucket,* Madeline Miller and menopause.

This year, the sparkling waters of Lake Geneva have been the perfect backdrop for a wonderful three days spent talking about our lives, our hopes, and—of course—our favorite books.

We're constantly emailing each other book recommendations, and we keep an Excel doc of hundreds of novels, with columns showing which of us has read what and how much we liked it. (Grace recently gave *Middlemarch* an A; Mariella said it was way too long and gave it a C-minus.) Like most book clubs, we spend about 5 percent of our time talking about actual books; the other 95 percent is taken up by talk of jobs, family, and gossip. The stuff of life. But books are our inspiration. So if I text Jamie, for example, at two o'clock in the morning because I just finished reading the most recent Tana French novel, she certainly won't think I'm weird.

We've had a few bumps in the road, of course. Some years, Mariella is too busy touring the world to stay in regular touch, and everyone gets a little offended. Grace was mad at me for two months when I canceled a planned meet-up at the Emily Dickinson Museum. And last year we got in an actual fight about whether *Station Eleven* was better as a book or a TV series. But 99.9 percent of the time, everything is great. These are the women that I rely on most in the world. I don't know how I'd survive without them.

Our girls are all wonderful friends with each other, too, and they've joined us for this particular trip. (I still call them girls; I can't help it.) And we are now, Mariella has declared, an official organization, because she has given us a name.

The Mother-Daughter Book Club. A.k.a. the MDBC.

Grace says we should have t-shirts made—*MDBC 4-Ever!* Her daughter, Merry, told her that this idea is "totally cringe."

Merry's probably right. But I'd wear one anyway. I'm too old to care about what anyone else thinks about my fashion choices.

We are so, so lucky, I think again. And then I knock on wood, just to be safe.

Mariella lifts a perfectly arched eyebrow at me. "Elin, why are you banging on the coffee table?"

I shrug and tuck my hand back into my pocket. "No reason."

I take a sip of peppermint tea and sigh. I don't want tonight to be our last night. For one thing, this weekend's been way too much fun, and I'm not ready to go back to real life yet. And for another, Mariella has just stood up and planted herself in the center of the living room. Judging from the look on her face, she's getting ready to make an announcement.

If I know Mariella—and I *do*—she's going to demand we all go skinny-dipping or play high-stakes Truth or Dare or something equally dramatic. She can't resist a grand finale.

"Ahem!" she says, and I watch as Grace and Jamie stop their chatter and snap to attention. As a corporate attorney, I'm used to being in charge at my job, but Mariella is definitely the one in charge when we're all together. Brassy, big-hearted, and bossy: that's Mariella Marciano.

"My loves, it is our final night," she says, "and for that reason we must do something very special."

See, I knew it.

She smiles slyly. "Which is why I have decided that tonight is the Night of Secrets."

"Not sure I like the sound of that," Jamie says. She pushes her coppery red bangs away from her forehead and takes a big sip of wine.

"If you are wondering what that entails exactly," Mariella goes on, "I will tell you: Each of us needs to confess something big. Something *juicy*."

Grace tucks her long hair behind her ears. She's the only

one of us who doesn't color her hair, but those silver waves look incredible on her. With her wide blue eyes, high cheekbones, and tall, girlish frame, she could practically be a Ralph Lauren runway model. "Don't we tell each other everything already?" she asks reasonably.

"Nobody tells people everything," Mariella says.

You're right. We all have our little secrets, I think.

And our not-so-little ones.

Jamie looks fidgety. "This could be dangerous," she says.

Yes, it could. I sink deeper into the couch, hoping I can make myself less visible. But Mariella points a perfectly manicured finger at me anyway.

"Elin," she commands, "you go first."

I hold up my hands like I can ward her off. "I plead the Fifth," I say.

"None of your lawyer-speak!" Mariella declares. " 'Fess up."

I glance into the kitchen, where I can see my daughter, Brigid, making popcorn, laughing with Merry and Zoey, two girls she's known nearly her entire life.

"I think Grace should go," I suggest.

"Grace is a woman of God, Elin," Mariella says patiently, as if I've forgotten that our friend's a minister. "How juicy can her secret be?"

When Grace laughs, her blue eyes sparkle. "I don't know, you might be surprised," she says.

"Wonderful! I look forward to it. Elin, you're still going first."

I could revolt. Say *"I don't think the Night of Secrets is such a good idea."* But I've learned from decades of experience that it's easier for everyone if Mariella gets her way.

Luckily, I've been mulling something over in my mind for months. It's not a *juicy* secret, but it'll have to do.

"I think I might leave my job," I say. I've been a civil litigator at a giant law firm for almost my entire career. Think seventy-hour weeks, lots of travel (we have clients from all over the US), and a high level of stress. I've been burned out for years, but I've never said the q-word. Admitting out loud that I want to quit actually makes me feel a little bit ill.

Hopefully that's just from the extra helpings of Grace's gooey brownies I had after dinner.

The room erupts in cheers. My daughter, Brigid, the oldest of the girls, pokes her head out of the kitchen. "What's going on out here?"

Zoey, Mariella's daughter, says blithely, "Oh, the Badgers probably scored a touchdown or something."

The rest of us look at each other in disbelief. "Zoey!" I chide, "it's summertime! Football season doesn't start until the end of August!"

Zoey shrugs. "I don't pay attention to sports."

Mariella throws up her hands. "I have told her all about how we looked forward to our epic nights in Camp Randall Stadium—the tailgate parties, the touchdowns, the Jump Around, the singing of 'Varsity,' the 5th Quarter. But her brain is filled up with skin care routines. There is no room for anything else."

Zoey does have beautiful skin—smooth and olive, not a wrinkle in sight. But she's still in her mid-twenties. "It's okay," I assure her mother. "Not everyone has to be a Badgers fan." Then I say to Zoey, "The cheering was because my friends are really excited about the idea that I might finally leave my job."

Brigid raises one eyebrow at me. "Are you serious?" she says.

"Serious as a heart attack," I say.

"Mom," Brigid says gently. "A heart attack is a medical emergency. Not a figure of speech."

"Dr. Mackenzie bustin' her mom," Zoey murmurs.

"I don't mean to be uptight," Brigid explains. "I just saw so many of them in ER rotations that—"

"That you know they shouldn't be taken lightly," I say. "And you're right."

"As usual," Zoey adds.

Brigid grins. "Well, I'll believe that Mom's leaving her job when she cc's me on the resignation letter."

"Ha! I'll make sure to do that."

"*Anyway,*" Mariella continues, "the four of us are telling secrets. Come join us!"

"My secret is that I didn't finish *The Covenant of Water,*" Zoey says.

"Please, that's no secret," says Merry, Grace's daughter,

who has appeared next to Zoey in the doorway. "But shouldn't we wait until Meg and Kathleen get back?"

Jamie looks startled. "What, the twins are still gone? I thought they were in the kitchen with you!"

I look at my watch. Jamie's girls had roared off in Meg's new Jeep to get ice cream at Kilwins almost two hours ago, even though we'd all gone there earlier to sample their legendary hand-paddled fudge (I'm partial to the sea-salt chocolate caramel). The town of Lake Geneva, a community of stately mansions known as the Newport of the Midwest or the Hamptons of Chicago, is less than seven square miles, so it's not as if the twins could've gotten lost. This isn't even unfamiliar territory to them. They grew up in the town next door. I can't imagine what on earth is taking them so long.

"Unless they're hiding in the pantry, they're not here," Zoey says. "But don't worry—we'll make them spill *all* the tea when they get back. We won't take it easy on them!"

Jamie looks out the window. The rain's coming down harder now, pounding on the skylight, slashing against the windows. "They'd better hurry up," she says.

"In the meantime, I'll go," Grace offers. As soon as she says it, she immediately starts to blush. Grace never wears makeup, but suddenly it looks like she's put an entire pot of rouge on her cheeks. She must have a real secret! But when she speaks, it's so quiet that no one can hear her.

"What?" Mariella cries. "Speak up!"

I wouldn't have thought it possible, but Grace gets even redder.

"I'm a virgin," she says a little louder.

My jaw nearly hits the floor. Of course I know that Grace had conceived her children—Meredith and her younger son, Luke—through IVF. And of course I know that she's never had a serious romantic relationship. But still, this secret is an absolute shocker.

"You lie," Mariella insists, though everyone knows Grace is the most honest woman in the MDBC.

Grace shakes her head. "Cross my heart."

I shoot a glance over to Merry. She's looking down at her lap, an embarrassed half smile on her face, but it's clear that her mother's secret isn't news to her.

"How did we not know this?" I practically screech.

"You know what this means, right?" Zoey says. "It means that Merry lost her virginity before her mom did!"

"Zoey!" Now Merry looks as if she'd like to hide under the couch.

"Well, you had that college boyfriend forever—I'm not saying you were a teen slut."

"Can you please just shut up?" Merry begs.

"You had a *virgin birth*," Jamie says to Grace, awed. "Like Mary. Are they going to make you a saint or something?"

Grace laughs. "I don't think the United Church of Christ is particularly interested in saint-making at the moment. And as for why I didn't tell you, I guess I was embarrassed. I mean, I tried to date for a while. But about three years ago, I just gave it up."

"Pretty sure you haven't missed much," Brigid says drily.

"Didn't you ever go on the apps?" Zoey wants to know. "Every single person I know is on them. Plus a few people who *aren't* single."

"Yes, I tried. But they weren't for me."

"Online dating is the worst. A cesspool of humanity," Brigid grumbles.

"My neighbor met her husband on Bumble," says Merry. "They're literally the perfect couple. And my friend Sally's been seeing a guy she met on Tinder for like a year."

"I've been seeing a girl I met online," Zoey says. "I don't know if TikTok counts as a dating app, though."

"Can we change the subject now?" Grace asks. "Please?"

"Fine," Mariella says. "My secret is equally astonishing." She pats her hips. "I have gained twenty-six pounds."

For a moment, everyone's quiet. Then Zoey snorts, which turns into a guffaw. And Merry starts giggling, and then Grace does too, and Jamie slaps her thigh and cackles. My dark secret vanishes from my mind as I laugh and laugh.

"What?" Mariella says. "What's so funny?"

Zoey, who's gasping for breath by now, says, "Mommy, I'm sorry, but it's not a secret if everyone can already tell!"

You can imagine some people being insulted at a moment

like this. Especially people who live in the public eye the way Mariella does. She sings all around the world, and her image matters. But Mariella loves to laugh at everything and everyone, including herself. So she starts hooting like the rest of us.

"I do not know why I spent all that money on extra-firm Spanx, then!" she says. "From now on I will let it all hang out! Zoey, bring me my sweatpants! And Jamie—it's your turn to tell a secret!"

2

Jamie,
mother of Meg and Kathleen

I don't want to go next.

When the others started sharing their secrets, I felt a knot tightening in my stomach. Because my secret is upsetting. Much more so than gaining a few pounds, or even being a virgin. I'd managed to push it out of my mind this weekend—well, mostly. What's that saying? *Be here now*? I really tried to: I swam, sunbathed, gossiped, read, drank palomas on the deck, all of it. I even flirted a tiny bit with the mail boat jumper, a cute Wisconsin grad a few years older than my twins, who spends his summers delivering mail around the lake by leaping from the US Mail boat to all the various private docks. I needed proof that I was still kinda cute.

Now, though, my secret's right in front of me again, and my heart aches at the thought of it. I get up quickly from the couch. "I think we need more wine, don't you?"

Maybe I can hide in the kitchen long enough that Mariella will forget I'm supposed to take a turn. Doesn't Zoey have a secret? Or Merry?

"I hope there's prosecco left," Mariella says. "I am in the mood for bubbles!"

I go into the kitchen, which is quiet and empty now that the daughters have joined their moms in the living room. The rain's falling even harder now. Big fat droplets hit the skylight with a sound like thunder. A few years ago, after a day of rain like this, some of Lake Geneva's streets turned into lakes of their own.

I pour myself a glass of water and gulp it down. I'm buying time.

Steeling myself to tell the truth. Because these are my best friends, and I should tell them what's going on.

What's taking my kids so long? That's what I'd like to know. *They've probably run into local friends.* But my phone's dead, so I can't text them. I left my charger at home, on the other side of the lake. My husband, Logan, and I bought a cute little 1950s Cape Cod in Williams Bay right before the girls started elementary school. It was supposed to be our starter home, but we've never had enough money to get a better one. We've never had enough money for a lot of things, honestly. Like, the next big purchase we'd talked about making was a new set of tires for Logan's truck.

Sometimes things just don't work out the way you think they will, you know?

Honestly, if my life had a motto, that'd be it.

Like how I was a junior at DePaul University when I found out that I was pregnant.

Or how Logan had to come back early from his study-abroad semester in Scotland because I was so scared and alone. (And *sick*. I must have thrown up three hundred times during that pregnancy.)

Or how, when we went to our first doctor appointment, we were told that we weren't just having one baby—we were having *two*.

Obviously, I wouldn't give up my daughters for anything. They're the best thing that ever happened to me. But sometimes I can't help wondering what life would've been like if things had gone differently when I was twenty-one.

"Jamie, did you get lost?" Grace calls from the other room.

I come back to the present with a start. "Sorry!" I open the refrigerator and grab the last bottle of prosecco. Back in the living room I pop the cork, refill everyone's glasses with the sparkling gold liquid, and sink down into the couch.

Zoey is in the middle of telling everyone her secret, which is that she went to Burning Man. She'd given herself the nickname Daffy Rat and ran around in a metal bikini that she'd made in some feminist metalworking class on the playa.

When I was Zoey's age, I had four-year-old twins.

"It was totally amazing," Zoey's saying, "and I totally never want to do it again."

"I should hope not," her mother says. "It sounds very unsanitary." Then Mariella turns to me and says, "Did you think I would forget you, my dear? It is time for your secret."

I nod. Everyone else has done it. I can do it too.

But I'm crying before I even say the first words. "Logan asked for a separation," I tell them. "Out of the blue. Or that's what it felt like anyway." I'd been in the backyard weeding when he came out to tell me. I was so shocked I couldn't even speak. "That says something, right? Maybe something about me?"

Not about whether I'm still attractive. More like, whether I'm still worth being married to. I can feel my friends' shock and sympathy even before I hear Elin say, "Oh, Jamie, honey," or Mariella proclaiming that this doesn't sound like the Logan she knows.

"I don't know," I say helplessly. "Things change. People change."

Now I'm glad the twins aren't back yet. I don't want them to see me like this, blubbering into a glass of prosecco. I've always tried to be strong for them, and this isn't strong. I reach for a tissue and blow my nose hard. "I can't believe I'm saying this. But I think Logan and I are through."

Elin comes over and sits beside me. She puts her arm around my shoulders.

I was her daughter, Brigid's, nanny (and Elin's cook and errand girl) for five years, but often she feels more like a mother to me than a friend or a former boss. Which is good, because right now that's exactly what I need. I lean into her.

"Whatever happens," she says gently, "we're here for you."

There's a loud pounding on the front door. Elin and I both jump at the sound.

"I'll get it," Mariella says.

What timing! It's Meg and Kathleen, of course. I wipe my eyes and blow my nose again. I hope I don't look like a total mess.

"Finally!" I say. "Probably their arms are so full of ice cream they can't even open the front door." I sit up and try to smile. "Twins! Double the fun, double the brain farts!"

"I'm going to tell them you said that," Zoey warns.

"Trust me, it's nothing they haven't heard me say before," I reply.

I'm smiling now, even though the sadness is still right there, big and heavy in my chest. I'm relieved my daughters have returned—the rain was making me nervous.

I hear Mariella open the front door, and I'm waiting for the sounds of them coming down the hall, bickering over whose fault it is that they took so long. Meg really does have a terrible sense of direction. And Kathleen can never decide between pistachio and mint chocolate chip. But there's only silence, and then Mariella says, "Jamie?"

Her voice sounds too high, and there's a waver in it. The blood in my veins turns to ice.

Something's wrong.

I'm up and running toward the door, which is wide open to the night. Mariella's standing there with her hand covering her mouth. Her eyes are wide with panic. I push past her. There's a policeman outside in the downpour, water streaming down his face. His mouth is moving. I think he's trying to tell me something.

I can't hear him. Roaring fills my ears. He reaches out to me, but I push his hand away. My heart pounds and adrenaline shoots through my veins like electricity.

I see flashing lights out on Snake Road.

Red and blue, whirling through the darkness.

I run barefoot through the slashing rain. The gravel driveway cuts into the bottoms of my feet. I can barely feel it. I think I'm screaming but I can't hear myself. All my focus is on getting to my daughters.

I'm living every mother's nightmare. I wish the rain could

wash the vision away, but nothing can do that. I'll remember this sight until the day I die.

The Night of Secrets has become a night of unimaginable horror. A hundred yards away is Meg's new Jeep, upside down and smashed into a tree.

Three Years Later

Lake Como, Italy

June

1

Mariella,
mother of Zoey

Everything looks perfect. And if everything looks perfect, then everything will be perfect.

Golden sunlight streams in through my living room's French doors, making the crystal chandelier sparkle and the Carrara marble mantel gleam. The elegant couches and matching chairs that I found last month in a Milan antique shop have been grouped to encourage conversation and relaxation. The silk throw pillows are arranged just so. And the enormous bouquets of pink and white roses from my garden offer a lavish final touch.

In a pair of four-inch heels that make me almost five foot five, I click over to my favorite antique mirror and gaze at my reflection. *"Toi, toi, toi,"* I whisper. It sounds like I'm spitting at myself, but it is the opera singer's version of saying "break a leg."

I need good luck because I'm hosting the first Mother-Daughter Book Club meeting in three years, and it must be *assolutamente perfetto*. I've had the house scoured from top to bottom. I've scheduled fine dinners and fun outings. I've lit candles for Saint Medard, the patron saint of weather, Saint Christopher, the patron saint of travelers, and Saint John, the patron saint of friendships (and authors!). I am taking no chances.

I swipe away a speck of dust from the mirror's gilded frame. Maybe it's too much to ask for the weekend to be absolutely, totally perfect. If I have to, I'll settle for a weekend with a happier ending than the last one.

I bend closer to the mirror to freshen up my lipstick. *"Toi, toi, toi,"* I say one more time.

"Mommy, are you talking to yourself again?"

My daughter, Zoey, has wandered into the room. Her hair's still damp from the shower and her tanned skin absolutely glows. She just signed a sponsorship deal with a French skin cream, but that glow doesn't come from a jar — it comes from youth. I know because I've been using that same obscenely expensive cream for years, yet no one would mistake me for twenty-eight. Or forty-eight, for that matter. Unfortunately.

Zoey goes over to the larger couch and starts rearranging the pillows that I've so carefully placed there.

"What are you doing?" Nerves make my tone sharper than I mean it to be.

"It's too fussy in here. Over-the-top," she says briskly. "I mean, jeez, did you hire the set decorator from La Scala?"

Her words sting. We bought this century-old villa perched on a hillside just outside Bellagio five years ago. My husband's grandfather grew up half an hour away, though he moved to America as a young man and made a fortune in real estate. The villa's paint was peeling and its plumbing was a disaster, but I've poured my heart and soul into renovating it, making it the perfect holiday home. Its decor reflects me perfectly: I've always loved crystal vases and gilt-framed mirrors, Persian rugs, and old oil paintings. I like things with glamour and history. Listen, if I could get away with wearing my favorite Violetta costume from *La Traviata*, I would.

"For your information, that couch was made for a nineteenth-century marble magnate, and it cost a fortune!" I say. "I sing old songs, and I love old things!"

"This is not news to me," Zoey says drily. "And, you know, you're kinda—"

"If you are going to say 'old yourself,' you'll stop talking right now if you know what's good for you!"

Zoey shoots me a sly grin. She *was* going to say that, the little minx. Now she inspects the dining room table, which I've already set for dinner.

"It's just a little try-hard," she says.

"A little what?" I ask.

"Oh, never mind, Mommy," Zoey says, tossing her long black hair over her shoulder. "Don't listen to me. It's your party."

"It's your party, too," I remind her. "Aren't you excited to see the girls?"

"Of course!" Zoey exclaims. "But it's not like we haven't *seen* each other. We have our virtual book club meetings. And I FaceTime with Merry, like, three times a week."

"I could live the rest of my life without ever having a virtual meeting again."

"You're just the wrong generation," Zoey says, grabbing a handful of the olives I've set out for our guests. "This stuff's like my entire *job*. Me and my friends are, like, chronically online."

"The 'wrong generation'?" I scoff. "There isn't anything wrong with my generation. *Yours,* however? That's something else. I mean, 'chronically' is *exactly* the right—"

"*Mommy,*" Zoey warns.

There's no need to start a fight ten minutes before our first guest arrives.

I make a quick pivot. "What's wrong with your generation is you have too much beautiful, youthful collagen," I say. "And you won't share it with us!"

Zoey rolls her eyes and grins. "You look amazing and you know it."

"Amazing for sixty."

"No. Just amazing. Full stop."

"Thank you," I say, smoothing my hair.

"So quit fishing for compliments," she adds. "It's undignified."

I pick up a perfect little throw pillow and actually throw it at her. "I wasn't fishing! Don't you have an influencer video to record or something?"

"As a matter of fact I do," Zoey says, "but it's more fun to tease you."

"What product are you going to talk about today?" I ask. "I hope it's a special kind of tape mothers can use to seal their daughters' mouths shut when they're being bratty."

"Mouth taping is surprisingly popular right now," Zoey replies with a raised eyebrow. "It's very good for sleep." She holds up the necklace she's wearing, a narrow gold cylinder on a delicate gold chain. "Actually, I'm going to post about this special item."

I wrinkle my nose. "It's not very special looking."

"It's not what it looks like, it's what it *does*."

"What do you mean?"

"It's a vibrator."

"No!"

Zoey snorts. "Oh, my God, don't act so shocked."

"But I *am* shocked!"

"No you're not. You're just being extra."

"I can't believe you're wearing a sex toy around your neck!"

"When did you become such a prude? You and Dad gave me the birds-and-bees talk when I was seven."

I'm about to throw another pillow at her when a heavy knock sounds on the door. We both jump, but Zoey recovers her composure first. She checks her phone and shows me the display. "It's noon," she says. "Elin did tell us she'd be here by now."

I slowly unclench my fists. For a second I'd been right back in that terrible night on Lake Geneva.

"Right." I smooth my hair again and adjust the scarf (Hermès, if you care) at my neck. "Someday, a sudden knock on the door won't terrify me."

Zoey smiles sympathetically. "I know," she says. "Same." She holds out her hand to me and I take it.

"I love you, you wonderful, obnoxious child," I say.

I never miss a chance to tell Zoey that I love her. That's something Lake Geneva taught me.

"And I love you too," she says. "In all your infuriating glory."

Together we go down the hall and fling open the door.

2

Zoey,
daughter of Mariella

"OMG!" I yelp in happy surprise. Because it isn't just Elin on the doorstep—there's also Grace, the minister, and her daughter, Merry, who I've known since I was born and who I love like a sister.

My mom squeals in delight and tries to hug and kiss everyone at once. She even grabs *me* and plants a kiss on each of my cheeks. "*Benvenute, benvenute,* my beautiful friends! *Sono così felice!*" she cries. She doesn't speak Italian well at all, but she loves to pepper her speech with it anyway. "Welcome, I'm so glad you're here! How was the flight? Was the customs line in Milan very long? Did you catch your train to Lecco all right? And your taxi—did he drive like a madman? They always do, it seems. Are you hungry?" She has a million questions, but she doesn't give them time to answer. Typical!

"I've missed you all so much," Elin says. "I'm so happy to be here, I can't even tell you. This landscape is stunning! I've never seen anything like it. The mountains! That cobalt lake! Even the clouds are more beautiful here. If I were you, Mariella, I'd never leave."

"I never want to! But of course we'll head home to San Francisco in September."

"Oh, poor you!" Elin says.

My mom laughs because there's nothing poor about her. That's what you get for marrying money. But she and my dad adore each other, and have ever since they first met. "I would have married him if he were a pig farmer," she always says, and I actually believe her. But I'm glad he wasn't a pig farmer. Growing up in San Francisco's Pacific Heights suited me in a way that growing up on a hog farm probably wouldn't.

Grace, whose name fits her well, says warmly, "You haven't aged a *day*, Mariella," and "Zoey, how did you get even more gorgeous?"

Now all the moms are laughing and wiping happy tears from their eyes, and Merry and I are looking at each other like, *Okay, Moms, sentimentality overload.* It's cute, though. I hope I still have best friends like that when I'm their age.

My mom has been planning this gathering for months, and she's been a ball of nervous energy the whole time.

Mariella Marciano is a well-known control freak, but I think she's convinced herself that if she plans out every second of our time together, then nothing bad can happen. I haven't had the heart to remind her that a tight schedule can't prevent a terrible accident.

"You do look incredible, Zoey," Merry says, pulling me in for a hug. "Like a real Italian!"

"*Grazie, cara!*" For the record, I don't speak Italian either. "Is it my new brunette color or my vintage Versace?"

"Both!"

"Luna found the dress in a Fort Greene thrift shop," I say. Luna, my girlfriend of three and a half years, is a costume designer with excellent taste. I'd invited her to our MDBC weekend, but she was off designing a shoot for some new California boy band, and we both agreed that was too good an opportunity for her to pass up.

"It's amazing, she's amazing, you're amazing," Merry says, laughing.

"Oh! Whoa! Hi, Meg!" I exclaim. I've just noticed Meg, the slightly younger—by ten minutes—of Jamie's twins, standing awkwardly behind Merry. She's watching the cab pull away like she wishes she was still inside it. "I didn't even see you there!"

I go to hug Meg, too, but for some reason she flinches. I drop my arms back down to my side. *Awkward!*

"Come on in, you guys," I say, trying to act like that wasn't weird. "Let's get this party started!"

"Lucia will show Elin and Grace to their rooms first," my mom tells me.

"Aye-aye, captain."

Lucia is our ancient Sicilian housekeeper. She comes over six days a week when we're here, but she spends more time gossiping with my mom than she does doing any actual housekeeping. Not that anyone really minds. She's a crazy good cook.

"This house is *gorgeous*," Merry whispers to me.

My mom can hear a compliment from a hundred yards away. "I bought it for a song!" she calls.

I roll my eyes. "Get it, you guys? A song, because she's a soprano?"

"Hilarious," Meg mutters.

"But honestly, most of it was Daddy's money." I hook my arm through Merry's; I hesitate before doing the same to Meg. She still feels stiff as I steer them toward the kitchen.

"Anyone who flies coach across the Atlantic deserves a drink," I declare. "How about Negronis? I mixed them up this morning—that's how thoughtful I am."

"I don't know what a Negroni is," Merry says, "but when in Rome…"

"We're four hundred miles north of Rome, actually," I tell her. "We're practically in Switzerland."

Meg has brightened at the mention of a drink. "It's five o'clock somewhere," she says. She glances down at her watch.

"Actually, it's five o'clock now, back home in Chicago — a.m., I think, but who's counting?"

"Exactly." I grab the cocktail carafe from the fridge. "On the rocks or up?"

"Up," Meg says decisively. "With an orange twist if you've got it."

"Of course."

Merry settles onto one of the kitchen stools. "My mom made a new gentleman friend on the plane."

I scoop ice into the crystal mixing glass. "Nice! I hope he was hot, and that they went and made out in the bathroom." I pour in the gin, sweet vermouth, and Campari mixture. "Oh, my God, what if she joined the Mile High Club?"

Merry laughs. "As if, Zo. My mom's not going to hook up with some guy she met on a plane. They were actually praying together because of the turbulence."

"That's not very sexy."

"I know, right? But he said he's going to go visit her church the next time he's on the East Coast for business."

"He should take her out to dinner, too," I say. "And then..." I waggle my eyebrows suggestively.

"And then what?"

"She can finally lose her V card."

When Merry doesn't say anything, I go, "Wait, *did* she?"

Merry shrugs, looking embarrassed. "I don't think so. But Mom and I don't talk about our sex lives that often."

"Fair enough." I give the Negronis another few stirs, then strain the ruby-red liquid into pretty little vintage cocktail glasses and add a twist of orange. "But isn't your mom the same age as mine? I think Grace needs to make this a priority."

"Why don't you tell her to put it on her to-do list," Merry says drily.

"Maybe I will!" I say. "Well, anyway, cheers." I clink my glass against Merry's, then Meg's.

"*Salute!*" Meg says. "*Santé, sláinte,* and *skål.*" Finally, she smiles. "I know how to say 'cheers' in every language on earth. That's the restaurant business for you."

"To an amazing weekend," Merry says. But she gives a quick anxious glance at Meg.

It's not just my mom who's worried about how the weekend's going to go. I think we're *all* nervous.

But we're going to act as happy and carefree as possible, of course. This weekend is supposed to be an escape, not a reminder of the terrible thing that happened the last time we were together.

I take a sip of my cocktail. *Delicious.* I can't help noticing that Meg's glass is already half empty. But she looks happier, so maybe that's okay.

My phone dings. I read the text out loud. "Brigid says, 'OMW—in by six.' Blue heart, airplane, blue heart." Right then is when I make my first mistake of the weekend. I ask, "When's your sister getting here, Meg?"

Meg instantly freezes. Then she slams her glass down and throws her shoulders back. "Where's your bathroom?"

I'm taken aback by her brusqueness. "It—it's down the hall," I stammer. "Second door on the right."

She goes stomping off.

"What was *that* about?" Merry asks me.

I shake my head. "I have no idea."

Halfway down the hall, Meg stops and turns around to face us again. "Kathleen's not my responsibility, you know," she says. "I have no idea where she is, and honestly, I don't even *care*."

3

Elin,
mother of Brigid

If I thought Lake Geneva—a.k.a. the Hamptons of Chicago—was lovely, Lake Como is something else entirely. The outside of Mariella's three-story villa is sparkling white stucco decorated with climbing roses, clematis, and jasmine, surrounded by fountains and carefully landscaped gardens. Inside, all the rooms look like they came out of the pages of a glossy home-decor magazine.

"Come, come, *per favore!*" says Lucia, Mariella's housekeeper, plucking at my sleeve to get my attention. She's barely five feet tall, with dyed black hair, skin like sunbaked leather, and dark, glittering eyes. She talks to me in rapid-fire Italian as she leads me to my room, which overlooks the gorgeous lake and the lush green mountains that surround it.

"*Avete la stanza più bella!*" she says proudly.

I have no idea what that means, but I smile and nod. With gestures and more Italian—peppered with brief snatches of accented English—Lucia shows me which drawers I should use for my clothes, and which pillows are for decoration rather than sleeping (at least I *think* that's what she's saying). Then she pantomimes how to turn on the shower in the en suite bathroom and caresses the towels to demonstrate how soft and luxurious they are. I see why Mariella loves Lucia so much. She's like a bossy, devoted grandmother.

I fall onto the bed the minute Lucia leaves. I'm achingly, overwhelmingly tired. But I can't nap—I don't want to miss a single moment of this weekend. After Lake Geneva, I wasn't sure we'd ever share another vacation again. But here we are, together, trusting that this time will be different. This time, there will be no tragedy.

I get up and drag myself into the pink marble bathroom, where I splash water on my face, smooth La Mer onto my skin, and dab a bit of liquid blush onto my cheeks.

Voilà! I almost look like I've slept. I almost look like I'm doing all right.

"Knock, knock!" It's Grace, smiling at me from the doorway. "This place is nicer than any hotel I have ever stayed in or will ever stay in," she says.

"Mariella has always had champagne tastes," I say. "Lucky for her, now she has the budget to match."

"Why didn't I have the good sense to marry rich?" Grace laughs. Then her face turns serious. "How're you holding up, Elin?"

I know that she isn't asking how I dealt with that crying baby across the airplane aisle for ten hours.

Keep it together. Only happy tears this trip, okay?

I sink down onto the bed, and Grace comes to sit beside me. "Talk to me," she says.

But instead of talking, I immediately start to cry. I don't care how old you are, it guts you when your mother dies. Lorraine Solie was such a big personality—such a force of nature—that part of me still thinks she's playing some huge joke. That on some future Sunday night, my phone will ring, and it'll be her on the other end, just like always. She'll tell me how quickly she solved the *Times* crossword that morning, share snippets of her latest bridge gossip, and ask after her favorite (and only) granddaughter.

"It's okay," Grace says softly. "Let it out."

I don't have any choice. Eight months after my mom's death, it still seems impossible to me that she's gone.

"Did you ever read *The Adventures of Tom Sawyer* when you were a kid?" I ask after I've cried for a while. "I was just thinking about that scene where Tom and Huck sneak back into town and watch their own funerals, and everyone's talking about how wonderful and good they were. My mom would've eaten that up!"

"Well, who wouldn't love hearing wonderful things said about them? But what you did for Lorraine was way better than a funeral," Grace says.

When I'd thought about what my mom would want for a service, the answer had come almost immediately: she'd want to go to a University of Wisconsin football game. Before she became a snowbird and moved from Wisconsin to Florida, she and my dad had had season tickets for forty years. Lorraine knew everything there was to know about three sports: Badger football, Badger basketball, and the PGA.

So I'd bought a bunch of tickets to the UW-Madison homecoming game. We'd kicked things off with a traditional tailgate celebration starring the classics: Johnsonville brats (with heaps of sauerkraut), squeaky cheese curds, cinnamon sugar doughnuts (fresh from the farmers' market), deviled eggs, and plenty of Spotted Cow beer and brandy old-fashioneds to wash it all down.

I know my mom would've loved the family and friends reunion, and the photos in the stadium with Bucky Badger. All the old stories shared. I even finagled a way to get a picture of my mom "toting the rock" up on the Jumbotron during halftime, bringing cheers from more than eighty thousand fans giddy over what turned out to be a pretty epic Badger win. Afterwards, we headed up to the Capitol Square for another Madison classic—dinner at the nostalgic Tornado Steak House. The night was filled with heartfelt stories, old family photos, toasts and tears, laughs and love. Glasses were raised through the night in honor of Lorraine Solie. Jamie, Grace, and Merry had all come to support me and Brigid, and Mariella, who was performing that week in Australia, had sent a bouquet of flowers as big as she is. Then she'd FaceTimed in to send her love despite the fifteen-hour time difference, singing "On, Wisconsin" like nobody else can do.

"That was a real celebration of life," I say. "I think my mom would've dug it." I pause. "Did I ever tell you about the morning she died?"

Grace hands me a box of tissues. "Tell me."

"She'd been in the ER for chest pains, so I booked a flight from Chicago to Florida. But all her test results came back great, and she was going to be released right around the time I arrived. Because I'd gotten ready so early—travel jitters, I guess—I took a walk over to the lake before heading to the airport. It was a really quiet Sunday. The sky was this beautiful deep blue, and there were all these puffy clouds, and Lake Michigan was glistening like diamonds in the sun. So I grabbed my phone and snapped a picture."

I blow my nose before continuing. "An hour or so later, I was on my way to the airport and my phone rang. It was Dr. Moskowitz, her doctor, calling to tell me that my mom had passed at 8:06 that morning. 'I'd just been talking to her,' he said, 'and then I stepped into the hallway for a moment, and when I came back, she was gone.' I could hear the shock in his voice, and the sadness. Everyone at the hospital had loved her. Everyone *everywhere* loved her."

Grace hands me another tissue.

"And here's the weird part," I go on. "Later, I noticed the time stamp on the photo I'd felt so compelled to take. She died at the exact moment that I took my picture. How could that be coincidence? My mom always used to say, 'You're going to miss me when I'm gone!' And she was right. She was so right."

"She sent you those sunbeams," Grace says. "As a way of saying good-bye."

"But there's something else. In the middle of the frame was this lone white gull. I swear it wasn't there when I took the picture. And I thought to myself, 'Well, there she goes. She's flying away.' And she flew over me as she went."

"That's amazing," Grace whispers.

"I cry all the time," I say. "Which my mom would hate. She just wanted me to be happy. But I miss her every single day. Tell me, how did you get through it?"

Grace's mother died two years ago. She'd been ill for a decade, and one might say that her death had been a mercy. Grace had long been preparing for it. But did that make her grief any easier to bear? I doubt it.

"'Blessed are those who mourn,'" Grace says gently, "'for

they shall be comforted.' That's what I told myself about fifty times a day." She gives a wry laugh. "Now I only say it about five times a day."

I recognize this as coming from one of the Gospels, but Sunday school was decades ago, and I can't say for sure which one.

"I also cried all the time," Grace adds. She puts a warm hand on my shoulder and then rubs it in small circles. When was the last time someone touched me to offer comfort? My husband, Charlie, gave me a peck on the cheek when he dropped me off at the airport. I can't remember the last time we even hugged.

But whose fault is that, Elin?

"Are you familiar with Naomi from the book of Ruth?" Grace asks.

I shake my head. I haven't looked at a Bible in years.

"She lost her husband and her two sons, which is an unimaginable pain. At first, she was bitter and broken. But she returned to a place of faith. She came to understand the blessings that hardship can bring." Grace smiles. "I know thinking about that kind of thing doesn't work for everyone. But it helped me."

I flash, for a moment, to Jamie. She nearly lost her whole family on one single, horrible night. In the aftermath of the accident, did it help her to think about how hardship can bring blessings? Somehow I doubt it. But I'm not sure it would help me, either.

"I didn't turn to the Bible. I turned to Chardonnay," I admit. "But I stopped that pretty quick, don't worry. I'm just shocked how lonely I feel, without my mom in the world."

"I'm lonely, too," Grace blurts.

The pain in her voice startles me. "Do you want to talk about it?"

Grace looks surprised by her outburst. Embarrassed even. She shakes her head firmly. "I think we should go find everyone else. And we should also find very large glasses of wine." She smiles. "You know, for our mental health."

I pull my friend into a quick, warm hug. "We need this weekend," I say. "And it's going to be wonderful. Absolutely *nothing* will go wrong."

Grace giggles against my chest. "From your lips to God's ears," she says.

"Amen," I whisper.

Please, God, let everything work out this time.

4

Grace,
mother of Merry

After my talk with Elin, I take a quick shower, change, and allow myself fifteen minutes of reading. It helps pull me back to equanimity. Plus my book, *Brat Farrar*, is delicious: an English country house crime novel that's based on a real-life court case and also a twist on the story of Cain and Abel.

When my fifteen minutes are up, I leave my bedroom and find Mariella and Lucia bustling around the kitchen, chattering in a lively mix of English and Italian as they put together a tray of savory snacks. It's loud and cheerful—the opposite of my own kitchen. Living by myself now that my children, Merry and Luke, are grown means that I can sometimes go weeks without hearing another voice in my house.

Maybe that's why I've started having long conversations with my plants.

It started with a simple "Good morning" when I was watering them, but before I knew it I was confiding in them. I know they can't hear or understand me—I'm not bonkers—but sometimes it still feels to me like my *Monstera deliciosa* knows more about me than my best friends do.

If I'm honest, that's because lately I've felt things that I don't want to admit to them. Like how life has felt utterly drained of color. Gardening, baking, taking walks, and all the other hobbies that used to bring me pleasure simply don't anymore. I feel like I'm going through the motions of life rather than actually living. I feel hollowed out. Numb.

Maybe I could tell my friends that; I know they'd be there to support me. But I definitely don't want them to know what it's like for me at night. How I lie there, waiting for sleep to come, and think about how maybe everything would be easier and better if I just didn't wake up in the morning.

Am I depressed? Am I just horribly lonely? Or am I both?

A dramatic sigh of exasperation interrupts my dark thoughts.

"I don't want the Tuscan olive oil!" Mariella exclaims. *"Voglio l'olio siciliano!"*

"Non so dove lo hai messo!! You had it last!"

Elin appears and lightly nudges me. "Maybe you and I should go outside. 'Too many cooks,' you know..."

On the beautiful stone terrace off the living room, the

afternoon sun is warm. A cool breeze swirls up from the lake. A bottle of prosecco nestled in a silver ice bucket is waiting for us, along with a platter of nuts, olives, and dried fruit for nibbling.

Mariella's impeccable hosting doesn't surprise me. What does surprise me are the dupes of the iconic sunburst chairs from the Memorial Union Terrace at UW-Madison. You can take the girl out of Wisconsin, but you can't take the Badger out of the girl. Instead of those chairs' traditional green, orange, and yellow paint, however, Mariella's are blue, teal, and turquoise—to match the lake, I'm guessing.

"If heaven's anywhere near as nice as this," Elin says, looking wistful, "then I think Mom's probably doing okay."

I pour us each a glass of bubbly and raise mine in a toast. "To heaven in the sky—and to heaven on earth, which is here and now." *And I'm going to try my best to appreciate it,* I think. *Relish it, even.*

Elin smiles. I can still see the sadness in her eyes. "Your congregation is so lucky. You are such a comfort. I don't know what I'd do without you."

"You'd soldier on," I tell her. "You're strong, Elin, don't forget that."

Elin puts on a pair of large, dark sunglasses, very Jackie O. Now you'd never know that she'd been crying. "We've come a long way from Madison, haven't we?"

I point to my damp gray hair. "A long way from eighteen, too."

"I can't believe we were ever so young," she says wistfully. "Me either."

Speaking of young, a French door opens, and I see a barefooted Meg step onto the terrace. Elin doesn't notice her, but Meg quickly spots us, frowns, and disappears back inside. *How odd. I wonder what's going on with her.* Meg was always on the shy side, but that was downright antisocial. I decide not to mention it to Elin.

"Do you know when Jamie's getting in?" I ask. I'm hoping she gets here soon, and that she can cheer up her sullen daughter.

"She's supposed to arrive tonight," Elin says. "But I don't know. She had to change her ticket once already—that's what Brigid told me. She's gotten closer to Jamie since the accident, you know. Sometimes I think the two of them talk to each other more than either of them talks to me." She sighs. "Things really are different, aren't they? Even Mariella isn't sure when Jamie's coming, and she's practically a one-woman surveillance state."

Jamie became very hard to reach after the accident at Lake Geneva. Understandable, considering what she was going through. So I'd called and left messages. *Thinking about you. Let me know if there's anything I can do. I'm keeping you in my prayers.*

"She *is* coming, though, isn't she?" I ask. "It wouldn't be like her to change her mind."

Elin gazes thoughtfully at the water. "I don't think she'd want to miss out on an all-expenses-paid trip to Italy," she says. "Mariella bought her ticket, you know."

"Still, it can't be easy for her—for all kinds of reasons."

"Sometimes it seems like nothing has been easy for Jamie Price," Elin says.

She might be right. Of all of us, Jamie's the one whose grand plans for her life didn't exactly come to pass. On the other hand, I'm doing exactly what I always wanted to do, and my life is hardly a barrel of laughs these days.

"I just want Lake Geneva to have never happened!" Elin blurts.

Me, too. I reach out and touch her hand. "I know."

I hear things like this from my parishioners every day. Everyone wishes they could go back in time and do better. They wouldn't say that cruel thing. They'd pay more attention to their spouse. They wouldn't choose work over family. They'd tell someone they loved them before it was too late.

Jamie, I know, would've asked the twins why they even needed to go out for ice cream when there were already brownies at the house. She'd tell them to just stay inside where it was warm and dry. And if they'd still insisted, then she'd have hidden the Jeep's keys.

What happened isn't her fault. But she must lie awake at night thinking about how she could have stopped it.

5

Merry, daughter of Grace

It's been half an hour, and Meg still hasn't reappeared. Zoey and I have given up on waiting for her and are doing a puzzle in the living room.

"What do you think her problem is?" Zoey asks, sounding huffy as she fits a border piece into its proper place.

I shrug. "Maybe it's a twin thing." I have a younger brother, and Zoey's an only child. Sisterhood is a mystery to us.

The moms wander into the room. Mariella eyeballs my luggage, which is still piled in the corner. "Only carry-on?" she asks.

She'd sent us a long list of instructions for the weekend, one of which was "no checked baggage." I don't think any of us asked why; it was easier just to obey her. Mariella seems to think she's everyone's mother — and boss, for that matter.

"Of course," I assure our hostess. "And presents for the gift exchange."

Mariella sighs dramatically. "If only my own child could be as responsible as you are."

"Hey!" Zoey looks indignant. "I only brought a carry-on, too!"

"But the only thing in it was makeup," Mariella says. "Tell me: How many tubes of Summer Fridays lip balm does one person need?"

Zoey addresses me. "Not bringing enough clothes gives me an excuse to go shopping."

"Shopping!" Mariella exclaims. "As if you and Luna aren't constantly shopping already! As if you didn't have a million dresses back in Brooklyn—"

"I packed way too many books," my mom interrupts. "Did I really think I'd read six novels in one weekend?"

She's just trying to keep Zoey and Mariella from bickering — even though it seems to be one of their favorite activities.

"So did I," says Elin, agreeing with Mom. "Has anyone read *Tomorrow, and Tomorrow, and Tomorrow*?"

The distraction works.

Mariella looks thoughtful. "I think I have it on my Kindle," she says. "I will look. But first..." She reaches into an ornate marble-topped cabinet and pulls out a stack of leather-bound books. "Look at the journals I found for us! They were handmade by a craftsman in Bologna. Aren't they *exquisite*?"

With a flourish, she hands me one the color of a sunflower. I run my finger across the buttery soft leather. It's absolutely gorgeous. It must've cost a fortune.

"In these journals we will write down all of our secrets! And then," Mariella says with a mischievous twinkle in her dark eyes, "we will share the very best ones on our very last night."

"You want to do the Night of Secrets again?" Elin asks dubiously.

"Of course I do!" Mariella says. "We can all sign nondisclosure agreements, don't worry."

"If you're going to ask me to draft the NDA," Elin says drily, "the answer is no. For one thing, I'm a trial lawyer, not a contracts lawyer. And for another, even workaholic trial lawyers occasionally take PTO." She notices Mariella's blank look. "Paid time off. A.k.a. vacation."

Mariella blinks her long dark eyelashes (ten bucks says she has extensions). "When you do what you love, your whole life is a vacation," she declares, and I can see my mom and Elin giving each other an almost invisible eye roll. We all know that Mariella's life is the most fabulous; we don't need to be reminded.

Zoey leans close and whispers into my ear, "Seriously, how long does it take a person to use the bathroom?"

As if on cue, Meg pokes her head into the room. Her eyes look red. She seems full of nervous energy. Zoey and I get up from our puzzle and go over to her.

"Are you feeling okay?" I ask.

"I'm fine," she says grimly. "Except I really don't want to be here."

"But Meg—"

"So I made some calls, and I'm leaving tomorrow." She thrusts her chin up defiantly. "And if you two don't want to be under your mommies' thumbs all weekend, you should come with me."

6

Brigid, daughter of Elin

The sun is setting by the time we pull into Mariella Marciano's cobblestone driveway. Right before Jamie gets out of the cab, she turns to me and grabs my sleeve. She looks me dead in the eye and says, "Remember our agreement."

"I'll follow your lead," I assure her.

"Don't say anything to anyone. Even if they ask. Not until the last night."

I nod. We've been over this before, but still, my pulse quickens. I'm good at a lot of things, but lying has never been one of them.

Jamie gives me a quick smile. "It's going to be fine."

It's like she can read my mind, the same way my mother

sometimes can. Maybe that's because Jamie was my nanny for five years back in Lincoln Park, when my dad was busy meeting *Chicago Tribune* deadlines and my mom was downtown working twelve hours a day. Jamie raised me almost as much as they did. For a while, the twins were like my little sisters.

"You'll do great, Doc," Jamie says. "Just keep your cool."

"I can do that," I say.

I mean, I *think* I can do that.

I pay the driver, and we pull our bags from the trunk. I wish I felt less jittery and nervous. I wish I felt like this vacation was going to be actually relaxing.

Jamie slams the trunk shut and turns around. She finally takes in Mariella's house. "Holy crap! Looks like something out of a freaking fairy tale," she exclaims. "That's a good sign, don't you think?"

I shrug. Is it? I'm a scientist; I don't believe in signs. "What makes you say that?"

"Because fairy tales have happy endings," Jamie explains patiently. "And that means the second meeting of the Mother-Daughter Book Club will, too." Her smile falters a little. "Fairy tales have happy endings, and lightning doesn't strike twice."

"Sure," I say. "Totally." I can think of several contradictory examples, of course, but I keep my mouth shut. I hope that in this case Jamie's right.

Mariella must've been lying in wait in the hallway, because she pounces on us the instant we open the front door, showering us with hugs and kisses while pulling us into the villa's huge main room.

Jamie laughs. "You act even happier to see me than my dog does," she says, her voice muffled in Mariella's ample bosom. "And he's so happy that he pees himself!"

Mariella takes a step backward, and with an utterly straight face, says, "My dear, I am so happy I could *explode*."

Once out of Mariella's embrace, Jamie scurries across the room to hug her daughter Meg. I don't see Kathleen, but everyone else is gathered in the living room. As I put down my bag and go to greet my mom and Grace and everyone else, I begin to feel the tension of travel drain from my body.

"Are you starving?" Mariella asks. "You must be starving."

I glance over at the dining room table, which looks like it's set for Thanksgiving, Christmas, and an Irish wake all at once.

"I'm famished," Jamie answers.

"You shouldn't have spent the whole flight doing lunges up and down the aisle," I tease her. "It burned too many calories."

My mom looks curious. "You two were on the same plane? How did that happen, when Jamie lives in Wisconsin and you live in Boston? Come to think of it, I don't know how you were even in the same *taxi*."

Jamie shoots me a warning look. Did I not literally just promise that I wouldn't give anything away? My cheeks flush. I stumble forward into what I hope will be a convincing fib. "Well, my flight—"

But Jamie interrupts me. "Of course we weren't on the same plane," she says quickly. "We just landed at Malpensa at the same time. And Bridge knows I'm all about fitness!" She flexes a very muscular bicep. "I'm actually getting a new personal training certification."

There's another reason Jamie needs to be physically strong, but no one's going to mention that now.

"*Everyone* should move around on long flights," I say, thankful that the subject has changed. Thankful that we can simply pretend we ran into each other at the airport in Milan, when in fact I'd been with Jamie in Wisconsin all last week. "It lowers your risk of deep vein thrombosis."

My mom gamely experiments with a wobbly lunge. "Like this?"

When Jamie starts to correct her form—"Keep your feet hip distance apart; no, don't let your knee go over your toes"—I know the moment of danger has passed. Our secret's safe. Even if I don't think it should be a secret.

That was close, though. I definitely need to do better about watching what I say.

My mom tries to get Grace and Mariella to do lunges, too, but Grace claims that she's glued to the couch.

"I'm wearing heels, darling," Mariella says. "I'd break an ankle. Anyway, it's time for something very special."

"Dinner?" Jamie asks hopefully.

"Not yet!"

I glance over at Zoey, whose face reveals a mix of pride and embarrassment. She comes to stand beside me. "You ready for some big diva energy?" she mutters.

Her mom kicks off her shoes and plants herself in the middle of the room, right under the crystal chandelier. That's when I realize that the world-famous diva Mariella Marciano is going to sing for us.

7

Jamie,
mother of Meg and Kathleen

Oh, *boy.* I hope Mariella's voice can drown out the sound of my rumbling stomach, which is growling like a stray dog. Brigid was telling the truth—I *did* spend the flight doing lunges, and squats in the galley while the flight attendants passed out drinks. It wasn't because I wanted to burn calories. I was just so nervous that I couldn't sit still. I haven't been away from home in years, unless you count a few afternoons in Chicago to see my daughters and once to have lunch with Elin.

It's good to be here, even if I'm a ball of nerves. I've been looking forward to spending time with these amazing women for months. Things have been hard lately, and I need the break.

And by "lately" I don't mean only the last three years.

Long before the accident in Lake Geneva, there were all those problems with Logan. And after... well, there were still problems. But they were new ones. Worse ones.

Things never work out the way you think they will.

I look at my phone. No messages.

Where is Kathleen? Wasn't she supposed to be here by now?

"My darlings!" Mariella calls. "You have heard the expression 'to sing for your supper,' yes?"

We all nod at her like obedient children.

"Well, I shall sing *before* your supper! This is an aria called 'O mio babbino caro.'"

Even though I'm about to faint from hunger, it's always exciting to hear my good friend, a world-famous opera singer, perform.

Mariella places her hand on her heart. I hold my breath in anticipation. Then she opens her mouth, and this huge, incredible voice comes pouring out of her throat. I gasp at the sound. It's loud. Overpowering. I don't even know how to describe it except to say that it's mind-boggling. One of the most beautiful things I've ever heard. The hair on my arms literally stands up on end.

O mio babbino caro

Mi piace, è bello, bello...

I don't really know opera. I listen to Zach Bryan on my back porch through a portable speaker I got for twenty bucks on Amazon. But somehow I know this song.

Mi struggo e mi tormento!
O Dio, vorrei morir...

Mariella's voice is an absolute miracle. I could almost believe that it could heal the sick, cure the blind, or mend the broken. And if it could...well, I'd kidnap her and take her home with me. There are a few miracles I'd like to see happen.

Babbo, pietà, pietà
Babbo, pietà, pietà...

When she finishes, we're too amazed to move or speak. We're all still holding our breath in awe. Then Mariella gives two loud claps, and I jump so high I practically fall off my chair.

"Yo yo yo," Mariella yells. And then she starts to *rap*.

Zoey jumps up from her chair and goes to stand beside her mom.

"I'm like four foot four, black hair to the floor / You didn't think a diva could rap hardcore," Mariella shouts. "I live on the lake, I'm always on the take / When shit gets real, well, then I like to *bake*."

Meanwhile Zoey is beatboxing. She's pretty good at it. Then it's Mariella's turn to handle the rhythm while Zoey starts to rhyme. "That's Mariella Marciano on the mic / Flowing like Puccini on a starry night / Her high notes hit the heavens, her trills are outta sight / But when the curtain falls, it's the *oven* she ignites!"

They take turns, rapping about opera, baking, and shopping. Grace and Merry start dancing, and Elin's rolling on the couch, literally weeping with laughter. Brigid's giggling and Meg's taking a video. "For blackmail," she jokes. When the rap's over, mother and daughter take a bow as everyone madly claps.

Mariella grabs her daughter and plants a big kiss on each of her cheeks. "Isn't she amazing?" the proud mama asks. "She could've been a star."

Zoey tosses her hair over her shoulder. "I *am* a star," she declares. "I have over a million followers on Insta and TikTok, and I practically created the clean girl aesthetic."

"I don't even know what you're talking about," Mariella says, as she motions for us all to decamp for the dinner table.

Are they going to start crabbing at each other again now? Honestly, I don't even care. I'm the first one to the dinner table by a mile.

8
Elin, mother of Brigid

I never get to eat like this in Chicago.

Insalata caprese. Prosciutto e melone. Fresh peas and tiny, lacy lettuces with rich, creamy burrata, served alongside crusty grilled bread drizzled with peppery extra virgin olive oil and flaky smoked sea salt.

And that's only the *appetizers*.

There are great restaurants in the Windy City, but I can't get my husband to go to them. Charlie's favorite restaurant is the Billy Goat Tavern, where he can get a Miller Lite and a "cheezborger" alongside all the other *Tribune* reporters. The Billy Goat's been a journalists' hangout for so long that the ghost of Mike Royko probably haunts it.

Jamie and Brigid sit next to each other at the far end of the table. I see my daughter whisper something to Jamie, who nods and smiles. Is it me, or does Jamie's smile look a little bit tentative? Nervous, even? I wonder if she's concerned about Kathleen. Or maybe she's worried about leaving home, when she has so many reasons to stick close by.

Not that Jamie's concerns, whatever they might be right now, seem to be impacting her appetite. She eats four slices of prosciutto-wrapped cantaloupe in about four seconds.

Meg, who's sitting as far from her mother as possible, is reaching for the wine. I watch as she pours what's left of the bottle into a goblet the size of a goldfish bowl. And she fills it practically to the rim. Her cheeks are rosy. Actually, her whole face is flushed.

"No word from Kathleen?" Grace asks Jamie. Her tone is light. Like there's nothing to worry about.

Jamie shakes her head. "Not yet. She'll be here, though. She said she would. And she always keeps her word."

At the other end of the table, Meg suddenly comes alive. But not in a good way.

"That's right," she practically spits. "Kathleen always keeps her word. She's soooo reliable. And everything's going to be so much more *fun* once she gets here. She's the best! Almost perfect, really. Which is why it's so weird that I'm such a complete fuckup. I mean, aren't we supposed to be genetically identical?"

I can see Jamie stiffen. "Meg," she says quietly. "I don't think this is necessary."

Meg takes a gulp of wine. "Actually, it is. I think it's about time you know how much it sucks to be the bad twin." She mimics her mother: "'Kathleen's studying law at the University of Chicago, isn't that wonderful? And Meg...well, Meg's still finding herself. She wants to be a writer, but she just works in food service right now.'" Meg takes another swig of chianti. "Well, I may not be 'living up to my potential,' but at least I know how to show up to places on time."

"That's enough," Jamie says through clenched teeth. "If you can't behave yourself, you may be excused."

It's exactly what she used to say to Brigid when my daughter was being a brat at the dinner table. Brigid would flush bright red, but then she'd calm down. She'd finish eating her mac 'n' cheese in peace. She was a rational, reasonable child.

But Meg isn't Brigid. She gets up, tosses her napkin onto her plate, and leaves the room. We all watch her go in shock.

Jamie whispers, "Sorry, guys. I don't know what's going on with Meg lately." She pauses. "I think she really misses her dad. They were always so close. And now..." She gives a helpless little shrug. "I don't know. She won't talk to me about it."

Grace pats her hand. "We all go through tough times. It's not your fault."

Jamie's eyes fill with tears. "Are you sure about that? Because I'm not."

My heart goes out to my friend. It seems like she has even more to worry about than I thought. And I'm worried, too. Because people are already crying and yelling, and the MDBC weekend has barely even begun.

9

Mariella,
mother of Zoey

This is not *how tonight is supposed to go!* I want to stomp my feet and scream this at the top of my lungs. I've worked for months to make everything perfect: the food, the music, the activities, the schedule.

You can't make the people perfect—that's the problem.

But if I don't turn this night around, the whole weekend is at risk. And then this will turn into the *last* meeting of the Mother-Daughter Book Club.

I stand up and refill everyone's water glasses. "Flying across the ocean is exhausting," I say, "*and* dehydrating," as if this might be the reason for Meg's little fit. "Speaking of long flights, has anyone read *The Great Circle*? It's about a woman who tries to fly around the world from top to bottom."

"It's on my to-read list," Grace says. She looks toward the kitchen. "Tell me there's more of the pasta."

I laugh merrily. *Fake it till you make it, right?* "In my house, there is always more food."

The *sugo di carne* is an old family recipe of Lucia's, beef and pork sautéed with a *soffritto* of onions, carrots, and celery, plus red wine and San Marzano tomatoes. It's been simmering on the stove for hours, perfuming the house with its rich aroma. Grace is not the only one to have seconds.

The rest of dinner goes well enough, *grazie al cielo,* thank heavens. All of the food is wonderful. I don't let myself eat very much of it, because there's only one pair of pants in my closet that fits. I had surgery to remove polyps from my vocal cords last year, and I ate a *lot* of gelato during my recovery.

But am I fully recovered? That is the bigger worry. Much bigger than whatever size I am these days. My vocal cords *are* my instrument, and there is no replacing them; I cannot buy new ones the way a cellist can buy a new cello.

After everyone but me has finished off the meal with Lucia's wonderful *budino al cioccolato,* I announce that it's time for the gift exchange. We move onto the terrace, which I've had lit by dozens and dozens of candles. It's so beautiful that I feel the tightness in my chest start to loosen.

Surely, everything is going to work out. Surely, we deserve a wonderful weekend.

"Merry, this is for you; Elin, this is yours; Grace, I'll set your present here..." Zoey is helpfully handing out all the packages while Grace pours us tall glasses of Chiarella mineral water. Meg is still sulking, and Jamie's pretending that everything is fine.

I am not the only one who fakes it until she makes it, it seems.

We'd picked names for a book exchange, Secret Santa style, but the first gift everyone opens is an extra one from me. I got us all the same thing: scoop-neck black t-shirts with "MDBC 4-Ever" spelled out in hundreds of twinkling rhinestones.

"Oh, I was talking about doing this!" Grace exclaims. "But Merry told me not to. She said, 'We don't need merch, Mom.'"

"Yeah, because we're not a *band*," Merry says.

Zoey cocks her head thoughtfully. "Is it me, or are the rhinestones giving Vegas stripper?" She grins. "Not saying that's a bad thing, of course."

"Shut up and put them on," I say, and of course everyone obediently tugs the t-shirts over their other shirts. "Oh, they look incredible. *Molto alla moda!* That means very fashionable." My friends seem very pleased with them, and I'm happy I got their sizing right. As for our daughters, *anything* looks good on them. "I have a book for Kathleen, too, but I guess that'll have to wait."

"Hopefully not too much longer," Jamie says. She glances over at Meg, who pointedly fails to meet her eye. What is *up* with that child?

Then Zoey dramatically unwraps a present from Merry, flinging paper everywhere. It's a book called *Anna K.*

"It's a glitzy retelling of *Anna Karenina*," Merry tells her.

"Perfect!" Zoey exclaims. "Since I didn't read the original when they assigned it in high school."

"I know." Merry laughs. "You told me even the *movie* was too long!"

Next, Grace gives Elin two Claire Keegan novels. "Because they're short, unlike you."

Elin laughs—she's five foot ten, a former All-American swimmer. "Unlike me is right."

"But," Grace says, "they are beautiful, *just* like you!"

This is very touching, and everyone murmurs happily. I'm feeling better. Things are looking up.

Next it's Grace's turn to open her present, which is from my daughter. When she holds up the book so we can read its title, my mouth falls open in horror. *"The Good Girl's Guide to Great Sex?"* I gasp. Why wasn't I more careful about who got whom in the exchange? My daughter has just insulted one of my most beloved friends. Giving Grace something like this is even more inappropriate than wearing a sex toy around her neck! "Zoey, you naughty, naughty child!"

Zoey chuckles and throws up her hands. "But I read it, Mommy! It's great! And it's for everyone—gay, straight, bi, whatever."

It's too dark to see if Grace is blushing. I'm sure she is, but she smiles and says, "Thank you, Zoey. This is actually a very thoughtful gift." She twists a strand of silver hair around her finger. "And who knows, someday it could be helpful. I mean, a good girl can dream, right?"

"It looks great," Elin says. "Can I borrow it this weekend?"

"*You?*" Jamie asks.

Elin grimaces. "Charlie and I are in a bit of a rut."

"I don't know," Zoey teases. "It depends on if you're the target audience or not. Are you in fact a 'good girl'?"

Weirdly, Elin goes pale. She melts back into the couch, tucking her blond bob behind her ears. "I think it's time for the next present, don't you?" she says.

Hmmm, I think. *Looks like we've got something juicy for the Night of Secrets.*

Elin doesn't meet my questioning eye as she composes herself and holds out a book wrapped in pretty gold paper. "For you, Mariella."

I accept it happily, pretending to be surprised that Elin picked my name for the exchange. This was the one intervention I did make in the present lottery: I made sure that Elin got my name. Everyone knows Elin gives the best books.

Which is why I'm so dismayed when I open it to find a copy of *Bel Canto*, by Ann Patchett. It's a novel about an opera singer—of *course* I've read it, three times at least. It's wonderful. But still. I wish she'd gotten me *Tom Lake*, which I haven't read but I know I'll love.

"Oh!" I say. "Why, thank you. This is so appropriate!"

"Open it," Elin says.

"What?" I think I'm doing a very good job of keeping the disappointment off my face.

"Look *inside*."

I open the cover. I see that it's a first edition. *Okay, well, I suppose that's nice.*

"Turn the page," Elin says.

I do what she says, and that's when I see the inscription.

For Mariella—

Your voice is big and beautiful, and now I know that your heart must be, too. It's not every day that someone drives 200 miles, one way, to ask me to sign a book for her dear friend.

Did I say "it's not every day?" I meant "it's extraordinary."

Music is the purest and most wonderful of blessings. So, too, is friendship.

I wish you many more years of both.

My hands are shaking. To get me this present, Elin must've traveled hundreds of miles, all the way to Ann Patchett's bookstore in Nashville, Tennessee.

I think Ann Patchett must've signed the book, too, but I can't read her signature through my grateful tears.

10

Merry,
daughter of Grace

After the book exchange, we somehow wind up debating the merits of rereading books. My mom says she reads the same P. G. Wodehouse novels whenever she's sick, and Elin admits to having read *Pride and Prejudice* six times. "It's a comfort read."

"I can top that," I tell her. "I read *The Hotel Cat* forty-three times in fourth grade."

She laughs. "That seems excessive."

"Or obsessive," I admit.

"I've only read *Sense and Sensibility* twice," she says, "but I always carry a copy of it in my purse."

"Emergency fiction rations!" Mariella says. "What a brilliant idea."

"Have none of you besides my mother heard of Kindle?" Zoey asks rhetorically. Then she goes on to say that reading a book more than once is ridiculous. "I don't even finish half the books I start! Why would I read any of them twice?"

I notice that Meg has nothing to add to the conversation, and that Brigid seems distracted. But at least she states an opinion: "*Love* rereading, don't have time for it."

Finally, the yawning moms head off to bed, and Brigid says good night too. Meg just vanishes.

When Zoey and I are the only ones left, she turns to me and says, "Time to go swimming."

I think she's joking until I follow her into the house and watch her grab towels from the hall closet and stuff them into a waiting beach bag.

"It's after midnight," I protest.

"So? The pool has lights."

"Wait, there's a pool? This place gets better and better."

Zoey grins at me. "Just wait, M. Your night is only beginning."

"I've been awake for nearly twenty-four hours already! I don't know how much more consciousness I can take." Besides, I just know my bed's going to be luxurious. I'm sure that Mariella has expensive mattresses and really nice sheets — the kind of stuff I can't afford, not on a social worker's salary.

But my doubts fall away as Zoey takes me down a garden path that ends in a lush stone grotto. Flowers, rocks, and reeds surround what looks like a large natural swimming hole.

Zoey presses something on her phone, and the water lights up, instantly becoming a brilliant blue-green. I gasp.

"Pretty rad, huh?" Zoey says. "My mom was like, 'Make me a swimming pool that looks like a duck pond.'"

I dip a bare foot into the water and sigh. It's the perfect temperature, cool and refreshing. I bet this particular luxury cost more than I make in five years.

"If this was *my* mother's house," I say, "I would never leave."

Zoey laughs. "Yeah, but your mom's mellow. Mine's crazy." She drapes her towel over a rock. "Ready to get in?"

"Hang on—I forgot my suit back at the house!" I blame jet lag for that not occurring to me sooner.

"Babe," Zoey says patiently, "we're skinny-dipping."

I shouldn't be surprised. Zoey has always been a free spirit. Me, though, not so much. She can see me hesitating.

"Here," she says. She reaches into her bag and pulls out a chocolate bar. She unwraps it, breaks off a sizable piece, and holds it out to me. "Have some of this first."

"No thanks. I'm still stuffed from dinner," I tell her.

"You need to eat it anyway," Zoey insists. "This is special chocolate. It's mushroom chocolate."

As in *magic* mushrooms.

I don't know what Zoey's thinking. I've never smoked pot. I've never even had a Negroni before today.

It's clear that Zoey finds me hilarious and totally square. She tells me that there's no law saying that I can't try mushrooms before marijuana.

"But isn't there a law saying that I can't try mushrooms at *all*?" I object. "And you can't either? Because *no one can*?"

"I think they're legal in Oregon," Zoey says, pressing a few squares into my palm. "But honestly, M, just shut up and try some."

I look down at the chocolate in my hand. I think about how all my life I've followed the rules and done the right things. If Zoey's spent her life being spontaneous and daring, I've spent mine being predictable and cautious. And where has it gotten me? Still living in the town where I grew up, working at a steady but incredibly hard job.

Not much time for fun.

The chocolate's in my mouth before I even realize I've made a decision. "It tastes weird," I say.

"The taste's not important. What's important is what it *does*."

What it does after a few minutes is turn the night air into a dark velvet cape that an invisible angel has lovingly draped over my shoulders. When I try to touch it, I can't tell if I'm caressing the breeze or my own skin. They've become the same thing.

The water is a prism. It breaks the pool lights into a thousand rainbows. I stare at a nearby flower, and I know exactly what it's like to have petals. To wave in the wind. To be kissed by bees. I realize that I'm a flower and a bee and the wind all at once.

Everything in the world is perfect and beautiful. I'm perfect and beautiful, too! I have petals. I have wings. Everything is glowing! Why have I never realized how wonderful the world is before now?

Zoey asks me how I'm doing. I don't know how to answer her. My thoughts don't seem to have words in them anymore. Instead, they have colors and smells and sounds. The flowers are singing. They sound like angels, but only I can hear them.

I slide into the gorgeous pool. I'm still wearing my dress. It floats around me like a cloud. I tip my head back and look up at the night sky. Stars are everywhere.

A word is coming to me now, coming from a long way off. It falls down to me like a meteor. It lands on my tongue.

"Incredible," I whisper.

I hear Zoey laughing. "Good," she says. "I was kinda starting to worry."

We're quiet for a long time. Hours maybe. I'm busy being a flower. A flower floating in a pool. A water lily! I love being a water lily.

Then a figure comes out of the darkness and stops at the edge of the grotto.

A bear.

A giant white bear, standing on its hind legs. But I realize that I'm not afraid. I love this bear. I love all the bears in the whole world.

"Zoey?" the bear says.

I didn't know bears could talk. And it has such a human voice!

"What are you doing in the pool?" the bear wants to know. "It's two o'clock in the morning, and you have yoga at seven. Your mother will kill you if you miss it."

"Oh, hey, Dad," Zoey says cheerfully. "Sorry, did we wake you up?"

I blink. The halo of white light around the bear dissolves. I realize that it's Mike Marciano. A rich, middle-aged father, not a wild animal. "I didn't even know you were here," I say, amazed.

"Yeah," Mike says. "I *live* here."

"Wow," I whisper. "That's incredible."

11

Kathleen,
daughter of Jamie

I don't want to be here.

But of course I came anyway. Because I'm the dutiful daughter.

That's what I'm thinking right as the tip of my cane gets caught in the cobblestones of Mariella's driveway. The next thing I know I'm falling. Free arm windmilling, grabbing nothing but air. Duffel bag and damn gravity pulling me down. I land on my knees. Hard. Pain shoots up my leg. I let out every curse word I can think of. Did you know that swearing helps with pain tolerance? Or so the studies show.

I climb awkwardly to my feet. I hoist my duffel bag up and keep going, more slowly now.

Take it easy, Kathleen. Don't break an arm. Or another leg.

My nosedive feels like just another sign that I shouldn't have come. I have a judicial internship back in Chicago this summer. I wasn't supposed to ask my boss for so much time off. But my mom begged me to give the Mother-Daughter Book Club a second chance. "There's going to be a surprise that you just can't miss," she promised.

When I asked her why she couldn't just tell me about the surprise over the phone, she said Brigid would never forgive her.

Mom, what does Brigid have to do with it? I'd asked. But she wouldn't say. She was all, *You'll find out.*

I almost trip again, right before I get to the front door. Someone should tell Mariella that her driveway's a total liability. She could be sued.

Maybe I'll tell her.

No I won't, I'm too polite.

Too bad I'm not speaking to Meg. *She'd* say something. She doesn't care about politeness at all.

The front door opens easily. *No worries about robbers here, I guess.* The house is dark and quiet, which figures since it's the middle of the night. I turn on my iPhone flashlight and limp my way down a hallway. I'm exhausted. Wrecked. I was sore even *before* I fell. Plane seats are not made for people with pins in their femurs. If I'd known how hard it would be to get here—that my flight would be delayed, my phone would die, and I'd miss the last train to Lecco, leaving me with a 150-euro taxi ride—I never would've come.

You're young, you'll be back to 100 percent in months, the doctors had assured me. But they were wrong. Three years after the accident and I still need a cane. I walk like an old lady and I eat Advil like M&M's, which gives me internal bleeding—but it's mild, apparently, so nothing to worry about.

I reach a large living room with two big couches, a love seat, and a handful of deep armchairs. Since I have no idea where I'm supposed to sleep, I decide to bed down on the nearest couch. I need to get off my feet. My duffel bag slips off my shoulder. It's heavy with law books, and it lands on the floor with a bang.

Oops, that was *loud.*

I prop a couple of throw pillows under my head and settle in. I wish I were in my own bed, with my little cat, Fern, curled up at my feet, the loud Chicago night out the window. But I'm here now, and I need to make the best of it.

I'm going to have fun, damn it, and I'm going to be a ray of freaking sunshine for my mom. Because life's hard for her these days. And unlike me, my sister never tries to make it any easier.

12

Grace,
mother of Merry

Something wakes me with a start. A noise like a window banging or a door slamming. I blink groggily. The clock by my bed says it's just after three. I lie still, listening. Hearing nothing now but crickets and the wind rustling the leaves outside my window.

I roll onto my back and take deep, calming breaths. But there's no way I'll get back to sleep. I slide out of bed. I'll go make myself a cup of chamomile tea. That helps sometimes. Certainly it's better to do something than to lie awake and wait for the anxious thoughts to start spinning through my mind.

My bedroom is on the second floor, so I tiptoe downstairs

and through the hall leading to the main part of the house. I hear voices coming from the living room and freeze. I prick up my ears.

"—flight was okay?" asks a low voice.

There's a sleepy-sounding grunt.

"Your leg didn't bother you too much?"

"I don't know, it's all right, I guess."

I know who's talking now: it's Jamie and her daughter Kathleen, who must've just arrived.

"You poor thing. Do you need ibuprofen?"

"No. I hit my daily limit hours ago." Then Kathleen's tone changes, and she says, "Is Meg here?" Her voice is sharp. Almost angry.

"She is. And she misses you so much, Kat."

"Bullshit."

"Don't say that."

"It's true. She called you a bunch of times and you didn't call her back. She told me."

"I was busy."

My mind starts to race. I'm trying to piece together what this means. The twins, who both live in Chicago, aren't seeing each other—they aren't even talking on the phone? For all the years I've known them, they've been inseparable.

"I really need to go to sleep, Mom."

"Let's get you into your bedroom."

"Can't move," Kathleen says. "Too tired."

"You poor thing," Jamie says again.

Kathleen doesn't answer.

I press myself against the wall, shivering in my nightgown. What am I doing, eavesdropping like some kind of spy? I know how to talk to troubled people. I do it with members of my congregation every day.

I tell myself that I should go out there and give Kathleen a hug before she falls asleep. I should tell her how glad I am that she's here with us. And I'll hug Jamie while I'm at it. I'll reassure her that everything's going to work out.

I'm optimistic. The Mother-Daughter Book Club weekend might be off to a rocky start, but there's nowhere to go but up, right?

Yet I can't make myself move. It's almost like I'm scared.

I hear Jamie putting a blanket over her daughter, telling Kathleen that there's a yoga teacher coming to the villa in the morning. Early. "It was Mariella's idea. I'm sure she'll be able to offer modifications," Jamie says. Then I hear her murmuring good night. Telling her daughter that she loves her. There's no answer from Kathleen.

I creep back to my own bed, where I lie awake until morning.

13

Elin,
mother of Brigid

I forgot how much I hate jet lag.

I'm staring at Mariella's fancy espresso maker and wondering how the heck it works. It's six o'clock in the morning in Lake Como. If I don't get caffeine into my system soon, I think I might actually die.

"Need help?"

It's Jamie. She's barefoot and still in pajamas, with her short red hair sticking up every which way. I'm so glad to see her, and not only because she seems like she might know how to make coffee. I miss her. We don't talk as much as we used to.

"I can't even tell how to turn the damn thing on," I admit. "You're a lifesaver."

Jamie starts pushing buttons and turning cranks, and two minutes later I've got a steaming cappuccino in my hands. I sip it gratefully while she makes one for herself.

"Sleep well?" I ask.

Jamie nods. But she has dark, puffy circles under her eyes, so I'm not sure this is the truth. I want to press her a little — why lie about something so minor? — but I don't. Instead I say, "Want to go look at the lake?"

We walk out onto the terrace. The air is cool and beautifully scented by Mariella's roses and jasmine. We lean against the railing, sipping our coffees. I don't know what to make of it, but the silence between us feels strangely heavy.

I watch my friend out of the side of my eye, wondering about the burdens that she carries so quietly.

"How're you feeling these days?" I ask. "How's—"

"I'm doing good," Jamie says, cutting me off. "We're all doing good. Really."

I'm not sure that's true, either, but I respect Jamie's right to not talk about things.

"Kathleen finally got here," she says, her gaze fixed on the lake.

"That's wonderful!"

"Sure is."

Her voice sounds a little flat. But maybe she's just overtired. Maybe she'll perk up after another cappuccino. Personally, I could drink ten of them.

"You're lucky you get both your kids here," I say.

"My girls are like oil and water these days." Jamie sounds glum.

"Even when they were babies they were very different. Remember?" Meg was quiet on the surface and fiery underneath, while Kathleen was sunny and even-keeled. "But they always got along so well. This must be a passing phase."

Jamie doesn't answer. I take another sip of my cappuccino. I'm starting to feel better now that the caffeine's entering my bloodstream. I want my friend to feel better, too.

"Jamie, you know you can talk to me," I say. "You can tell me anything."

She turns to me, a strange expression on her face. "Can I, though?" Then she looks back toward the water. "You were my boss for five years, Elin. And I think that's kept me from being completely open with you. When a person signs your paychecks, you just can't tell them everything."

I immediately start to protest. "But we talked *constantly*! We spent so much time together—you, me, and all of our kids—that Charlie started calling our house the Commune. How can you say we weren't close?" *You were like a little sister to me.*

"I'm not saying we weren't close. I'm just saying that maybe we haven't always told each other everything."

I open my mouth to argue, but then I shut it again. Because I haven't told Jamie everything either, have I? If I had, she'd know there was a time when I thought my marriage was over.

She'd know that last year I'd fallen in love with someone else. That his name was Edward, and that he was another lawyer at my firm. We'd had an affair that lasted six wonderful, terrible months and ended the night before New Year's Eve, with the bottle of Veuve Clicquot I smashed against his black marble counter. It wasn't my finest moment, not by a long shot. But I was devastated and furious, and I knew that if I tried to stay with him, my heart would end up breaking into more pieces than the damn bottle.

Am I really supposed to admit that to her? Maybe. But I'm not ready to yet. I don't even like thinking about it myself.

"If there's been any distance between us," I say resolutely, "we'll fix it—starting today." I smile. "And who knows, maybe there'll be all sorts of good things that come out this weekend."

Jamie smiles back. "I guess that's why we're here."

"I thought we were here to talk about books."

"As if," Jamie says. "You know we spend most of our time just *chatting*."

"Life does seem to get in the way of literature sometimes."

"It's just a lot more complicated. Books don't have feelings, you know?" Jamie shrugs. Then she holds out her arms. Gives me a lopsided, sleepy grin. "Whatever. Now give me a hug, bitch."

And so I do.

14

Mariella,
mother of Zoey

Dio mio, coaxing feral cats into a bathtub must be easier than getting jet-lagged women to an early morning yoga class. It's not even 8 a.m. and we're already behind schedule. At this rate we'll be having dinner at midnight, and I am too old for that.

The yoga teacher, Silvia, owns a studio in Bellagio, but she does private classes for the rich and famous — and for me, too, although I'm poor by Lake Como standards and famous only in certain circles.

Grace, the only one to show up on time, tells me that I need to relax. "Maybe I could relax in the damn yoga class, if it ever even starts," I say.

Jamie shows up next, followed by one — no, both — of her daughters. "Kathleen," I cry, "you're here! Welcome, welcome!"

She says, "It's great to be here," although if you ask me, she does not sound convinced. I wonder what is going on with these twins and their strange attitudes. I hope I don't have to wait until the Night of Secrets to find out. More importantly, I hope they shape up, and quick. The weather is lovely and I don't need any black clouds.

Then Elin arrives with Brigid, who's already gone for a run. (As Zoey would say, *Overachiever alert!*) But it's another ten minutes before my beautiful, exasperating daughter staggers in. Merry slouches along behind her, yawning, bleary-eyed, and still in her striped pajamas.

"What did you two get up to last night?" I demand. "You didn't sneak out, did you? I know those Ricci boys are home."

Zoey blinks innocently. "We were just up late talking, Mommy!"

I know there is more to this story. She's lucky that class is finally beginning, or else I'd shake it out of her.

Silvia welcomes us with a bow and a smile and quickly begins class. "Bring your palms toward the center of your heart in prayer position," she says. "Close your eyes, and bring your awareness to your breath." Silvia's voice is a soothing alto. She speaks English well, with a beautiful Italian accent. "Take a deep inhale in through your nose, and feel it flow down into your belly."

I can feel my body releasing tension already.

"Now, I would like to invite you to set an intention for today's practice," Silvia says.

I intend for today to be perfect. No, wait, that's not right. I intend to relax. To stop worrying and loosen up. I intend to—

Bang!

I nearly jump out of my skin.

"Sorry," Kathleen calls. "I dropped my cane."

My stress comes back, multiplied. Her *cane*! Why on earth did I make Kathleen get up for exercise she can't even do?

But then I see that Silvia has already set up a folding chair, and she's directing Kathleen to sit. "You can do all the poses from here," she assures her. "I'll show you how."

Kathleen nods and thanks her. Crisis averted.

Everything's going to be fine, I think. *My intention for today's practice is to believe this to be true. Also, to relax. Yes.*

Back at the front of the room, Silvia instructs us to exhale and fold forward, keeping our spines straight. "Bring your hands to the mat beside your feet. On your next inhale, step your right leg back into a lunge..."

All my focus goes into my breath and toward following Silvia's gentle instructions. I feel my galloping thoughts slow. My body is stiff at first, but soon it starts to loosen up. I glide from Cobra pose into Downward Dog, then push forward into another lunge.

I'm already sweating. Yoga is hard! I'm grateful for my

thick, sturdy legs and my strong arms. I wish that I could always focus on what my body can do instead of what size pants it can fit into.

"Remember that yoga is not a performance but a *practice*," Silvia says gently. "And I believe that how we show up to our mat is how we show up to our lives."

We flow into Warrior II pose. She makes us hold it.

I want to show up to my life with hope, not worry, I think. *With love, not fear. But if she doesn't let us break this pose soon, I'm going to scream.*

We do Triangle, Half-Moon, Tree. I breathe, sweat, and stretch my muscles to their max. I can't think of anything else but making it to the end of class.

We finally get to lie down in Savasana. I'm completely spent. But I feel calmer than I have in months.

I should do yoga more often. Yoga is marvelous for singers: it improves breath control and it helps keep us strong and limber. People don't imagine that singing opera is tiring, but trust me, it is.

"Relax," Silvia tells us, "and let your inhalations and exhalations flow effortlessly into one another."

I close my eyes and breathe. Silvia puts on lovely harp music. Beside me, my daughter starts to snore.

15

Jamie,
mother of Meg and Kathleen

After yoga we have strong coffee and sweet Italian pastries on the terrace overlooking the lake. I devour a soft bun filled with whipped cream—a *maritozzo*, Mariella calls it—and then split a *cornetto*, a delicious Italian croissant, with Brigid.

"I'm officially ruined," I say, brushing crumbs from my shirt. "I'll never enjoy a bowl of Grape-Nuts again."

"But did you ever *truly* enjoy Grape-Nuts?" Elin muses as she slices another *cornetto* in half. "They're like a bowl full of tiny pebbles."

"They're like the gravel that kestrels eat to help them digest their prey," Kathleen calls.

I notice that my daughters have taken their pastries to opposite ends of the terrace. Kathleen is reading; Meg seems to be writing in her journal. *What will it take to bring them back together?* If I knew what to do, I'd do it in a heartbeat.

If only their father was around to help me.

After we clear our plates, Mariella announces that the next official MDBC activity is a boat ride on Lake Como. "So everyone put on your sunscreen and swimsuits and meet me in the driveway in thirty minutes!"

Elin and Grace nod like they know this already, and I wonder: Did I miss a memo? Or did Mariella just forget to tell me? I'm not one of the OG friends, so I understand.

Or I try to, anyway.

But there's an actual *problem* with going on a boat ride. I wonder who's going to say it first, me or Meg.

The answer is Meg. "I have adult-onset motion sickness," she says.

Mariella crosses her arms. "I have never heard of such a thing."

"I wish I was making it up. It started in college. I got a bunch of migraines my freshman year, and the next thing, I couldn't go on our boat without getting seasick," she says. "The last time I went out, I barfed like that girl from *The Exorcist.*"

Believe me, this is barely an exaggeration. But I also noticed — though I pretended I didn't — how much wine Meg drank last night. And a hangover on a choppy lake is hell on earth. Ask me how I know.

For a second, I think Mariella's going to freak out because Meg's messing with her painstaking planning. But she must be blissed out from yoga, because she says, "All right, no worries! In that case we will take a hike!"

I clear my throat uncomfortably. Who's going to point out the obvious issue this time?

Kathleen gives a quick, awkward laugh. "Um, I'm sorry, but I'm not so great with hiking these days," she says.

Mariella instantly pales. "Oh, my dear—what is wrong with me?" She shoves the end of a *cornetto* in her mouth and chews it quickly.

"Why don't we split up?" Elin asks sensibly. "Those who want to walk, walk, and those who want to sail, sail."

"The logical lawyer saves the day," Grace says.

"I am *sail*, 100 percent," I announce. There's nothing like flying over a lake on a summer day, wind and water and sun in your face. I had to sell our boat after the accident. It was Logan's baby—he'd bought it at auction and refurbished it himself—but I miss it to this day.

"I want to hike," Zoey says. "I know this amazing trail up into the hills right above Varenna. You guys will love it." She turns to Meg. "We have to take a super quick ferry ride to get there, but you *can't* get seasick on a ferry, I swear on my Jimmy Choos."

Meg grins. "Does that mean if I barf you have to give them to me?"

"Totally," Zoey says.

"Sounds good to me."

"Well, I am choosing the boat ride, because this is vacation," Mariella proclaims. "On the boat there will be cushioned seats and a cooler full of cold drinks. On a hike there will be bugs, dust, and tap water from an ancient canteen."

"I'm going to burn calories," Zoey counters. "You're just going to *consume* them."

"Fine! I will hike too!" Mariella hollers.

Before they can really start bickering, Grace says, "I think a boat ride sounds incredible."

And Elin goes, "Boaters are best!" and I yell, "Damn straight!" And then Brigid and Zoey start teasing us, calling us lazy, and everyone is laughing and getting excited for the next activity.

Well, almost everyone.

Who's about to have the most fun is a friendly competition between everyone *except* my daughters. They barely even look at each other.

I ask myself for the thousandth time: *Why does tragedy bring some people together and tear others apart?*

16

Brigid, daughter of Elin

I already ran five miles and did an hour of yoga, so what I'd most like to do is park my butt on a boat. But Jamie's going on the boat trip, and it's a bad idea for us to be in close proximity right now. She thinks keeping her big secret is going to be easy, but I know Jamie: she won't be able to resist asking me for reassurances that I've handled everything correctly, and that all is going according to plan. And then eagle-eyed Mariella will get up in our faces, and she'll demand to know what we're whispering about, and one of us is going to crack. Probably me.

Jamie would be furious if I did, but sometimes I think I should just tell everyone what's at stake. The whole situation is so complicated, and I don't know the best way to handle the information. Medical school taught me all about the human body but much less about emotions in times of hardship. What I *do* know is that if I were Jamie, I wouldn't be keeping any of this to myself.

But I made my promise and I'm doing my best to keep it, which is why I hopped onto the ferry with Zoey, Mariella, and Meg (who did not get seasick) and am now dragging my tired body through the narrow alleyways of picturesque Varenna instead of sipping sparkling mineral water in the middle of a sparkling lake.

I have to admit, though, the walk is fantastic. Zoey is leading us from the picturesque Piazza San Giorgio to the Castle of Vezio, high on a bluff above this pretty town. She's a very good tour guide.

"Vezio is an ancient military outpost, built by a queen called Theodolinda," she calls over her shoulder. "And FYI, it's absolutely *crawling* with ghosts."

Meg stops in her tracks. I run right into her back. "Count me out, then," she says.

Mariella, who's huffing and puffing behind us but nevertheless looking glamorous in a white sundress and Dior sunglasses, cries, "Zoey, enough of your nonsense."

But Zoey just smiles mischievously.

"Come on, Meg," I say gently. "Speaking as a scientist — and a doctor who's seen a lot of dead people — I promise, you're not going to see any ghosts."

"Wait a minute. How *many* dead people? Aren't doctors supposed to keep their patients alive?" Zoey teases.

"My track record is excellent," I tell her. "Don't worry."

Meg grimaces. But then she sighs and starts walking again.

Heading steadily uphill, we pass a tiny walled cemetery full of flowers. It's so colorful and pretty, I have to stop and take a picture. (Only in Italy would a cemetery look like the perfect place for a picnic.) After we climb a set of ancient stone stairs, my quads are really starting to burn. I try to ignore them as we wind through trees with narrow, almost silvery leaves and tiny black fruits.

"These are actually the northernmost olive groves in Italy," Zoey says. "Olives have been cultivated in the Lake Como area since the first century BC." She plucks an olive off a tree. "Here, try one."

I laugh and shake my head. "Raw olives aren't edible, Zoey."

She flashes a wicked grin. "I know. But I was hoping you didn't."

I turn around. The sapphire-blue lake glitters below us. I shield my eyes from the sun to get a better view. "Beautiful, isn't it?"

Beside me, Meg just shrugs.

"Beautiful, yes, but I can see nearly the same view from my terrace, and I don't have to break such a sweat to do it," says Mariella, stopping to catch her breath. "*Dio mio,* I hope we get there soon."

Except after we get to the castle, we're heading into the hills, climbing high enough to get panoramic views of Lake Como, the Grigne mountains, and maybe even the Swiss Alps. At least that's what Zoey says. "Don't you dare tell my mom," she'd whispered to me earlier. "She'll die."

I wonder how many secrets one weekend can hold.

After another set of steps, we come to the top of the bluff. We've made it to the grounds outside the ancient walls of the Castello di Vezio. I stop under the shade of a big larch and stretch out my aching calves. Meg looks to the right and gives an ear-piercing shriek.

A white, faceless ghost is perched on a railing overlooking the lake.

My heart does a little flip. *What the —*

Zoey skips over, grinning. "Amazing, right? Every year, people drape volunteers in gauze and plaster. They sit there until it's dry, and then—voilà!—a plaster ghost!" Then her voice gets quiet and dramatically spooky. "But people swear that Queen Theodolinda's heart and soul remain inside the castle, and at night her specter wanders through the cold stone halls…"

Mariella swats her daughter with her sun hat. "Oh, hush, child," she says. She turns to me. "Doc, isn't there something you can give my daughter to make her less of a pest?"

I laugh. "Sorry, I'm not aware of any prescriptions for that."

"Well, I hope you'll start looking into the possibilities

immediately." She takes off her oversize sunglasses and looks me right in the eye. "What *are* you working on these days, darling? Any fascinating new research projects?"

I feel a flare of anxiety in my stomach. I absolutely cannot tell Mariella the truth. So I keep my answer vague. "Well, back in the Boston lab, we've been doing work on regenerative medicine and tissue engineering."

"Tissue engineering—is that as gross as it sounds?" Zoey asks.

But before I can answer, she whips out her phone. "Okay, everyone, gather up and strike a pose. Pics or it didn't happen!"

She squishes us together and proceeds to take at least fifty photos—with the ghost in the background, of course—and then scrolls through them, trying to decide which ones to post to whichever social media account needs content. You gotta love Zoey Marciano: she's got the charm of a beauty queen and the attention span of a gnat.

Mariella is still focused on me, though. She's not as distractible as her daughter is. My little flare of anxiety grows bigger.

"Go on," she says.

Just keep it vague, Brigid. "The brain is an amazing organ," I tell her. "As a neurologist, I feel very privileged to study it. And to *wonder* about it. For example, how can a few pounds of squishy gray jelly allow us to experience and enjoy all this incredible beauty?" I point to the gorgeous sky dotted with cottony clouds, to the flowers buzzing with bees.

"Yes! And how does this squishy jelly make us hike up endless Italian hills?" Mariella asks. "Even when we don't really want to?"

"Well, the motor cortex sends signals to the muscles in your legs," I say, "and to the other parts of your body involved in walking, which include—"

Mariella interrupts me. "But what happens when those signals can't get through? When the brain can't talk to the legs anymore? What do you do then?"

I know exactly what she's asking me. And I know what she wants me to say. But even though it's my area of expertise, it's not my story to tell.

17

Elin,
mother of Brigid

I've gone boating a hundred times before, but never in a craft this luxurious. The *Dolce Vita* seats eight and is the Bentley of boats. It's got a wine-red lacquered hull, and its bench cushions are white leather. There's even a small but comfortable cabin, with polished wood and brass detailing, should we want a little shade.

As I settle back into my seat, with the golden sun on my face, I'm practically maxed out for pleasure — and we're still in the no-wake zone.

How did I get this lucky?

I know that I shouldn't ask that question. The last time I did, something terrible happened. Three years later, we're still feeling its effects. But today is so wonderful. Am I supposed to pretend like it isn't?

As we glide away from the dock, the village's colorful buildings grow smaller behind us. The boat picks up speed. My hair tickles my cheeks. Deliciously cool water droplets land on my arms. I'm entranced by the beautiful view. But Grace is entranced by our captain.

"Kind of an Italian stallion, isn't he?" Grace says to me, nodding at his broad back.

I give a surprised laugh. Grace is generally quite proper — not the type to make thirsty comments. But I have to admit, I definitely noticed him when we boarded, and I agree with her. "He kind of looks like a more mature version of the guy who seduced Jennifer Coolidge in season one of *White Lotus*."

Grace nods. "I can see that. Although that guy got less appealing in season two when he tried to kill her. So all in all, I think our captain's much hotter."

The captain cuts the engine and turns around to smile at us. Grace's eyes widen. Mine, too.

"Did he overhear us talking about him?" she whispers.

"Don't worry," I whisper back. "His English probably isn't that great."

At least I hope it isn't.

My hopes are quickly dashed when the captain begins speaking without a trace of a European accent. "Well, ladies," he says, smiling, "my name is Daniel Asher, and it's a perfect day! Are you ready for an incredible tour of Italy's most gorgeous, romantic lake?"

Grace blurts out, "You're not *Italian*?"

And Merry goes, "*Mom*, be quiet! What does it matter?"

As for me, well—I just have to laugh.

Daniel's dark eyes flash with amusement. "You're right, I'm not Italian. I'm actually from Vermont. Which is a very beautiful state, but not nearly as beautiful as this." He gestures toward the blue-green water. "Lake Como is the deepest lake in all of Italy, and one of the deepest lakes in all of Europe. It was created during the last ice age, when multiple glaciers pushed down from the Alps, carving out deep valleys that later filled with water."

"Fascinating," Grace says.

"There's probably close to six trillion gallons of water in it. The temperature is usually between sixty-eight and seventy-five degrees Fahrenheit in the summer—perfect for water sports."

"You don't say!"

Grace is clearly going to hang on his every word. I try to catch her daughter's eye—I want to see if she's noticing this too—but Merry's busy scanning the sky through Kathleen's binoculars. I remember Kathleen mentioning that she'd gotten into bird-watching in the wake of the accident. Her mother, Jamie, meanwhile, is taking a million pictures with her phone. I suck in my stomach in case I'm in any of the shots.

"This whole area was under the ocean in the Mesozoic era," Daniel goes on. "But about sixty-five million years ago, the Alps started rising, and eventually they rose above sea level—and now look at them."

"Do people ever find marine fossils in the rock?" Grace asks.

I doubt she truly cares. She just wants to keep this handsome man talking.

As for me, I let my mind wander. I'm not interested in the unique composition of the region's sedimentary rocks. But I am *very* interested in a Lake Como flirtation between my beautiful single friend Grace and a handsome sailor with no wedding ring on his finger.

A love affair is too much to hope for, obviously. But I'm going to do it anyway. Why not? Maybe at this gathering of the MDBC, something that's life-changing in a *good* way can happen.

"Hey," Kathleen exclaims, "I think that's a short-toed snake eagle!" She grabs the binoculars from Merry.

I glance skyward and see a pale winged shape soaring high over our heads.

"The Italians call them *biancone*," Daniel says. "It means big white. But I think short-toed snake eagle is a much better name."

"Oh, definitely," says Grace.

Rein it in a little, Grace, I think. But the captain seems charmed by her attention. He smiles broadly at her before turning back to the wheel. Maybe he's reached the end of his Lake Como geology and ornithology knowledge, and Grace will have to find some other topic to draw him out again.

We fly along the eastern shore of the lake's upper branch, passing stately villas and charming cottages nestled among lush gardens and emerald-green trees.

After a little while, the boat decelerates, sliding through the water with barely a sound. We're approaching a shore lined with beautiful stone buildings. A village of red-roofed homes clings to the steep hillside behind them.

"Get ready for something truly spectacular," he calls over his shoulder.

I look over at Grace and grin. "'Truly spectacular' would be Captain Daniel taking his shirt off," I whisper. "Don't you think?"

She flushes bright pink. Giggles. Nods *yes*.

He steers the boat underneath an old stone bridge that arcs over a ravine, connecting two of the waterfront buildings. Suddenly we're in a small, shadowy gorge. Steep cliffs rise dramatically from the water on either side of us. Lush greenery clings to the rocks. The temperature has dropped five degrees.

"This," he says, "is l'Orrido di Nesso. It's a natural gorge formed by the waters of two streams."

"It's so beautiful," I say.

"Isn't it? Though *orrido* actually means horrid."

"It's the most amazing thing I've ever seen," Grace says in an awestruck voice.

A waterfall at the end of the gorge pours white froth into the blue-green water. Behind us I hear a splash as someone jumps off the stone bridge into the lake.

Daniel tosses an anchor over the side of the boat, then turns to us and grins. "All right, ladies, who's ready for a swim?"

18

Zoey, daughter of Mariella

I don't know what Meg's problem is, but I'm going to get to the bottom of it.

I sidle up alongside the younger Price twin as we hike the wooded trail behind Vezio Castle. "Sorry about the ghost thing," I say.

"No worries," she says. "I've just watched too many horror movies lately."

"Luna and I order pizza and watch horror movies every Sunday night. We just streamed *Longlegs*. Have you seen it?"

"Yeah, it got under my skin for sure."

I wait a beat, then ask, "How's it going, like, in general these days?" I keep my tone light, as if it's a totally innocent question. Which it isn't. I'm dying to know why she was so pissy yesterday. Why did she say she was going to leave? And how come she didn't?

I'm glad Meg stayed, of course. My mom would've freaked out if she'd left, and it would've ruined Jamie's weekend completely. Plus, I actually love Meg, even if I'm not as close to her as I am to Brigid and Merry. That's because, while the age difference doesn't matter now, back when Bridge was twelve and Merry and I were ten, we thought the twins, who were six, were babies. It wasn't until recently that it started feeling like we're all basically the same age.

Anyway, Meg doesn't answer my question. We keep climbing the gentle slope. When we pass the crumbling ruins of a stone cottage, I'm tempted to make another ghost joke. Or mention how we're not far from the Villa de Vecchi, a.k.a. the Ghost Mansion. A woman was brutally murdered there in the 1800s, and unlike Vezio, I think it might be haunted for real. But maybe that's not the best way to get her talking.

I try again. "Seriously, Meg. Is everything okay?"

She lifts a shoulder, a kind of half shrug. "'Okay' sounds about right. I wish it was better."

Better? There's literally nothing better than Italy in late June! Meg clearly brought her problems, along with her carry-ons, to Lake Como. "I'm sorry," I say. And I really do mean it. "Is there anything I can do?"

"You can fix me a big drink when we get back to the house." She smiles at me, but it looks a little forced.

"Done," I say. I know we're all on vacation — and I started it with the Negronis yesterday — but something about her attitude has me wondering if Meg often day-drinks like this back in Chicago. I push a little more. "I definitely have more cocktails when I'm around Mariella. Stress relief, you know?" I laugh. I glance back at my mom, who looks like she's being dragged up the hill by Brigid. I feel a sharp stab of love for her. Love mixed with frustration. She needs to exercise more. This hike isn't that hard. "Families are tough sometimes," I add. "Even on vacation."

"I just... I just feel like I lost my best friend," Meg blurts out.

I'm so surprised by this confession that I actually trip on the rocky path. But I don't fall, thank God, and I don't think Meg even notices.

I know if I sound too eager to hear more, she'll clam up. So I say softly, "Really? I'm sorry."

It seems like that's all she wants to say. But I'm good at getting people to open up. My graduating class voted me Most Likely to Become Oprah. My voice is gentle when I say, "I'm guessing you mean Kathleen."

Meg nods. "We were so close."

"I remember."

"You know how some sets of twins have, like, a special

private language? We never did, because we didn't need one. We literally just knew what the other one was thinking."

"Like ESP or something?" I'm dubious.

"Almost! We were so *connected*. Even when we went away to college, we talked every night, and we texted a hundred times a day."

Meg pauses. Meanwhile we keep climbing along the sun-dappled path, with little white butterflies flitting around us. We're almost to the top of the hill. This time, I don't have to prod her to go on.

"But after the accident, *everything* changed," she says. Her voice sounds thick. She blinks away tears. "And it's all my fault."

"How could that be?" I ask, incredulous. "It was an accident, Meg. You weren't even driving!"

Out of the corner of my eye I can see Meg's lips pressed together in a hard, thin line.

"I just fucked up, Zoey," she says fiercely. "I fucked up big-time."

"What do you mean?"

She shakes her head. "I can't talk about it anymore. I'm sorry."

We crest the hill in strained silence. At the top, we turn around in slow circles, taking in the view as we wait for Brigid and Mom to catch up. I know I should be appreciating all this insane beauty—the wildflowers, the azure sky, the freaking *Alps*—but I can't stop wondering about what Meg meant when she said it was all her fault. I'm trying to figure out how to ask her when my mom comes over, sweating, panting, and hollering, "Group hug, group hug!" at the top of her giant opera-singer lungs.

My mom is so, so extra. I pull Meg close to one side of me and my mom to the other, and then Brigid puts her arms around all of us.

"We made it, *grazie al cielo*!" my mom cries. "We are badass mountaineers!" She mops her brow dramatically. "And now let's get off this damn hill and go eat some *lunch*."

"Not quite yet, Mommy." I let go of Meg and pull out my phone. "You know what I always say: Pics or it didn't happen!"

But less than a minute later, Meg bolts.

Literally.

She takes off like she's running an Olympic one-hundred-meter dash.

I'm left standing there, thinking *WTF*? And so is everyone else.

19

Jamie,
mother of Meg and Kathleen

A chance to swim? The captain doesn't have to tell *me* twice. I'm the first one in, though Elin and Merry quickly follow. I dive from the side of the boat, plunging deep. I swim down, down, down. The cold lake gets colder. The water pressure increases. I'm being squeezed by the lake. It's like a full-body hug. When my lungs start to burn, I swim up and break the surface. I take a deep breath and then dive back down and do it all over again, four, five, six times. I can't see anything but my own hands in front of me, white as ghosts.

Underwater, phrases come rushing back to me. Things that the doctors said after the accident in Lake Geneva. *Buoyancy reduces the force of gravity on the immersed joints. Hydrostatic pressure assists in the dissipation of edema.*

Doctors have fancy terms for everything. What they meant was: being in water is relaxing. It reduces swelling.

And they're right. It helps. But it doesn't *fix* anything.

The patient's prognostic trajectory remains indeterminate at this juncture.

A spectrum of outcomes are possible, contingent upon evolving clinical parameters and therapeutic responses.

It took me a while to realize what they meant. Here's my translation: *Even though we're doctors, we don't have any fucking idea what's going to happen next.*

That was just one of a million things that sucked.

I'm running out of oxygen now. I turn back toward the surface, pushing myself toward sunlight and air. I come up gasping.

Kathleen's leaning over the side of the boat, looking worried. "Mom! I was just about to send Captain Daniel in after you!"

"It's beautiful," I tell her. "You should come in!"

"I'll dip my toes in later."

"But Kathleen, water is so good for—"

"Mom," she says, her voice cold and annoyed. "I'll get in when I'm ready."

My poor, angry daughter! I would give anything to make her feel better. If only the universe worked that way.

I grab the ladder and pull myself out, shivering and dripping. Everyone else is back in the boat by now. Elin hands me a thick, soft towel. I bury my face in it.

"Ready to continue the tour?" Captain Daniel asks.

I nod, shivering.

As our captain maneuvers the boat back into the main part of the lake, I carefully reapply sunscreen. Then I hold out the bottle to Kathleen. With our pale Irish skin, we burn quickly. "Don't end up looking like a cooked lobster."

"I'm not a *child*, Mom," she says, sounding mildly aggravated. "I already put some on."

"Sorry," I say. "Old habits die hard."

My pretty, freckled daughter smiles at me; I'm forgiven. But I remember when I could do no wrong in her eyes. I remember when she called me Mama and held my hand in the grocery store. Now when I see mothers in the park with their little girls in their little pink dresses, I'm jealous. And when I see women strolling down the street with their husbands, I'm jealous of that, too.

But I don't want to think about the past. Just for once, I don't want to think about Logan.

As we speed along, Captain Daniel tells us that Bellagio is known as "the Pearl of Lake Como." He slows down to point out the Villa del Balbianello, which appeared in *Casino Royale*, and the Grand Hotel Villa Serbelloni with its adjacent Villa Serbelloni, now known as the Rockefeller Foundation

Bellagio Center, which Mary Shelley, the author of *Frankenstein*, praised in her travels.

"What if we'd all lived in a place like the Villa del Balbianello, Jamie?" Elin asks. "Look at those terraced gardens. That ornate stonework. Those huge windows overlooking the lake. It's too much! Can you imagine being that rich?"

I can barely imagine feeling like I've got enough money to pay the bills, so no, I can't imagine it. But I don't want to spoil the mood. I smile. "It's so enormous that we never would've been able to find our kids!"

"We wouldn't have to," says Elin, laughing. "Our servants would find them for us. We'd just ring a bell and *poof*, there they are."

"While we're sunning ourselves in the garden."

"Exactly."

Maybe, in that fantasy life, Elin and I would've just been *friends*. Without the lingering boss and employee labels. But I feel closer to Elin now, having said what I did earlier. I didn't know how badly I needed to get that particular secret off my chest.

20

Grace,
mother of Merry

"Look at her go," Captain Daniel says, watching Elin race through the water like Katie Ledecky at our second swim stop. "She claimed she didn't even want to get in."

"She was like that in college, too," I tell him. "She never liked cold water. She dreaded that first dive into the pool at practice. But you should've seen her at a meet! No hesitation there. She'd win her event by a mile."

"Impressive. But how come you aren't swimming?"

I can hardly tell him the truth, which is that I want to keep talking to him. "I just ate all that cheese and crackers. It hasn't been half an hour."

"You know that's a myth, right?"

"It is?"

"Yep. Also, reading in dim light doesn't damage your eyesight."

I laugh. "That I knew. I take my reading very seriously."

He squints out over the water, making sure his passengers are safe. We're the only ones left on board. Everyone else is in the lake. "What are you reading right now?" he asks.

I count them on my fingers. "Well, let's see, there's *Brat Farrar* by Josephine Tey, and *The Hunter* by Tana French, and *A Start in Life* by Anita Brookner..." I pause. "I know I brought at least two others, but for some reason I can't think of what they are."

"That's even more impressive," he says. "I used to read a lot. Now, not so much."

Well, he can't be totally perfect; that would be ridiculous. I'm trying to figure out what to say next when Jamie hauls herself up the ladder and comes into the boat, dripping water everywhere.

"That was amazing," she says, reaching for a towel.

Captain Daniel turns to me. "Last chance."

I shake my head. "I'll stay dry, I think." *And next to you.*

But then he checks his watch and realizes the time; he calls everyone back to the boat to continue the tour. "I'm booked to take a bunch of Texans out this afternoon," he explains.

We zip along, dodging speedboats and slow double-decker ferries. The view is never less than spectacular, and Jamie takes about a million pictures. I want to keep talking to our captain, but Daniel's focused on steering, and the wind is loud, and I can't figure out how to keep our conversation going.

All too soon, Captain Daniel informs us that it's time to return to the dock.

"Tutte le cose belle devono finire," he says. "All good things must come to an end." He smiles wistfully.

Does his gaze linger on me just a second longer than it needed to?

No, no—that's wishful thinking. The fantasy of a lonely romantic. I may be depressed, but at least I'm not delusional.

The closer the dock gets, the heavier my heart feels. Even my stomach's unsettled. For a while I chalked it up to motion sickness. But it didn't go away when the water was smooth. It didn't go away when Captain Daniel stopped the boat. And it didn't go away when we sailed around the beautiful lake. So now I have to call it what it is: the physical symptom of a sudden, intense crush.

Leave it to me to fall for someone who lives four thousand miles away. Someone I barely know anything about.

I tell myself that Captain Daniel's this charming to every boatload of ladies. It's part of his job. It means bigger tips. It means great reviews on Google.

He's probably got a beautiful Italian girlfriend.

But there isn't a wife, or an ex-wife. I know this because Elin flat-out asked him. Lawyers are used to asking people blunt questions, I guess. She said, "How come somebody hasn't snapped you up?"

And the way he answered gave me pause. He hesitated for a moment, and then he said that he'd come close to marriage once. "But it wasn't to be." And the way he said it made it sound like he hadn't been the one to end things. Like he'd had his heart broken.

I've talked to so many brokenhearted people in my line of work. Believe me, I wanted to put my arms around him right then. Partly out of habit—I'm a hugger—and partly out of desire. Instead, I just wrapped my arms around myself, like I was trying to keep warm.

I wish this boat ride would never end, but Bellagio, with its pastel-hued grand hotels lining the lakefront, is growing ever nearer. And all too soon, we're coming up on the dock. Captain Daniel ties the *Dolce Vita* to its berth. Then he clambers out and reaches down to help us out of the boat. I linger on the luxurious bench seat. I'm going to be the last member of the MDBC to put my feet on dry land. The last one he says good-bye to.

When it's my turn to disembark, I reach up to take Captain Daniel's hand. Touching it, I feel an almost electric shock, a thrill shooting through my entire body. I suppress a gasp. Daniel smiles down at me. Did he feel it too? I have no way of knowing. His skin is warm and calloused. He gives a gentle tug, and I step up onto the worn wooden dock.

"Thank you," I say warmly. "That was the boat trip of a lifetime."

He smiles. The corners of his eyes crinkle. "It was my pleasure. I enjoyed talking to you, Grace."

My friends and my daughter have already walked off the dock and are back onshore. I can sense them watching me.

"Same." I don't want to leave. But they're all waiting for me. "I guess I should go," I say. My cheeks are burning hot. I don't know why.

Oh, yes you do, Grace Townsend!

Captain Daniel's dark eyes sparkle. "Or... you could stay and have lunch with me."

I'm so surprised by this offer that the first thing that comes out of my mouth is the opposite of what I mean. "Oh, no," I say, "I couldn't."

He cocks his head. Looks at me quizzically. "Are you sure about that? You could tell me all about the books I ought to read."

I'm uncertain, wavering, and he can see this. He hooks his thumb behind him, gesturing to a large sign that reads LA GOLETTA. "It's a great restaurant," he says.

I give another glance over to my friends. Then I turn back to Captain Daniel. "On second thought," I say, "yes. I'd love to."

This goes against my entire nature. I'm not spontaneous like Zoey, or a planner, the way her mother, Mariella, is, but I am and always have been extremely, extremely cautious. But suddenly, here I am in Italy, about to throw caution to the wind.

"Great," he says. "But there's just one thing. And it might be a deal-breaker."

My heart gives a lurch. He *does* have a girlfriend. "What is it?"

"You have to call me Dan. Or Danny."

I start laughing. That's *it*? That's the deal-breaker? I try to compose myself. I look very serious when I say, "Those terms are acceptable. But then you have to call me Reverend Grace."

The captain's smile—I mean, *Danny's* smile—widens. "Absolutely," he says.

Then he holds out his arm, and I tuck mine through it, and we walk toward the restaurant with the blue, blue lake glittering behind us.

21

Meg,
daughter of Jamie

The group hug is annoying, but I deal with it. It's Zoey Marciano, Little Miss Influencer, who sends me over the edge.

Thumb-typing, she chirps, "Hashtag *hike*, hashtag *Summer Fridays lip gloss*, hashtag *girl squad*. Ladies, this is perfect. And now....*post!*" Grinning, she shows the rest of us her phone screen.

My face goes hot with anger. I'd thought Zoey was taking pictures for Instagram, but she was taking a video. She captured her mom collapsing onto a rock. Brigid moaning as she massaged her calves. And me cursing my blistered heels and sweating last night's booze out of every pore.

To make matters worse, she'd cut a lightning-fast edit and put it on TikTok, set to a clip of Benson Boone's "Beautiful Things." I hate Benson Boone even more than I hate TikTok.

Everyone else thinks the video is hilarious. I'm practically shaking with anger. I didn't really want to come on the hike in the first place, and I *definitely* don't want to be part of Zoey Marciano's social media content.

"You okay, Meg?" Zoey asks, peering into my face.

She doesn't get an answer. Because I'm done. I'm sprinting away down the path. I hear them shouting after me, but I don't care. Despite my blisters, it feels good to run.

By the time I'm nearing the castle, running doesn't feel good at all anymore. My muscles are aching. My lungs are screaming. I'm dying to stop but I keep going. Running away from all of them.

Wishing I could run away from myself.

I'm so sick of how messed up I feel. And how messed up my life's been for the past three years. I don't know what I'm doing or where I'm going. I struggle to write, even though I want to do it more than anything.

When I get to the edge of the village, I bend over to catch my breath. Next thing I know, I'm sobbing. What the *hell*? I stand up again, start walking. Slowly. I've got a cramp in my side. Tears and snot are streaming down my face. Italians are looking at me like, *What's wrong with that tourist?* Not that they really care. I'm just another stupid American to them. I only stand out because of my misery.

I find the ferry, but afterwards I can't remember how to get back to Mariella's. I get lost somewhere in the winding streets and end up outside the gate of a white stone mansion. Guard dogs bark furiously. They'd tear my throat out if they could get to me, and I almost wish they could.

I retrace my steps. Take a different narrow road. I'm still lost but at least I'm not crying anymore. Pretty soon I think I see a familiar gate. *Finally.* It feels like it took forever, but I'm still the first one here.

Mariella's husband, Mike, is in the kitchen with Lucia. I try to sneak by, but he spots me.

"Well, if it isn't Meg Price, hello, hello, kiddo! Long time no see!" Mike exclaims. He hurries toward me, wiping his hands on a long linen apron. The next thing I know I'm getting bear-hugged by Zoey's sweet, paunchy dad. He smells like sautéed garlic and raw onions. It's a familiar, comforting smell. Add in a whiff of cigarettes, and Mike would be the olfactory copy of every line cook at Giovanni's, the old-school fancy restaurant where I work.

When he lets me go, he takes a step back and peers at me. "You all right?" he asks.

"Yeah," I say, turning my face away so he won't be able to see my red, puffy eyes. "Just a little tired." My stomach growls.

"I bet you're hungry, too! Lucky for you, my dear, lunch is ready!"

"Shouldn't I wait for the others?" *Say no,* I think, *please say no.* I suddenly realize that I'm starving. Food will make me feel better.

"They must be right behind you. Please, sit down."

Mike pulls out my chair. I sink down at the table set for ten, and he immediately starts bringing me plates of food.

"Here is some stracciatella and prosciutto, if you want. Do you like olives?"

My mouth's already full, but Mike isn't going to wait for my answer anyway. He comes back with a beautiful bowl of multicolored olives brightened by thin curls of orange peel.

"Flavored with coriander seeds, bay leaves, garlic, and *arancia del Gargano,*" he tells me. "My secret recipe."

A moment later, he brings a plate of pasta. "This is *gnocchetti alla chiavennascha.* Little gnocchi made with breadcrumbs."

"It looks amazing."

"It tastes even better, I promise."

I almost feel like crying again. But this time it's out of gratitude. I can't remember the last time someone took care of me like this. So calmly and effortlessly. My mom tries to when I visit—she'll shoo me out of the kitchen and refuse my offer to help—but then she'll burn the rice or forget to take the salmon off the grill in time. She's perpetually wound up because she has so much on her mind.

As for my dad? Well, the last time he could take care of me was more than three years ago.

Mike keeps coming out from the kitchen to check on me while I eat. In between bites, I tell him how great it is. Mike's lunch makes the food at Giovanni's taste like Olive Garden in comparison. Which, don't get me wrong, has its place—but fine dining it ain't.

I'm just mopping up the last of the gnocchi sauce with a sliver of crusty bread when I hear the front door open. The sound of laughter. Excited chatter. And my mother's oh-so-familiar voice.

I quickly stand up. "Thank you, Mike, I think this was the best lunch I've ever eaten."

And then I'm out of there, before the boat ride group even makes it halfway down the front hall.

22

Merry,
daughter of Grace

I feel crispy from the sun and the swimming, and I'm dying to take a shower. A nap would be great, too, because I was up all night, believing that I was a flower. How embarrassing! Though I'm a little surprised to admit that I don't regret it.

But it's soon clear that neither a shower nor a nap is going to happen anytime soon. Zoey, Brigid, and Mariella are back from their hike, walking in right behind us, and Zoey's dad is in full hosting mode.

"Welcome back! Time to eat! *Mangiamo,*" Mike exclaims, beaming at us. He darts into the kitchen, reemerging with Lucia, both of them carrying heaping plates of food.

"A feast worthy of a Roman emperor!" Elin says giddily.

"That reminds me—did anyone read that book about them by Mary Beard?"

"I only read novels, you know that," Mariella chides.

"I heard an interview with her," Elin says. "She talked about an emperor who smothered his dinner guests to death by showering them with millions of rose petals."

Mike looks alarmed as he sets an antipasto platter down. "We keep our rose petals in the garden, don't worry."

"Where is..." Lucia points to her dyed black hair. "Pretty lady, with silver?"

"She's probably been kidnapped," I say.

Lucia looks at me blankly. Mariella explains. "She is having lunch with the man who took us on our boat tour," she says. "She is fine."

"But we don't know that for sure," I say.

I'm still trying to decide whether to be happy for my mom—or worried about her sanity. I mean, who is this Captain Daniel guy? He could be a total psycho for all we know. I'm used to her making friends with people wherever she goes. That always happens. But she doesn't go off and have private lunches with them in countries she's never been to before. I don't know what to think.

"Okay, beautiful ladies, your attention please." Mike points to the platters in front of us. "This is tagliatelle with cured salmon, black garlic, and ricotta cheese. And this is poached sturgeon with fennel and herbs. Over there is little baby gnocchi, and of course, a salad made with radicchio, wild arugula, and shaved Parmigiano Reggiano."

"Incredible. How many Michelin stars does your kitchen have, Mike?" Elin asks.

"Eleven!" Mariella cries, which is ridiculous, and causes us all to burst into laughter. Not that I've ever eaten at a Michelin-starred restaurant—there aren't any in Bridgeport, and I couldn't afford it if there were—but even I know that the most you can get is three.

I help myself to the tagliatelle. It tastes even more incredible than I'd imagined: creamy, salty, perfectly *al dente*.

"He deserves twelve stars," I say, and Mike takes a happy bow.

Mike is a food snob, he'd be the first to admit. But there's nothing snobby about him otherwise, even though he inherited a family fortune at age twenty-five. Instead of living off that, though, he worked his way up through the film ranks to become a cinematographer. One of his movies was even nominated for an Oscar. But he got tired of the long shoots, the endless scramble for funding, and the constant travel. He retired early and started helping manage Mariella's career.

And he took cooking classes. A *lot* of them. So now he Face-Times with Ina Garten, and he's been on two episodes of Stanley Tucci's *Searching for Italy*.

He asks how the boat ride went. Elin and Jamie are right in the middle of telling him how amazing it was when I blurt out, "Seriously, what if he takes her somewhere and holds her for ransom?"

Everyone turns to look at me. I can feel my whole face and chest getting hot. Just like my mom, I flush easily, but I don't care. "She just went off with him!" I insist. "We don't know anything about that guy!"

Kathleen's looking at me like I'm nuts.

"Did you watch *White Lotus,* too?" Elin asks.

"What are you even talking about? How do we know we can trust this guy?"

"He's a *tour guide,*" Kathleen says. "From *Vermont.* He's paid to take care of rich tourists. Not kidnap them."

Elin pats my hand. "I know, it seems out of character for your mom. But don't worry, she's fine. In fact, I'm willing to bet she's having the time of her life."

"You are too young to be so suspicious," Mariella says.

I realize I'm holding my shoulders tight up around my ears. I let them drop with a sigh. But I can't relax. "I know you think I'm crazy. But I'm also a social worker. Every single day, I see people get hurt—by someone who's supposed to love and take care of them. A husband hits his wife. A mother burns her son with a cigarette. A teen father locks his toddler in the basement because she spilled a cup of milk."

I can feel tears threatening to well up. "Every. Single. Day," I repeat. "Do you know how hard it is to see things like that? It makes me feel like it's impossible to trust anyone." I brush the back of my hand across my eyes; it comes away wet. "And that includes boomer boat captains, however handsome they may be."

Elin comes around the table to put her arms around me. Hugging me from behind, she smells like lake water. Like sunscreen. Like a mom.

But not *my* mom, who went off with a hot rando without even warning me. "Honey," Elin says quietly. "I hear you. And now I want you to hear me, too, okay? Your mom is fine. I promise. I never would've let her go if it was in any way unsafe."

I take a deep inhale. Of course Elin's right. But my mind's still spinning, imagining everything that could go wrong. Maybe he's a total creep. Maybe he seduces all the lonely women he meets. Maybe he really is married.

My mom's been down lately, I can sense it. She's vulnerable, and he could take advantage of that.

"You see people during the hardest times of their lives, Merry," Elin goes on. "That doesn't make everyone in the world bad. It doesn't even make *those* people bad. It just means they're struggling, and sometimes they really screw things up."

I hear what she's saying, I do. But the truth is, some people *are* bad. I've met them. I've been afraid of them, and I've been furious at them, and I've still tried to help them. Every single day.

"You trust me, right?" she asks.

"Of course I do." Elin's like an aunt to me. I've known her for as long as I can remember.

"So trust me when I say that you can relax, sweetie. Captain Daniel is a fine man."

Elin gives me another squeeze and then lets go. As she walks away, I start to wonder if my worry is really about my mom at all. Reverend Grace has always been able to take care of herself. But I can't say the same about a lot of the clients I work with at my job.

While I'm here in beautiful Lake Como, the kids I serve are still stuck in their daily lives, some of which are horrific beyond imagining. "I'm not used to being away from my cases," I admit. "Maybe part of the reason I'm on edge is that I'm trying not to think about my clients, but deep down I'm still worried about them."

"Of course you are," Elin says. "But they're surviving without you. And they'll be there when you get back."

"Will they ever," I say grimly. I stab one of Mike's special olives with my fork. "Part of me dreads going back. And another part can't wait to be there to start fixing things again."

"You're just like your mother," Jamie says. "You both want to make things better for everyone."

"My mother's a good person to be like." I try my best to smile.

"Hmmm, if you're so similar, maybe you'll have a Lake Como romance, too."

"I'll call the Ricci brothers," Zoey says. "If I liked boys, I'd totally have the hots for them."

"No you will not call the Ricci brothers," says her mother, and the two of them bicker good-naturedly through the rest of lunch.

23

Grace,
mother of Merry

Captain Daniel—I mean Danny—leads me from the bustling dock toward the lakeside restaurant, which is part of the gorgeous Grand Hotel Villa Serbelloni. The smiling host greets Danny as if they're old friends (*Maybe they are!*), and then seats us at a table overlooking the hotel's turquoise pool, which is ringed by comfortable lounge chairs occupied by the well-heeled guests of the hotel. Past the pool, the lake shimmers cobalt blue. About thirty yards from shore, a narrow platform with a diving board rises up out of the water, and I watch in amusement as a young boy climbs the platform's ladder, runs down the length of the board, and then flings himself into the air, flipping twice before landing with a giant splash.

"This is wonderful!" I gush, and Danny smiles at me, and suddenly I feel terribly shy. I unfold my napkin and stare intently down at the menu. It's easier than meeting Danny's eyes. Also, Italian food is my absolute favorite cuisine, so reading this menu is nearly as fun as reading a novel.

"I suppose we *have* to get the Focaccia Villa Serbelloni," I say.

"Order it for the name, devour it for the burrata," Danny agrees. "I can also recommend the *patè di cavedano del nostro lago*."

I read the description in English. "I'll have to trust you on that, since 'patè of chub fish from our lake' is not the most appetizing thing I've ever heard of."

Danny laughs so merrily that I finally find the nerve to look up at him. "You can't go wrong here," he says, "no matter what you order."

"The bucatini?"

"Get it. I'll have the *linguine alle vongole*. And we should probably have wine, don't you think?"

I nod. "Definitely." I hope it will calm my nerves a bit. I don't know what this lunch tête-à-tête means exactly, but it *feels* like a first date.

Of course, for all I know, he picks a new passenger to flirt with every day, and I'm just the latest dope who thinks she's caught his fancy.

When the waiter glides over, Danny orders for us in what seems to me like flawless Italian. Our wine comes quickly, and as we sip it, we share basic facts about our lives.

I learn that Danny is a former high school history teacher. He's also a hobby gardener and an avid hiker. Thanks to an Italian grandfather, he spent many summers in Rome and now has dual citizenship. He moved to Italy after a painful breakup, which he doesn't really want to go into. "Water under the bridge," he says.

"The bridge of l'Orrido di Nesso," I suggest, and he smiles. He thought he'd stay for six months; now he's been here for five years. He has a little house in the hills above Varenna and a cat named Mitz.

"Mitz is the name of Virginia Woolf's marmoset," I tell him.

"Well, that's who she's named for."

"Really?"

He shakes his head and grins sheepishly. "No, not really. I just thought you'd like it if that were true."

I laugh. "I suppose I'd take it as a good sign. Virginia Woolf is one of my favorite writers."

"I'll check her out," he says, and I choose to believe him. "But then you have to watch *Lazzaro Felice*, a wonderful movie set in Inviolata, which is outside of Rome."

"Done," I say firmly. "I love an assignment."

Danny raises his wineglass, and we clink ours together. "What about you, Reverend Grace?" he asks. "Tell me everything. Where you were born, what you wished for when you blew out your birthday candles, where you went to school, what you thought you'd be when you grew up, where you are now — all of it."

I can't help but be surprised by his eager interest. I haven't gone on *hundreds* of dates or anything (if that's even what this is), but in my experience, people don't ask so many questions. Usually they just want to talk about themselves while I nod and smile, practicing my active listening skills.

"Well, if you really want to know," I begin, "I was born in Bloomington, Illinois, and I've lived in Bridgeport, Connecticut, for thirty years. When I was a little girl, I wished for a horse every single birthday. I never got one, but I did get to take riding lessons for a while thanks to my grandma. You already know I'm a minister. I got my master's from Harvard Divinity School—"

"Harvard? Very impressive."

"Oh, but I'm a Badger forever," I add quickly. "University of Wisconsin-Madison. That's where I met my best friends, including the ones I'm here in Italy with now. Let's see, what else? I already told you about my kids. I have zero pets but a lot of houseplants. My hobbies are reading, reading, and reading, with occasional monstera and begonia propagation. I'm mostly Norwegian on one side of my family and

German on the other, and when I was little, I wanted to be a fireman. Or firewoman, I guess I should say."

"I'm sure you would've been great at it," Danny says. "You strike me as the kind of person who's good at everything she does."

"Thank you," I say, flushing a little. "I guess you seem like that kind of person, too."

Neither of us knows what to say next, but thankfully the waiter appears and deposits the appetizers between us. It's been hours since breakfast, and my attention is immediately drawn to the plate of warm focaccia. Creamy burrata is tucked between the slices of bread, and ribbons of prosciutto are piled artfully on top. Danny and I each select a triangle. I take a bite, relishing the milky cheese, the soft bread, and the salty ham. It's wonderful. Next I sample the patè, which is salty and fresh-tasting—a truly unique dish, with its crumble topping and apple puree.

While I'm savoring the food, I also appreciate the poolside view... and the warm smile of my companion, who seems to enjoy watching me delight in La Goletta's fare. A small silence settles between us as Danny and I eat. But soon, for some reason—nerves, I suppose—I feel a great need to break it. And then I hear myself say something terrible.

"So, I've just got to ask, Danny: What's up? Is there something secretly wrong with you?"

Danny nearly chokes on his focaccia. "Excuse me?"

I'm horrified. "That didn't come out like I meant it to."

He lifts his eyebrows skeptically. "How *did* you mean it to come out?"

If I could crawl under the table and hide I would. "Believe it or not, I was trying to pay you a compliment—"

He laughs and interrupts me by saying, "You should try a little harder, then."

"I'm sorry. What I meant was that you seem so…" I hesitate. I've only just met him. If I tell him he just might be humanity's best example of what can be done with a Y chromosome, he's going to think I'm nuts. And I would have to agree with him.

I take another sip of wine. I take a deep breath. I try again.

"You seem like you have absolutely everything going for you. You love where you live, you're happy in your job, you're smart and kind and so easy to talk to…" I shrug. "I couldn't help wondering why you aren't attached to some beautiful woman. Do you have some deep, dark secret?"

Danny looks at me frankly. "Like what?"

"You're emotionally unavailable, or you're wanted by the FBI, or—"

"Well, I am a cannibal," he says, deadpan.

We stare at each other. He's the first to laugh. "I hope I don't have to tell you that that's a joke."

"Of course not," I say. "I just…" My voice trails off. What am I trying to say? "I just meant to say that you seem so wonderful. Perfect almost." My voice sounds small and lonely. "And no one on earth is perfect."

"You're absolutely right," Danny says.

The waiter returns with our pasta, but for the moment, we ignore it. Danny reaches into the little vase on our table and plucks out a tiny purple flower. He holds it out to me. "But sometimes," he says, "when the stars and the sharp-toed snake eagles align, two very imperfect people can realize that they could be perfect for each other." He smiles. "For an afternoon, anyway."

My heart swells. And it cracks. That's all we have, isn't it? One golden afternoon.

24

Jamie,
mother of Meg and Kathleen

A normal person would let her guests rest after such a carb-tastic three-course lunch, but Mariella is not a normal person. She is a micromanager. A cruise director. And a dyed-in-the-wool diva.

"Now, Mike, Zoey, and I are going to do a little work in the garden," she informs us. "As for the rest of you—"

Zoey interrupts her. "But I just got a manicure!"

"That's what gloves are for, darling," Mariella says sweetly, and Mike adds, "You're working off that Pucci dress you bought with my credit card."

Zoey hangs her head. Sometimes she seems so young still, though she's four years older than my twins. "Fine."

"Hashtag *busted*," Merry says with a giggle, and Zoey laughs and sticks her tongue out at her.

The rest of us, Mariella announces, can choose between a massage or an appointment with a person she describes as "a very special artist."

Elin wants to know what kind of artist, but Mariella won't say.

"It's a surprise," she says coyly.

"I'll take the massage," I say. There are enough unknowns and surprises in my life already. "Bridge," I say, "you should get one, too."

Brigid looks reluctant. "I don't know if that's a good idea."

"Since when is a massage *not* a good idea? Get off your fanny," I say, just like I used to when she was little. "You're coming with me."

She wouldn't have dared roll her eyes at me back then, I'll say that. But she's too grown-up for me to scold her. Too accomplished. She's an MD, while I'm just a certified personal trainer.

"Fine," she says. She follows me back up the stairs to Mariella's third-floor yoga room.

Sunlight pours in through the windows, making big golden squares on the floor. Relaxing piano music comes from speakers I can't see. Two massage therapists, a man and a woman, are waiting for us. They're dressed in white uniforms, like nurses, and standing beside two large, thick mats on the floor.

"Where are the tables?" I whisper.

"Are we going to be half-naked together?" Brigid whispers back.

"*Buon pomeriggio,*" the woman says, bowing slightly. "Welcome. I am Stefania. Have you had Thai massage before?"

Brigid and I shake our heads. "I have never even heard of it," I admit.

Stefania explains how it works. Brigid and I will lie on the mats on our backs, fully clothed, while our therapists use a combination of stretching, pressure, and body adjustments to relax us.

"Thai massage improves flexibility," Stefania says, "and invigorates, how do you say it—ah, the *energy system* in the body." She smiles at us. "Yes?"

"And it much calm you," says the other massage therapist. He points to his chest. "Luca. Sorry. My English is not so good."

Luca's English may be iffy, but he's very cute. Besides, how many Italian words do I know? Two. *Grazie* and...damn, I forget the other.

Brigid looks skeptical. Doctors probably don't think in terms of energy systems, whatever that might mean. But she smiles gamely. "Sounds great," she says. "Like yoga, maybe, but without the effort."

"And without having to get up at the crack of dawn," I add. "Don't tell me Mariella's going to make us do that again."

"She's certainly going to try," I say.

When we lie down, Luca and Stefania move to the bottom of our mats to begin with our feet. I close my eyes. Stefania lifts up my heels and gently rotates my ankles. It feels nice. She slowly swings my legs side to side, like a pendulum. It's weird, but I like it.

I can hear Brigid stifling giggles. Luca must still be working on her ticklish feet.

I want to relax. I want to not think.

Not worry.

Not plan.

But of course it's impossible. Plus there's something I need to know.

"Are you avoiding me?" I ask Brigid.

"What? No, of course not."

"I feel like every time I walk into a room, you walk out of it."

She sighs. Even when Brigid was young, she could never lie to me. "It's been very hard not to say anything," she admits. "So maybe I've been trying to keep my distance a little."

I get it. It's been hard for me, too. "I asked the twins if they wanted to be a part of this with us. But they're so closed off, they didn't even ask me what 'this' is."

Stefania presses down on my quadriceps with both of her warm, strong hands. *Ow!* I can feel those airplane burpees.

"It's only the biggest thing that's happened to us in three years."

"If it works, that is," Brigid says.

"It'll work," I say. *It has to.*

I open my eyes for a moment and see Luca literally *sitting* on Brigid's lower leg. He's got it tucked between his calves and his hamstrings.

"Does that feel good?" I ask, incredulous.

"Amazing," says Brigid. She moans. "I think my energy system's really getting invigorated."

I shut my eyes again. I try to relax. But my mind's going like one of those lottery hoppers with a hundred balls bouncing around. Instead of numbers, the balls have words. Like *mothers and daughters. Resentments. Secrets. Accidents.* I just wish I could stop thinking.

I say to Brigid, "Tell me about the mice again."

I can hear the smile in her voice as she complies. (She's told me this story a hundred times.) "Once upon a time, researchers wanted to find out if it was possible to repair the spinal cords of paralyzed mice. So they fed the mice a very special diet. And they gave them specific drugs to promote the regeneration of nerve tissue. And they also stimulated their spinal cords with electricity."

"And then?"

"And then, after some time, many of the mice were able to walk again."

"And they all lived happily ever after," I add. Then I grunt as Stefania digs her elbows into my hips. It hurts, but in a good way.

"Of course they did," Brigid says.

"Any more good stories?"

"Well, more recently, certain gene therapies have restored mobility in mice with severed spinal cords. But of course, the *problem* is that—"

"You can skip that part," I interrupt. "I know all about the problems, remember?" Brigid knows I'm not talking about mice anymore.

"The human body is a very complex machine," she says. "Far more complex than that of a laboratory mouse."

"And nothing works out like you think it will. That's my life's motto, you know. It keeps the wild hope in check."

I look over at Brigid again. Luca's got her twisted like a pretzel. I can't imagine that feels good, but she looks happy. "I just wish the twins would talk to me."

"Or each other," Brigid says.

She's right. They used to be so close. But these days it seems like the only person either of them ever talks to is the one person who can't talk back.

25
Elin,
mother of Brigid

Mariella tells Kathleen and me that we are to meet her "very special artist" in the library, which is in the villa's north wing. I barely make it two steps into the room before I have to stop and gape at the books on Mariella's floor-to-ceiling bookshelves. I run my finger along the nearest spines: Anita Brookner's *A Start in Life* and *Hotel du Lac;* all seven of the Brontë sisters' novels; Barbara Taylor Bradford, Bill Bryson, and—

"Earth to Elin," Kathleen says, giving me a little nudge.

"What! Oh! Right." I cast a final longing look at the *Br* shelf before turning to greet a slender young woman with kohl-lined eyes who's seated at Mariella's writing desk. "So sorry," I say. "I'm like a kid in a candy store with all these books."

"I understand completely," she says warmly, with hardly a trace of an accent. "Please, sit. My name is Francesca Bernardi, and I am a friend of Mariella's."

I surreptitiously glance around the room, looking for signs of Francesca's "very special" art. I don't see anything other than books, furniture, and a beautiful antique globe in the corner.

"Mariella tells us you're an artist," Kathleen says. "What's your medium? Are you a painter? Sculptor? Dancer? A conceptual—"

"Forgive the cross-examination," I interrupt. "Kathleen's a law student." Francesca smiles and shakes her head. Tiny golden bells on her earrings jingle. "I work in ink, actually."

"So, drawings? Sketches?" Kathleen asks.

More jingling bells. "No. I am a tattoo artist."

What? My grip tightens on the arms of the chair. "That definitely wasn't what I was expecting you to say," I admit. I hope I sound cheerful as opposed to alarmed. Were the rhinestone t-shirts not enough for Mariella? Are we all supposed to get matching tattoos?

"Do either of you have any tattoos already?" Francesca asks.

I notice that she has a bracelet of stars tattooed around her wrist. On the smooth skin of her inner forearm, I see a line of three small swords. On the inside of her other wrist is the symbol for infinity.

"Absolutely not," I say. "I'm too old."

"A cleanskin!" Francesca says, delighted. "But I must correct you: one is never too old for a tattoo."

Kathleen hesitates. "I have one." She looks uncomfortable.

"You have a tattoo?" I exclaim. "Where? I just saw you in a bathing suit!" A very skimpy bikini, I might add.

"A violet-green swallow near my hipbone. It's my favorite bird. My mom doesn't know I got it."

I grin and elbow her lightly. "Something for the Night of Secrets!"

"Only if I can't think of a better one."

"Can I see it?"

Kathleen stands and pulls down the elastic waist of her skirt a couple of inches. Sure enough, there's a tattoo of a dark bird with arched wings.

"That's lovely," I say, not certain if I mean it or not.

"It's covering up a scar," she says.

"From the accident?" I ask this without even meaning to.

"I crashed my bike when I was twelve. The scars from the accident are more... internal."

"Oh, I see." I don't know what else to say.

Francesca pushes a binder toward us. "Please," she says, "have a look. These are some of my designs."

There are pages upon pages of intricate drawings: flowers, vines, koi fish, hummingbirds, fat little winged putti. She's a very skilled illustrator.

"You have a wonderful way with lines," I say.

"Maybe you want to pick one out," Francesca suggests sweetly.

Rather than saying what first comes to mind, which is *hell no,* I deflect. "Kathleen, maybe you should get a tattoo of a short-eyed snake eagle—to match your swallow."

"Short-toed snake eagle, and no, I don't think that's a great idea."

"Ah, I see, you are both uncertain," Francesca says. "You believe this is too much, too soon."

"Well, Mariella might've warned us," Kathleen points out.

No kidding. I don't want a tattoo because I'm sure I'd eventually come to dislike the design. I can't trust my taste anymore. It'd be like the dress I bought for this trip: I loved it when I brought it home, but two weeks later I hated it. And while I can return the dress or give it to Goodwill, I can't exactly get rid of my arm.

Francesca lifts the sleeve of her black t-shirt to reveal a beautiful daisy, in the style of an old-fashioned botanical drawing. "A tattoo can be a very meaningful thing. This is for my grandmother, Margherita. Margherita means daisy. Although she's gone, she is always with me." Then she points to the swords. "These come from the Three of Swords card in tarot. They remind me that challenges are part of life. That it is possible to learn from pain. And that resilience leads to growth."

"That's actually kind of profound," I say. "What's that quote—"

"'What does not kill me makes me stronger,'" Kathleen says. "Nietzsche."

"Right!"

"I call BS, though. What didn't kill me *hurt* me very much, maybe permanently, and it also made me bitter."

But I can tell by the set of her mouth that she doesn't want to talk about the accident. She just wants to toss it into the middle of a conversation like an unexploded grenade. There's an awkward silence as I try to figure out what to say. Finally I turn to Francesca and say, "I'd love to hear more about your art."

Francesca inclines her head; yes, she will tell us more. "Tattoos honor our memories, our passions, and the people or animals that we love," she says. "They're art which we carry with us always." She smiles. "My skin is a living canvas, a representation of my dreams and hopes and wishes. And a testimony to everything and everyone that I love."

"You're almost convincing me," I tell her. I'm not sure this is true. But I'm not sure it's *not* true, either.

Kathleen asks, "What would you get, Elin?"

Surprisingly, I know the answer. "If I had to get one, and I had to do it right now, I'd get the most cliché tattoo in the world. A heart on my upper arm, with the word 'MOM' inside it." My throat tightens as I say this. I miss my mom so much.

And if I got a tattoo like that, she'd be spinning in her grave like a top!

"I have done many such tattoos," Francesca says. "In fact, if you look closely at my daisy, you will see the word NONNA in the yellow center. *Nonna* means grandma, of course."

"I dare you, Elin," Kathleen says. "Be spontaneous and irresponsible!"

The last time I was spontaneous and irresponsible I slept with my colleague. "I tried that. It didn't work out."

Kathleen's eyes widen. "Do tell!"

I shake my head. *No way.*

"That's for the Night of Secrets, then," she says.

"Oh, sure." More like for *never*.

Francesca says, "It is a big decision. I understand. But I cannot send you away with nothing." She fans out a large deck of cards on the desk. "So I will offer a quick tarot reading. Please, point to a card that calls to you."

"You are a woman of many talents," I say.

Francesca winks at me. "In my experience, that is true of all women." She cocks her head thoughtfully. "Men, not so much."

I tap a card, and Kathleen does the same. Francesca turns them over and smiles to herself.

"The Three of Cups for Elin and the Star for Kathleen," she says. "Very good. In tarot, the Three of Cups symbolizes a time of friendship, festivity, and communal joy. See these three women with cups of wine? They're having the time of their lives!" She winks. "As I suspect you are, too."

"You better believe it," I say.

"And the Star card," Francesca goes on, "is all about hope, inspiration, and renewal. Lovely, right?" Then she leans close and speaks with quiet urgency. "The Star suggests that you must forgive yourself, and that you must also forgive others."

Kathleen's face darkens. "Interesting," she says.

It is a strange and surprising reaction. *What's that about?* I turn to Francesca, worried that Kathleen's stony response might have offended her. "Thank you so much for your time," I say. "You're obviously so talented. And wise."

"Do you know what else the cards tell me?" Francesca asks.

"No." Do I want to know?

She offers us a brilliant smile. "They say you each have a tattoo in your future!"

26

Grace,
mother of Merry

Once I get over my stupid gaffe, lunch turns wonderful again. Seagulls float by in the warm breeze, and a little sparrow lands near my feet, begging for crumbs. My tomato bucatini is the epitome of summer, the ripe and sweet tomatoes contrasting with salty, funky, shaved Parmigiano. Danny offers me a bite of his *linguine alle vongole,* which is garlicky and briny in the best way.

But even better than the food is the conversation. Danny and I talk and talk. Getting to know each other. Experiencing the giddy delight of discovering a kindred spirit.

I've always found it easy to talk to people; it's a big part of being a minister. But talking with Danny is different. It feels less like conversation and more like *dancing*. We whirl from topic to topic, leap from one story to the next, laughing, interrupting each other, sharing our memories, impressions, and opinions.

We're in the middle of bonding over our favorite bands from our high school days when Danny suddenly sits up straight in alarm.

"Sorry, I'll be right back," he says. Before I can respond, he rushes out of the restaurant.

Since the restaurant is open along one wall, I can see him stab at his phone and then press it to his ear. He paces back and forth in agitation until whoever he's called answers, and then he starts talking a mile a minute. I can hear snippets of what he's saying, but since he's speaking Italian, I can't understand it.

"*Mi dispiace,*" he says, "*è troppo tardi...Sì, sì, certo...*Texans..."

My ears prick up at that one English word. And I remember Danny saying that he was supposed to take a group of Texans around the lake this afternoon.

It's 2:45.

I quickly stand, catch our waiter's eye, and make a sign for "check." "*Per favore,*" I mouth. Maybe if Danny sprints, he can still make it to the dock on time.

He comes back inside, tucking his phone into his pocket, looking pained.

"Everything okay?" I ask.

"Well, the bad news is that I messed up, and Franco's going to make me pay," Danny says. Then his expression brightens. "The good news, though, is that I've got the rest of the afternoon off. So — what do you say to a little bit more of a tour?" Before I can answer, he adds, "Unless you're going to tell me that you need to get back to your friends."

"My who?" I quip. Then I smile. "I think a tour sounds wonderful."

"Great." Danny quickly counts out some euros and lays them on the table, calling to our waiter, *"Grazie mille, Enzo, è stato bello vederti."*

He gently places his hand in the small of my back, steering me out of the restaurant and into the sunshine. "I want to take you to Varenna," he says. "In my opinion, it's the best town on the lake."

"How far away is it?" I wonder how long I can stay out before Mariella gets fussy.

"As the crow flies, two miles. As a car drives, twenty-seven."

"How could that be?"

He points across the water. "Varenna's right there, just to the northeast. But because Bellagio is situated where the lake splits into two, you have to drive all the way down and around the eastern fork and then back up again to get to Varenna. So it's best to have wings...or a boat." He grins.

"How lucky for us that we've got the latter!"

The boat ride is less than fifteen minutes—I wave as we speed right past one of the double-decker ferries—and in a matter of moments we've arrived at a picturesque town with a colorful waterfront and tall clock tower.

Once we dock near the tiny harbor, Danny leads me along Varenna's beautiful promenade, lined with a brilliant red metal fence. "It's called the Walk of Lovers," he says, with what might be a hint of embarrassment. On one side of us are the wisteria-draped old stone walls of the town; on the other, the glittering water.

"It's the prettiest walkway I've ever seen." I pull out my phone to take a picture, but my battery is dead. I sigh.

"I guess you'll have to remember it the old-fashioned way," Danny says as we walk past a big red metal heart framing a view of the lake.

I laugh. "True. But I don't think I'm in danger of forgetting any part of this day."

After the promenade, we head uphill along narrow cobblestone streets toward the town square. Everywhere I look, flowers spill from earthenware pots and window boxes. Cats nap blissfully in the sun. Tiny shops display pretty paintings, handmade leather goods, and unique ceramics.

Danny sees me admiring a jade-green ceramic bowl through a shop window. "Would you like to go in?" he asks.

"Oh, I'm not much of a shopper," I reassure him. "I'm more of a window-licker."

"A *what*?"

I can't help laughing at the startled look on his face. "It's a French expression," I explain. "*J'aime faire du lèche-vitrines* means 'I like to window-shop.' Except that it's literally 'window-lick.'"

"Did Duolingo teach you that?"

"I minored in French in undergrad. I'm pretty rusty by now, though."

"Sounds like a trip to Paris is in order."

"If only!"

"It's a ninety-minute flight from Milan," Danny says. "You could do it tomorrow."

I nod. "Yes, I could. But I'd have to be an entirely different person. Ditching my friends to have lunch with you is about as wild and spontaneous as I get."

Danny grabs my hand, gives it a quick squeeze, and then lets it go. "You never know. You might surprise yourself."

My cheeks flush. My hand tingles where he touched it. "Believe me, I already have."

As we walk along, Danny tells me how Varenna was founded by fishermen in the eighth century and later became an important center for trade and military defense. "Now, of course, it's just a pretty little tourist town. But back in the twelfth century, you would've seen ships burning in the harbor while poor villagers held off their attackers by pelting them with stones." He stops to pet a calico cat lolling in the sun. "The twenty-first century has plenty of problems, but I'll still take it over any other."

"Tell me about it! Whenever I read historical fiction, it's all bloodletting, poisoning, trench warfare, and people dying of the plague." Then I laugh. "I read happy books, too, of course. You can't beat P. G. Wodehouse for a comfort read with a happy ending."

"I'll have to put him on my list, too."

"You should."

27

Mariella,
mother of Zoey

Elin comes downstairs from the library looking scandalized. "I can't believe you were trying to make me get a tattoo!" she exclaims.

I blink innocently at her. "But, darling, a good tattoo is like jewelry you never lose, and that you never have to take off." I hold out my hand with its bare pinkie finger. "Look. I bought the most beautiful signet ring in Paris, but I lost it on my last tour."

"Where's *your* tattoo, then?" she challenges.

I give a secretive little grin. "Wouldn't you like to know."

The truth is that I don't have a tattoo. But I am planning to get one. And I know exactly what it'll be.

Elin opens the fridge and pulls out a mineral water. She looks around to make sure we're alone and then whispers, "Kathleen has a tattoo that she never told Jamie about."

I glance over at Zoey, who's just come tromping inside wearing her gardening shoes. She probably has secret tattoos, too, along with the two the whole world can see (a deer on her inner bicep and a harp near her ankle, don't ask me why).

"Well, if you want to talk about naughty daughters, *mine* is wearing a sex toy around her neck." For the record, I do not whisper this. "She's also getting mud all over the floor."

Zoey sighs theatrically. "Mommy, vibrators were invented before vacuum cleaners. And up until the 1920s, they were considered a *medical device*. Doctors used them to treat 'female hysteria' — in other words, any problem that a woman had that a male doctor couldn't explain." She kicks off her shoes. "And let's not forget that absolutely *no one* cared about the female orgasm back then."

"Thank you so much for the history lesson," I say. "Speaking of vacuum cleaners, go get ours so you can clean up your mess."

Zoey rolls her eyes, but she goes to fetch the Dyson.

Elin smiles. "She's a sweet kid. I mean, a sweet *young woman*."

"She drives me to distraction. But you're right. She is sweet, and I love her to absolute pieces. I love her girlfriend, too. Luna is an absolute doll." I put the kettle on for tea. "Whittard Earl Gray or Yorkshire Gold?"

"Oh, surprise me," Elin says.

"Surprises are for the Night of Secrets," I tell her. "I'm giving you Yorkshire."

I pour us big mugs and add generous splashes of whole milk. Together we go sit in the shady part of the terrace.

Elin tucks her long legs under her, just like she used to do when she studied on the couch in the student lounge. Suddenly I can see her, age nineteen, blond hair twisted into a bun and held in place by a number 2 pencil. I imagine Grace on the other end of the sofa, wearing one of her vintage dresses, her cat-eye glasses slipping low on her nose. I take a sharp inhale, overwhelmed by nostalgia for our college years together. I can't believe it was over forty years ago. Elin must be having similar thoughts.

"Remember Terrace season?" she asks. Each spring, UW-Madison's famous sunburst chairs—like the ones I've got outside—were returned to the Terrace overlooking Lake Mendota, and everyone immediately flocked there to snack, study, gossip, and flirt.

I sigh. "That was always the best part of spring. And we'd walk out to Picnic Point, and—"

"And you'd never wear the right shoes," Elin interrupts, laughing, "and you'd complain about how long the walk was."

"Shut up!" I exclaim. "I looked amazing in my cute little sandals and my ankle-zip Guess jeans, and you know it."

"You were twenty," Elin points out. "You would've looked amazing barefoot in a potato sack."

I pat my soft, round hips. "That is true. But now I must wear my years, and my deep love for carbohydrates, proudly."

Or if not proudly, then at least good-naturedly.

I hope.

"Speaking of carbs, how about the Babcock Dairy Store?" Elin says dreamily. "Oh, my God, what I would do for a scoop of that ice cream."

"Badger Blast! The best flavor."

"Sorry, but Orange Chocolate Chip was the best," Elin says. "Two scoops minimum."

"You could eat three, as I recall."

"I was in training!"

"You ate like a linebacker. You pledged Gamma Phi Beta because they served fudge-bottom pie at Rush."

"That is *not* why I pledged them, and I don't recall any linebackers having pictures of themselves in a Speedo hanging in a booth in the Big Ten pub!" Elin exclaims. Then she smiles ruefully. "You know, I was embarrassed about that back then. Now I'd commit crimes to have that body again. And that metabolism. I could eat all the ice cream and cheese curds I wanted."

She glances down at her long, muscular legs. If you ask me, they still look pretty good. A lot better than mine, anyway.

"Remember traying down Bascom?" Elin says.

"I remember the time you knocked me over like a bowling pin!"

Whenever it snowed, we'd steal dining hall trays to sled down steep Bascom Hill. It was a campus tradition. On one particularly cold evening, when an officer tried to stop Grace from taking her run down the hill, she charmed him so thoroughly that he ended up borrowing my tray and racing her to the bottom.

"Those were good times," I say wistfully.

"The best."

I take a sip of tea and regret that we don't have cookies to accompany it. *This is why my pants don't fit, but who cares?*

"But this weekend is the best, too," I say. "Right? Everything's going good, isn't it?" I can't keep the nervousness from my voice.

Elin nods reassuringly. "This weekend is incredible. Sure, there's been a little tension here and there. But what can we expect? We're strong-willed, opinionated women."

"True. I just think that every year is the best year, whenever we're together."

Elin smiles fondly at me. "You're such a sap."

28

Meg,
daughter of Jamie

Seems like everyone's pretty much having the time of their lives around here. Me, I just keep waiting to feel different. Like being in a new country's going to make me feel like a totally new person. But of course it hasn't worked. I don't know why I thought it would.

My dad used to have a saying: *Wherever you go, there you are.* Meaning you can run but you can't hide, not from yourself, anyway. That's why I didn't split after the first night, the way I said I was going to. What would be the point? It would devastate my mom. It'd piss off Mariella. And it wouldn't make me feel any better.

At least at Mariella's the food and drinks are good. And free.

I pull the journal she gave me out of my backpack. Mine is a deep blue, the color of Lake Como in the evening. She'd walked by as I was turning its blank pages earlier. "Remember, that's for all your secrets," she'd said, winking at me.

"Sure," I'd said. "You bet." But I have only one secret, and I'm not going to write it down.

Instead, I sit on a bench in the garden and doodle around the margins of the first page. Then I draw one of Mariella's rosebushes. I sketch some little Italian bird hopping along the path. An Italian lizard, sunning itself on a rock.

I'm crosshatching the shadows in my picture when my mom appears. With her blue dress and red sneakers, she's got a real Dorothy from Oz vibe going on. Inwardly I sigh. *Is it possible to be alone here? Ever?*

"Well, hello, you," she says, acting like she came upon me by accident. I don't buy it.

"Hi," I say, closing my journal.

"We missed you at lunch."

"Sorry. Mike insisted on feeding me earlier."

She nods. "Mike is a lovely man," she says. "And very patient." She sits down beside me.

"He'd have to be, to put up with Mariella."

"Don't be unkind about our hostess."

"I'm being honest. Mariella is a *lot*. You can admit it."

My mom chuckles. "She and Mike complement each other." She pauses. "The way your dad and I used to."

I can feel myself tensing up. I really, really don't want to talk about my dad. I'm having enough trouble holding things together as it is. I rub my temples like I'm getting a headache. Maybe I *am* getting a headache. Maybe my mother's giving it to me. Or maybe it's from the pressure of keeping my secret.

"You doing okay, Meg?" my mom asks.

I shrug, and together we stare off into the garden. The lizard's gone now. Mom scared him away.

"I wanted to talk to you about tomorrow night," she says after a while. "Mariella's Night of Secrets. I don't want to spoil her fun. But also I'm not sure I should be keeping secrets from my kids. I was hoping to get you and your sister together. I thought you might want to know what's up."

I stand quickly. "It's okay," I say, my voice full of false cheer. "Just surprise me!" And before my mom can say anything else, I hurry away.

Later, in my room behind a closed door, I take out my journal and reconsider my drawings. Nothing looks right.

I used to be a good artist. A good student. A good writer. A good daughter. I used to be a lot of things.

Across the pictures I write: *I don't want to say what I have to say.*

And then I scribble everything out until it's nothing but black.

29

Grace,
mother of Merry

"Now I want to take you someplace special," Danny says.

"More special than the Walk of Lovers? Or that wonderful restaurant?"

He squints at me in the sunlight as he takes my hand. This time he doesn't let it go. "Well, I guess you'll have to be the judge of that."

His palm is warm against mine as we thread our way through the narrow passageways. There are no actual streets in the old town; on either side of us, steep skinny alleyways decorated with hanging plants beckon, as if calling me to get lost in this picturesque place.

Soon we arrive in a pretty, sunlit square, the Piazza San

Giorgio. On the far end, there's a gray stone church with a rose window and a tall fairy-tale tower on its right-hand side. Behind it there are dense trees and the steep rise of the hillside.

"That's the Church of San Giorgio over there," Danny says. "It was consecrated in 1313."

More than seven hundred years ago. Wow! "You know, I never think about how young the United States is. But what's our oldest building? Some Jamestown church?"

"Well, as a former history teacher, I can tell you that there are Pueblo dwellings in what's now New Mexico that date from about 750," Danny says. "But you're right—in Europe, history seems so much more *present*. The architecture keeps reminding us of who and what came before. But come this way, we're going over here."

He then turns me around and leads me just a few feet to a tall and narrow pale-yellow building with a pair of carved double doors. "Here we are," he says proudly.

I'm nonplussed. "This is the special thing? What is it?"

"It's the Church of Santa Maria delle Grazie," he says. "Or in English, Holy Mary of *Grace*." He knocks a pattern on the door, and a few minutes later, one heavy side creaks open. "By appointment only," he says, grinning.

He greets the old woman who opened the door warmly and then ushers me into the cool interior. It's much smaller inside than I would've guessed from the exterior. The woman says something softly in Italian and then returns to her work of dusting the frame of a large oil painting. On the far wall, an ornate golden altar gleams. To my right and left, niches hold beautiful old statues of saints.

"Are you bringing me here because I'm a minister?" I whisper. "Like you think I might be going through God withdrawal?"

Danny laughs quietly. "No, no—it's because this church honors important women in the Catholic Church. There's the Madonna and child, of course. And in the niches here in the nave, the statues depict Mary as Blessed Virgin of Sorrows, Saint Teresa d'Ávila, Saint Gertrude, and Saint Eurosia."

I walk slowly around, admiring their Baroque forms; the statues are truly beautiful. We don't pray to any saints in the United Church of Christ. But I know my Catholic history and theology, and I'm moved to be in the silent spiritual company of these women.

Then I sit down in one of the wooden chairs in the nave and bow my head. *Dear God,* I think—as if I'm writing Him a letter. *Creator of our past, our present, and our future, we thank you for the many blessings you bestow on us each moment of our lives.* It's a United Church of Christ classic.

I look up to see Danny watching me. Smiling faintly, I shrug. "As long as I'm here, I might as well say a quick hello to God."

"I'm glad you did," he says.

I stand up. "Thank you for bringing me here. It does feel... well, holy, I guess."

"Do you want to walk around some more? Or go find a gelato?"

I know what I want to do next, but I can't say it until I'm outside the church, blinking in the bright sunlight.

I can't say it until I've worked up my nerve. Until I can tell myself that God isn't listening.

Because what I want to say next is *very* unlike me.

For one thing, it's brash.

For another, it's a lie.

I say, "Actually, I'd really like to meet your cat."

Don't get me wrong. I like cats as much as the next single lady. But Danny's feline is purely an excuse to get an invitation to his house.

He looks surprised. But pleasantly so. "Done," he says. "I warn you, though, Mitz is a fickle beast. How do you feel about riding a motorcycle?"

He sees my obvious hesitation. "It's more of a glorified moped," he says reassuringly.

"Still, it sounds much scarier than a boat!"

He laughs. "Unfortunately I can't drive the boat into the hills. The bike gets me to the Varenna harbor every morning." He takes my hand, presses it, and then lets it go. "Don't worry. All you have to do is hold on."

What he means, of course, is that I have to hold onto *him*.

We walk a few streets over to where he's parked an ancient-looking scooter. I swing my leg over the seat and wrap my arms around Danny's waist.

"Scooch closer," he says. "For safety reasons only, of course," he adds.

I can hear the smile in his voice.

I press myself closer. I feel the heat of his skin through his shirt. My heart thuds hard inside my ribs. I wonder if he can sense it.

"*Andiamo,*" he says, and hits the gas.

We take twisting, narrow roads out of Varenna and up into the surrounding hills. I'm probably squeezing Danny half to death, but I don't dare loosen my grip. It's less from romance and more from caution, I tell myself. The wind whips my face. The ride is exhilarating. The great blue lake gleams on my left, then my right, as we take hairpin turns skyward. Butterflies startle out of wildflowers on the side of the road and flitter like tiny angels in the air. The clouds seem to chase us.

When he finally comes to a stop in front of a sweet white stucco cottage tucked into a hillside, I breathe a giant sigh of relief and dismount on wobbly legs. Danny grabs my arm to steady me.

"You made it!" he says.

"Barely!" I reply, laughing.

The air smells like orange blossoms. A lizard skitters across a stone wall half hidden under clematis vines. From the deck of Danny's house, I can see Lake Como sparkling below, tucked into its ring of blue-green mountains. It's so beautiful it almost hurts.

"If I lived here," I say, "I don't think I would ever leave."

"I was extremely lucky to get it. It only happened because I was doing work on it for the old couple who lived here. When they decided to move to Milan to be with their daughter, they sold it to me."

Danny clicks his tongue, and a small black-and-white cat comes running. She's purring like crazy, winding around his legs, but when he tries to pet her, she shrinks away. "I found her in a dumpster when she was a kitten," he says. "I saved her life! But she never acts particularly grateful."

"I guess I don't think of cats and gratitude as going together."

"Yeah, me either, I guess."

We sit side by side on the deck's love seat. Danny props his feet up on the railing. I tip my face to the sun. For a moment, neither of us speaks. The silence isn't awkward, though. It's comfortable. Then Danny's pinkie curls around mine. Somehow this is different from holding hands while walking through the streets of Varenna. My breath quickens.

"You're really easy to be around," he says quietly. "And before you tell me that that doesn't sound like much of a compliment, let's recall that your version of a compliment was assuming something was horribly wrong with me."

"I'm *still* sorry about that."

"What I want to say is that...well, I've been alone for a long time."

Me too, I think.

"My job is to charm people. To become their dear friend for a few hours. And then that's it. I never see them again. Which has suited me just fine. A fun time that *ends.*" He gazes out over the lake. He frowns a little, like he's concentrating. "But then I met you. And it sounds crazy, but I thought to myself, *This can't be the end.* The thought of watching a good woman like you walk away from the boat, knowing I'd never see you again—I couldn't handle it. So I took a chance." He pauses again. Turns to me. "Believe me, it's been a long time since I've done anything like this."

"I'm really glad you did." *More so than I could ever admit.* Then I laugh. "How do you know I'm a good woman?"

"I think it's obvious, don't you?"

"I don't know. When you spend your life trying to help people, you probably do give off a lot of benevolent vibes. But don't you think good is boring?"

"Not at all."

He takes my hand in his. His fingers are warm and strong. Waves of pleasure roll through my whole body.

"But if you think bad is more exciting," he says slowly, "what would being bad look like?"

"Take me inside," I say, "and I'll show you."

No, that's not true.

I say it only in my mind.

In real life, I simply bite my lip. I'm thrilled and scared and I don't want to mess this up. "I don't know. Being wanted by the FBI?"

"Just like I am," Danny jokes.

"Exactly." Then I give a yelp of surprise, because the cat has launched herself into my lap. Her purr's so loud it vibrates her whole body. "Hello, Mitz, make yourself at home."

"She *never* does that," Danny says. "It must be a sign."

Mitz turns in a few circles and then settles down on my legs. "A sign of what?"

He shrugs too. "I don't know. But it's got to be something good."

"But not boring."

"No," he says. He brings my fingers to his lips and kisses them ever so lightly. "Definitely not boring."

30

Zoey, daughter of Mariella

My mom, a.k.a. the Bossiest Woman Alive, has put me in charge of cocktails for tonight's official MDBC meeting. I'm totally tempted to troll her by making weird drinks that went viral on TikTok. Can you imagine Mariella's face if I walked out with a tray of Parmesan espresso martinis and cotton candy margaritas?

She would *die*.

The problem with that idea is that we'd all be stuck with disgusting cocktails. Plus my mom would immediately come back to life and kill me for messing with her perfectly planned weekend.

So I do a little internet research, and then I sit and ponder things for a moment, and then, just like that, it comes to me: the Como-politan. It'll be like a cosmopolitan, but instead of lime juice, I'll use lemon juice and limoncello, the famous liquor of southern Italy. I quickly mix up a sample drink. *Squisito!* Exquisite.

I also grab a couple of bottles of sparkling wine and the ingredients to make Aperol spritzes, just in case, and I bring these out to the terrace along with little bowls of salty, crunchy, and smoky almonds that my dad made last night.

I do a quick head count. Grace is still missing. "No word from your mom, M?" I ask, handing Merry a Como-politan.

Merry shakes her head. "She goes off with Captain Handsome and doesn't even bother to check in! I called her but it went straight to voicemail. Her phone's probably dead."

"She's fine," Elin says, for what is probably the millionth time. "I swear." She takes a sip of her drink. "This is delicious, Zoey. What is it?"

I list the ingredients, and she nods approvingly. "It's a far cry from wapatoolie punch, I'll say that."

Mom groans, and Elin explains to me and Merry what wapatoolie is. "You take a garbage can, line it with a trash bag, and then fill it with fruit punch and every kind of liquor you can get your hands on. Voilà! Wapatoolie punch."

"Sounds disgusting," I say.

"It tasted like candy," Mariella says. "Like a liquid Jolly Rancher—"

"That could send you to the hospital."

Merry clears her throat. "Anyway," she says, "we all agree my mom's not in mortal danger, right?"

"Yes," everyone exclaims.

But it is weird that Grace isn't back yet. I can tell my mom is unnerved by it, though whether she's actually concerned about her friend's whereabouts or just the integrity of her carefully planned schedule, I couldn't say.

And I wonder how many of us are thinking about the last MDBC meeting, when we were all waiting for Meg and Kathleen to get back with the ice cream. When we thought they'd just gotten sidetracked on the way home.

Obviously, none of us could've imagined what actually happened. We had to see it for ourselves—and then wish we could unsee it.

But I don't want to dwell on that night, not now. "Which book are we talking about first?" I say brightly. I pop an almond in my mouth and crunch.

"First we will make our presentations," Mom says imperiously, "in the assigned order—a copy of which you all received—and *then* there will be open discussion."

Whoops, I forgot. But can I be blamed for ignoring my mom? She'd sent so many emails. What size bag to bring. The best sunscreen to pack. The right footwear. Blah, blah, blah. I think I ought to be forgiven for skimming the email that included the extremely detailed meeting agenda for tonight.

Too bad Mariella isn't exactly the forgiving type. If she knew that I can't even remember what book I'm supposed to talk about, she'd be madder than if I'd served martinis made with Parmesan *and* cotton candy.

Well, I never was great at homework. But I've always been pretty good at winging it.

My mom opens her journal and turns to the page where she's written out the schedule. "First, we have Jamie Price, talking to us about *Hello Beautiful*."

Jamie gives a quick, awkward smile. "Is it weird I'm nervous? I'm not great at public speaking."

"This isn't public speaking," Elin assures her. "This is *us*."

Jamie glances down at an index card. *Bless her*, I think, *she made notes*.

"Okay. So. *Hello Beautiful* by Ann Napolitano follows the life of the Padavano family over several decades in Chicago," she says. "The characters are so vivid, they practically leap off the page and land next to you on the couch. The story is heartwarming, and also a little heart*breaking*. It'll make you laugh, cry, and text your mom." She puts her card down. "Was that okay?" I can hear the hope in her voice.

"It was excellent," my mom says. "A-plus." She checks her agenda again. "Zoey, darling, you're next."

Crap. "Uh, what's my title?"

"You're joking!"

"Of course I am!" I cry. "I totally know that I'm supposed to talk about…" I look desperately over at Merry.

"Where'd You Go, Bernadette," she whispers.

I flash her a grateful smile. No prob, I can do this. "You guys, I loved *Where'd You Go, Bernadette*. It's kind of like a scavenger hunt for this girl's missing mom. Bernadette Fox is a genius architect with a touch of the crazies, kind of like someone else we might know. Someone whose initials are M.M." I nod toward my mom, and everyone, including her, laughs. "It's chaotic, super funny, and a bit *too* relatable. I'd call it a must-read for the mom drama and the epic fails."

"I've read it twice!" Meg says. "I didn't love the movie, though, even though I love Cate Blanchett."

"She's iconic," Jamie says, beaming at her daughter. I think it's the first time this weekend that Meg's spoken without being specifically asked a question. Usually she's silently scowling or writing in her journal, off in some corner.

"What's Zoey's grade?" Brigid wants to know.

My mom narrows her eyes at me. "B-plus," she says.

"What?" I throw an almond at her. It lands on her ample chest.

She picks it up and tucks it into her mouth. "Thank you, darling," she says. "I'll take another when you have a chance."

"I should throw the whole bowl at you," I grumble.

"No, what you *should* do is prepare your book talk in advance."

Dang it. How could she tell I hadn't?

Now it's Elin's turn to give a little speech; her book is *This Is the Water*, which is about a girls' swim team, a serial killer, and the mom who vows to stop him. Then Brigid talks about *Lessons in Chemistry*, and Kathleen says a few words about *Everything I Never Told You*, by Celeste Ng. My mom wants to sing her mini-review of *The Whispers*, but when I threaten to post her on TikTok, she backs down.

The conversation gets louder and tipsier as the meeting goes on. Meg doesn't even make a presentation, because by the time her turn rolls around, we're too busy arguing about whether Bernadette is a toxic mother and if books like *Women Talking* or *A Little Life* (which is basically 750 pages of trauma) should come with trigger-warning stickers.

Then my dad appears out of nowhere, wearing a full-length apron that looks like a dress, and informs us that dinner will be ready in half an hour.

"Dinner!" exclaims Elin delightedly. "I forgot we had that to look forward to."

"There are *many* things we have to look forward to," my mom assures everyone.

Even in the shadowy evening light I can see Meg roll her eyes.

And I can see Merry anxiously checking her watch.

And I can see Jamie and Brigid exchanging a long and extremely mysterious look.

31

Elin,
mother of Brigid

How does Lucia do it? Tonight's table setting could be a photo spread from *T* magazine: "A Soprano's Sophisticated Summer Soiree," or maybe "A Diva's Divine Dinner Party." Bouquets of roses fill elegant glass vases. Pink taper candles in terra-cotta holders cast a warm glow over creamy Italian linens and hand-painted Tuscan ceramics. Also, the smells coming from the kitchen are out of this world.

"Lucia is a miracle, and I am going to kidnap her," Jamie says.

I laugh. "I know, right? But careful, don't make any kidnapping jokes around Merry."

Poor girl, she keeps looking anxiously toward the front

door. Checking her phone, too, even though her mom's has probably gone dead. I gave up on trying to reassure Merry hours ago. As she pointed out, just because something's wildly unlikely to happen doesn't mean that it can't. Lake Geneva was proof.

My tall, gorgeous daughter pads into the room, and I stop my dark thoughts before they get started. "Bridgie, come sit by me," I say. "I feel like I haven't seen you all weekend."

She drops into the chair next to me and leans her head ever so briefly on my shoulder. "Love you," she murmurs.

"Love you more," I tell her. "Isn't this trip amazing?"

There is a slight but noticeable pause before she says, "Yes."

"You know what? You work too hard," I say, giving her a quick, sympathetic hug. "You have to relax, honey."

She shrugs. "But I love my job. *You* work too hard, and you can't stand yours."

"That's not true," I protest.

"Yes, actually it is," she says.

I feel myself flinch a little. Hearing it stated so bluntly is surprising. Am I that obvious?

I told the MDBC three years ago that I was going to leave my job. So what the heck is keeping me there? Habit? Inertia? The colleague I was sleeping with?

All bad reasons to stay.

"I'm going to make some changes," I tell her. "You'll see."

She nods sleepily. "Okay. Keep me posted." Then she yawns.

"No napping at the dinner table!" Mike chides. He's standing at the head of the table with his arms lifted like a conductor's, holding a wooden spoon like a baton. "Dinner will be served in a moment. I must warn you, your fare is slightly more humble tonight, since Lucia has the night off."

"So *you* set this gorgeous table?" Jamie blurts out.

"Yes, I did," Mike says. "Don't look so shocked. There will be tomato panzanella and wild mushroom fettuccine, as well as my very special tuna à la Marciano—"

"Hey, I make tuna à la Price!" Jamie exclaims. "It's baked tuna casserole with Campbell's cream of mushroom soup, just like my mom used to make."

Meg grimaces at her mother's enthusiasm.

"It's better than it sounds," Kathleen says loyally. "But what was really good was her hamburger stroganoff."

"She got that recipe from me!" I exclaim. "And I got it from *my* mother!"

"Anyway," Mike says brightly, "my version features fresh tuna steaks wrapped in prosciutto and sage, with a balsamic brown butter vinaigrette, and a side of fava bean puree drizzled with some smoked olive oil from an estate in Tuscany."

My mouth's watering long before Mike sets the beautiful bowl of wild mushroom fettuccine in front of me. If my husband cared even one-tenth as much about food as Mike does, I'd be thrilled. But I can't compare my life or my relationship to Mariella's; they will always seem less glamorous, less wonderful. I'm okay with that.

Mostly.

Mike eyes the empty Negroni pitcher. "Should I assume that all the alcohol you need is already in your stomachs?"

"Only barbarians fail to serve wine with dinner!" Mariella cries. "Go get three bottles of Brunello from the cellar."

"You're going to pay for them in the morning," Mike warns her. "Then again, *bevi di più, ridi di più, ama di più!*"

"That means 'drink more, laugh more, love more,'" Mariella translates as he goes to fetch the wine.

"He sure is good to you," Jamie says wistfully.

"Mike's a wonderful man," Mariella agrees. Then she leans forward and smiles her famous, fabulous smile. "But I *did* have to train him. Literally."

"What? How?" We all want to know.

"Using techniques that people use to teach dolphins," Mariella says.

I burst out laughing; I can't help it. So does the rest of the table.

"Mommy," Zoey chides. "Seriously."

"I am completely serious. I read a whole book about it. You borrow strategies from exotic animal trainers to train your spouse."

"Tell me you still have your copy," I say. "I want to borrow it."

Brigid raises her eyebrows. "What do you want to train Dad to do?"

I shift uncomfortably in my seat. What am I prepared to admit? "I'd like to encourage him to try restaurants other than the Billy Goat, for one thing."

"And for another?"

"Let's not talk about this now, honey."

Or ever.

"Charlie's wonderful," Mariella says loyally. "We all know that."

"So's Mike," I say.

"Of course he has his flaws," Mariella says. "But I've got mine, and happily they complement each other."

I lift my glass. "Hear! Hear!"

Then I glance over at Jamie, who's staring down at her pasta without seeming to see it. I know what she's thinking about.

She's thinking about husbands. About Logan.

About how he was always the life of the party. How he was the first one in the lake and the last one out. How he grilled the best steaks we'd ever tasted, every Fourth of July.

And about how someone saying that they want to leave you isn't even close to the worst thing that can happen.

32

Merry,
daughter of Grace

I was hoping we were all going to go to bed after dessert. Not that I'd nod off right away. Even though I'm exhausted, I can tell that I won't be able to sleep until my mom gets back.

But Mariella has other plans anyway. Even though it's 11 o'clock at night, she kicks off her heels and crouches down low in the center of the living room. She wraps her arms around her knees and makes herself as small as possible.

"Hiding!" Zoey shouts. "Cowering!"

Mariella lifts her head to shake it *no.*

"Squeezing! Ball?"

No.

"Small!"

Mariella nods *yes*, signs *more*.

"Tiny! Little!"

Mariella shoots back up to standing and grins triumphantly.

"Okay, first word: *Little*," Zoey says. "I know, *Little Fires Everywhere*!"

Mariella shakes her head. She points to Elin, Kathleen, and Brigid.

"*Women!*" Zoey shrieks. "*Little Women!*" She puts her hands on her hips. "Mommy, that was *way* too easy."

Mariella ignores Zoey's scolding and turns to the rest of us. "How come my daughter is the only one playing?"

I know why I'm not: I'm stuffed and tired and worried. Meanwhile Elin and Kathleen look like they've melted into the couch. Brigid seems to have fallen asleep in an armchair. And I don't even know where Meg is.

Jamie says, "The hikers are exhausted, and the boaters are sunburned."

"But charades is on the schedule!" Mariella cries. "Can't we play just one tiny round?"

Poor Mariella. She's worked so hard to make this weekend perfect. And so far it's been great. Before she disappeared, even Meg seemed like she was finally having fun.

"Fine," I say, "I'll go."

Mariella practically bounds over with the hat, and I pull out a strip. I grimace when I read it. How am I supposed to act out *The Unbearable Lightness of Being*?

But I'm saved by the entrance of my mom.

She's not alone.

Behind her, with a nervous grin on his face, is Captain Daniel.

The wave of relief I feel gets swamped by a tidal wave of anger. I'm on my feet. I'm suddenly wide awake. "Where were you?" I demand.

I know I'm acting like the mother whose teenager stayed out too late. My mom looks taken aback. I haven't spoken sharply to her in years.

"I took your mother to lunch," Captain Daniel says.

"For *ten hours*?" I don't care how rude I sound.

"We thought you'd been kidnapped," Mariella says.

"Well, Merry did," Kathleen clarifies.

"Yeah," I snap, "I pretty much did."

"I'm so sorry, my dear," Mom says to me. She turns to Captain Daniel. "Danny, let me introduce you to the others you haven't met. This is Zoey, Brigid, and Mariella, our hostess."

So he's Danny now? Well, *Danny* looks slightly embarrassed to be the center of everyone's attention.

"You have a beautiful home," he says to Mariella. "I love your sense of style."

Mariella shoots a victorious look at Zoey. "See? *He* doesn't think it looks like La Scala in here."

Zoey shrugs one tan shoulder. "Or maybe he does but he likes that kind of thing."

Mariella squeals in mock rage and throws a pillow at her daughter. Zoey ducks. The pillow sails through the open French doors and lands on the terrace. Mike appears out of nowhere to pick it up and put it back where it belongs before vanishing again.

"But really," Mariella presses, "what did you two do all day?"

I watch as Danny and my mom exchange a quick furtive glance. *They have a secret*, I think. Whatever they tell, it won't be the whole truth.

"Danny showed me around the hills above Varenna," my mom says. "Did you know that the Como area is the silk capital of Italy? Although silk was brought to Venice first—by Marco Polo, actually."

Maybe she's trying to prove that Danny still knows history, despite quitting his teaching job to drive tourists around in boats. Or maybe she's trying not to answer the question of what they did all day.

I want to press her. But I stop myself. Because I realize that my mom is glowing.

Sure, she got a lot of sun today. But that's not what's causing it. I notice how close she's standing to Danny. How comfortable and relaxed she seems.

I see my mom every week for Sunday dinner, and I haven't seen her look this way in months.

Maybe years.

Maybe *ever*.

Everyone else is looking at the two of them, too, and I can tell they're all biting their tongues. They're dying to know more, but they don't want to embarrass my mom, and they don't want to freak out Danny.

The silence starts to get a little awkward.

Mariella, of course, is the one to finally break it.

"Tell me, Danny," she says, "how do you feel about charades?"

33

Kathleen,
daughter of Jamie

I slip out of the room when Captain Handsome's taking his turn at charades. It's obvious that he's acting out *The Da Vinci Code*, but for some reason none of the ladies from the MDBC have figured this out yet.

The night air is warm and velvety. It's so much softer and sweeter than the air in Chicago that it feels like a different substance. As I walk into the garden, the sound of Mariella's giddy laughter gets quieter and I can feel the tension in my shoulders start to lessen. I adore all those women, I do. But I'm more of an introvert than I used to be. I blame it on the accident.

I blame a lot of things on the accident.

I decide that I should go find the pool. If I can float for a while, I can give myself a break from gravity. In the water, I no longer limp, and I no longer need a cane. I remember what it's like to feel perfect and whole.

Ahead of me, the path forks. Which way is the pool? *Eeny, meeny, miny, moe...* I go left. At the next fork, I head to the right. I keep a close eye on the ground as I go. I have to be careful about tree roots, cracked flagstones, or anything else that might catch my cane and throw me off-balance.

Mariella's garden is way bigger than I thought. The path keeps splitting and meandering. By now I can't even see the villa.

I take another left. *Did I pass this dolphin fountain already?*

I've been paying too much attention to the ground and not enough to where I'm going. It's even possible that I've been walking in circles. My hip is aching, and I don't know how much farther I can go. Fatigue weighs down my bones.

Am I really lost in Mariella's garden? How stupid would that be?

I sit down on the rock that I may or may not have passed by before. I'm so tired. I picture myself curling up in a flower bed instead of a queen-size memory foam and just going to sleep. It's a ridiculous image. I don't know whether to laugh or start to freak out.

One thing I know I'm *not* doing: yelling for help. No way. This is too damn embarrassing.

I should start walking again. But which direction? *Eeny, meeny, miny —*

I hear a twig snap.

"Hello?" I call softly.

No one answers. The hairs on my arms stand up.

"Hello?" I say again. "Is someone there?"

I hear the crunch of gravel. Footsteps. And they're getting closer. But I can't see anyone yet.

"Hello?" I say, louder now.

Silence. Then another footstep.

Why aren't they answering me? I'm lost, I'm in pain, and now I'm about to get attacked by an Italian prowler. I grip my cane like it's a sword.

And then, out of the darkness, my sister appears.

"It's you!" I cry, as the shock of adrenaline dissipates. "You scared me to death! Did you not hear me calling out?"

My sister calmly removes an earbud from her ear. She says, "What?"

I can't tell if I'm more relieved or more furious. I clench my jaw so hard my teeth ache. "Oh, my God. Never mind."

Meg takes out her other earbud. Looks at me quizzically. "What are you doing out here?"

I turn away from her. If I don't answer, maybe she'll just leave.

"Kath?" she says. "Are you all right?"

"I'm fine. I'm going swimming," I say curtly.

Meg snorts. "You're nowhere near the pool."

Damn it. "Yeah, well, I got lost."

"Seriously?" She laughs.

That she finds this funny infuriates me. "I must've missed a turn. Unlike *you*, *I* have to watch the ground when I walk. I'm held together with metal pins, remember?"

Meg takes a step backward. Like my words have literally struck her. When she speaks, her voice is quiet and cruel. "Aren't you sick of people feeling sorry for you, Kathleen?"

My grip on my cane tightens. How *dare* she. "I'm sick of walking with a goddamn cane, that's what I'm sick of!"

"You weren't the only one hurt, remember?"

I know I wasn't! But as far as remembering—well, I can barely recall anything about that night. There was rain. The shriek of brakes. The world spinning too fast. The sky in the wrong place.

"Well, *you* walked away with barely a scratch!" I cry.

Meg sinks down on a rock on the other side of the path. Her shoulders slump.

"Why are we still fighting?" she says. Her voice catches in her throat. Suddenly she sounds as broken as I feel. "I mean, we should *talk*, Kathleen. The way we're avoiding each other—it's absurd."

I know she's right.

But I'm not ready yet.

"Just tell me where the pool is."

Meg stares at me, her face in shadow. "Wow," she says. "Okay, then." She stands up. Hooks a thumb over her shoulder. "It's down that path. Take a right by the nymph statue, then the next left."

I stand up, too, suppressing a grimace. I'm in a lot of pain, but I don't want her to see it. "Great," I say flatly. "Thanks."

I limp in the direction she told me. In another fifty yards, I find the pool.

Its surface is as smooth as glass. In the trees, an owl calls.

I slowly take off my clothes. Then I slide into the water. Its cool smoothness calms me. I paddle gently from one side of the pool to the other. Fireflies blink off and on beneath the trees. I let the anger and the bitterness wash themselves away.

How dumb it was for me to be scared of being murdered in Mariella's beautiful garden. Why be afraid of a stranger when it's the people you love who hurt you the most?

34

Mariella,
mother of Zoey

I'm the first one awake, as usual. The sun's rays are just beginning to touch the mountaintops as I tiptoe down to the kitchen. Miraculously, I don't feel tired. I don't have a hangover. I don't even have blisters from hiking.

So far so good, Mariella; your plans have been working out. Is there a saint of weekends? I will light a candle for her.

I make myself a double espresso and curl into my favorite chair with a book, as per my morning ritual. I'm almost to the end of *28 Summers*. "Make sure you have Kleenex," Grace warned me, and I have a box just in case. I'm just getting to a really good part when I glance at the clock and realize that it's almost time for our yoga session.

Mannaggia!

I toss the book aside and hurry upstairs to the yoga room. I open all the windows, letting in fresh air and birdsong. I make a mental note to ask Kathleen what bird makes that operatic trilling, and then I fetch the broom. I know Lucia swept yesterday morning, but I also know that her eyesight's not what it used to be. I'm sweeping and humming Mozart's "Vedrai carino" to myself, happy as a lark, when Zoey comes in, yawning.

"I should *not* have had that third glass of wine last night," she says, unrolling her mat. She lies down on it and closes her eyes. "Let's just stay in Savasana the whole time, okay? 'Corpse pose' feels extremely appropriate right now."

I set my mat down beside my daughter's and perform a few gentle stretches. Butterfly, Pigeon, Forward Fold. As my voice teacher used to say, "Your body is your musical instrument, and you must work to keep it in tune."

Zoey, I notice, seems to have gone back to sleep.

After a little while I nudge her. "What time did I say yoga was?"

"Seven," Zoey murmurs, her eyes still closed.

"It's 7:29! Where *is* everyone?"

"Well, they're sane, Mommy, so they're probably still in bed."

"But they know the schedule!" I lift my arms skyward. I need to start my sun salutations. I didn't realize it was so late.

"Mommy, these are grown women," Zoey says. "You can't make them do exactly what you tell them to do all the time."

I fold forward, keeping my breathing long and slow. Yoga is important, but so is making this weekend wonderful. And I know the exact right way to do it. "Didn't Elin specifically put me in charge?"

"Actually I think you might have put yourself in charge," Zoey says.

A flash of sudden worry flickers through me. "Are you telling me I'm too bossy?"

"You, bossy?" Zoey laughs. "*You*, who made the entire Cleveland Orchestra do the Macarena with you last year?"

I lift my head up a little, then fold forward again. My hamstrings are sore. "But it was my birthday. And they loved it," I say.

"You made the whole audience do it, too," Zoey adds.

"We got rave reviews. They were all over the internet, which is surely how you know about it." I walk my hands out so I'm in a plank position. "Even though you haven't seen me perform live in years."

"Okay, fine. So what about the fact that you've made Dad play servant this whole weekend? Don't tell me *that's* not bossy as hell."

I lift my hips so I'm in Downward Dog. *God, my calves are tight, too.* "He doesn't mind! In fact, he loves it."

"Argh," Zoey says in obvious exasperation. *She knows I'm*

right. "You're still the bossiest person any of us knows. Admit it."

There's a weird fluttering feeling in my stomach. Is it because I'm upside down, and maybe I *am* a bit hungover after all? Or does it mean that I've gone about things all wrong, and something bad's about to happen?

Breathe in, breathe out, Mariella. Stay calm. Everything is fine.

"I'm a terrible hostess. That's what you're saying."

"No, Mommy, I'm not saying that," Zoey says. "I think you're amazing. But maybe you should ask other people what they want to do for once."

I bristle. "Well, I can't ask them if they won't even get their fat lazy butts out of bed!"

Zoey makes a warning noise in her throat. Still upside down, I turn my head toward the doorway, where Elin, Grace, Jamie, and their daughters are watching me.

O, merda.

Elin folds her arms across her chest. "Whose butts are you calling fat and lazy?"

35

Elin,
mother of Brigid

If any of us thought Mariella would be flustered by our lateness or the fact that we just busted her insulting our derrieres, we were dead wrong. She sounds as imperious as a queen, even while still in Downward Dog with her own ample butt sticking up in the air.

"Why are you still in pajamas, Grace?" she demands. She turns her upside-down eyes toward yours truly. "Elin Mackenzie, you can't do yoga in a *sundress*!" She walks her hands back to her toes and hangs, bent over, for a count of three. Then she straightens up and stomps over to us, hands on her hips, dark eyes flashing. "*Per carità,* what is going on?"

"We can't do yoga, Mariella," Grace blurts.

"What do you mean y—"

"Of course, we *can*," I clarify. "It's just that we don't want to."

We'd all stumbled out of our bedrooms twenty minutes ago, and almost without speaking we'd come to an agreement. No yoga today, no thank you. Grace and I would be the ones to break it to Mariella, since we've known her the longest and we've disappointed her before. Like when we wouldn't pledge the sorority she was obsessed with back in college. Or when, in our twenties, we couldn't drop everything to catch a flight to Iceland on two hours' notice (she'd wanted us to see the northern lights with her). Or when we refused to read *50 Shades of Grey* for our book club.

She got us back for that one, though. She'd dictated *pages* of it into our voicemails.

"We'd really like to relax," Merry says now. "Because it's vacation."

Mariella's sculpted brows furrow. Not very much, though, thanks to a one-two punch of La Roche-Posay retinol serum and a few dozen units of Botox. She gets the latter every two months, because—and I believe this is the correct quote—*I must not look like a wrinkled old bag under the spotlight!*

"I don't understand," she says now.

I smile fondly at my friend. "We know you don't understand relaxing, honey. Divas don't do downtime. But we can probably show you how it's done." I walk over to her and tuck my arm through hers. "Come on," I urge. "Let's go down to the kitchen. Jamie will make us her famous pancakes."

Mariella casts a panicked glance back at her daughter. "Zoey, it's a mutiny!" But Zoey's giggling and taking a video. "Please," she begs us, "I need a *Real Housewives* catfight. It'll be so good."

Grace shakes her head firmly. "Zoey, darling, we don't want to do yoga, and we definitely don't want to be part of your internet content," she says in her special minister voice.

Zoey knows this voice must be listened to. She turns off her camera. I'm trying to pull Mariella toward the door, but it's not working.

"Jamie will make pancakes," she repeats. "And then what?"

"Then we will *eat* them," I tell her. "And after breakfast, we're all going to read in the sunshine. Or maybe some of us will dip our feet into the pool."

"But for how long?" Mariella cries. "Thirty minutes? An *hour*?"

I can see her fingers twitching. She wants her notebook so she can put this into the schedule.

"I think we're going to play it by ear," I say.

She stares at me like I've just told her I'm a serial killer.

The sound of clapping comes to us from the hallway. When I turn around, I'm startled to find Mike standing right behind us. For a large man, he's extremely stealthy.

"Defy her," he says. "Be stronger than I am."

"Geez, Mike," Jamie says, obviously surprised too. "You could be a spy."

He chuckles modestly. "Maybe there's still time for a new career. But what's this I hear about a mutiny? And pancakes?"

Mariella tugs at my sleeve. "Elin, darling, there are so many things I have planned today—"

I put my arm around her shoulders. "I know. You're the best planner in the world, Mariella! And we love you. But today we want to follow *our* rules."

Jamie steps forward and gives a mock salute. "And the first rule of the Mother-Daughter Book Club is that *there are no more rules!*"

Zoey gives a little hop of delight. "I love this for us," she says. She goes to the other side of Mariella and wraps her arm around her waist. "Mommy, you've done the most amazing job. It's not your fault that the rest of us lack your vision and your stamina."

Zoey clearly knows that a compliment is the way to her mother's heart.

Mariella sighs and flings up her hands. "What can I say? You are grown women! I cannot make you do exactly what I tell you to do all the time."

"Did I not just tell you that *exact* thing?" Zoey says.

I smile at Grace over Mariella's head. "See? She took it well. Nothing to be afraid of."

Grace smiles back. "Not yet, anyway."

"Not yet is right," Mariella says, with more than a hint of mischief in her voice. "I will soon be planning my revenge."

36

Grace,
mother of Merry

Jamie and I race down to the kitchen, giggling like teenagers let out of school early.

"Eggs, flour, butter—where do you think Mariella keeps her cinnamon?" Jamie asks. She's yanking all of Mariella's cupboards open, one after the other. "I like to put cinnamon in my pancakes. It has anti-inflammatory properties."

In a pantry next to the refrigerator, I find enough spices to stock an aisle at Whole Foods. "Do you want Ceylon cinnamon? Or maybe cinnamon from Vietnam or Sri Lanka?"

Jamie laughs. "Shoot, my cinnamon comes from Costco!"

I grab the Ceylon jar just as the other women come in. We cluster around Jamie as she starts mixing her ingredients.

Jamie's pancakes are legendary. Brigid and Elin have been talking about them for years.

"You use whole milk?" Mariella asks her. "Or, wait—is that buttermilk?"

"Is the butter salted or unsalted?" Elin wonders.

"Out!" Jamie cries, laughing. "You know what they say about too many cooks!"

"But we aren't cooking," I point out. "We're *spectating*."

"You're spying!" She brandishes a wooden spoon at us. "Out, this is my secret recipe!"

"Good. You will share it on the Night of Secrets," Mariella says.

Jamie takes a playful (I think) swipe at her with the spoon. Mariella dashes from the kitchen, screeching.

We go and sit at the big oval table, and everyone drinks coffee, and as the warm breeze blowing in through the French doors tickles the back of my neck, I feel a sense of relaxation and well-being stronger than any I've felt in ages.

Ironically, this happiness brings the prickle of tears to my eyes. I discreetly dab at them with a corner of the tablecloth. No one notices. Zoey and Mariella are now arguing about whether *The Secret History* or *The Goldfinch* was better. Merry and Kathleen are talking bird sightings. And Elin's asking Meg about how her novel's coming along. I didn't know Meg was working on a novel; I wonder what it's about.

"You okay, Grace?" Brigid asks.

Well, okay, *someone* noticed. I turn to her and smile. "Couldn't be better. I think I just got a little pollen in my eye."

"I've got eyewash in my first aid kit if you need it."

Of course she does. "You're a good doctor," I tell her. "Like I always knew you'd be."

For some reason, she quickly looks away, seemingly uncomfortable. But I don't have time to ponder why because Jamie appears with the pancakes, and everyone exclaims in delight, and thirty seconds later I've got two big golden pancakes on my plate.

"Oh, my God, I've missed these," Elin says with her mouth full.

"I used to make them for everyone after church on Sundays," Jamie tells the rest of us. "It was a ritual. Sometimes I made them on Monday mornings, too. They made going back to work and school a little easier."

"Sometimes she'd even have whipped cream," Brigid says. "But we had to make it ourselves, with a whisk, because she claimed it was better that way."

"It is," Jamie insists. "You can taste the difference."

Her pancakes are as good as Elin says they are. And they taste even better because I'm eating them with the people I've loved for most of my life.

It's not something you think about when you're single in your twenties, but breakfast in a one-person household is very quiet. Especially when it's just you, your cold cereal, the newspaper, and a few houseplants.

I give myself a visible shake, brushing off the dark thoughts that have been my constant companion these past few months. If anything can make me feel better again, it's being with the Mother-Daughter Book Club.

And Danny, says a tiny voice.

I'm startled, but that voice isn't wrong. Being with him yesterday made me feel like a bigger, brighter person. And as if the whole world had grown bigger and brighter around me, too.

"Remember, Grace?" Elin says, nudging me.

I snap back to attention. "Sorry — what?"

Mariella gives me a sly look. "She was thinking about Danny. Captain of the speedboat and captain of her heart."

How could she tell? I roll my eyes at her, pretending she's wrong.

"I was saying," Elin says patiently, "remember when Merry and Brigid read *From the Mixed-Up Files of Mrs. Basil E. Frankweiler* and decided that they were going to live in the art museum?"

"I do remember. I still can't believe they plotted it. They lived nearly a thousand miles apart!"

"I was so slick, I just talked my way onto the bus," Brigid says. "That Greyhound driver was ready to take me to New York!"

"It was a *twenty-hour ride*," Elin says, clearly still aghast. "How could he have let a little girl like her on alone?"

"Meanwhile I couldn't get four stupid blocks away from my house before all the neighbors started calling my mom," Merry says.

I remember that, too. How Mrs. Klein from up the street had called to tell me, in her wavering little old lady voice, "Grace, your daughter is standing on the street corner with a suitcase."

"You know what they say—it takes a village." I laugh. Truth be told, I couldn't have raised Merry and Luke without the help of those neighbors.

Elin leans toward me. "Let's get back to this 'captain of your heart' business."

I shake my head. "There's really nothing to say. We had a lovely afternoon together."

"That can't be the end," says Mariella. "Because that would mean a very disappointing plot."

"Life is rarely as exciting as fiction," I point out.

I'd put my info into Danny's contacts, but I didn't get his number. For one thing, my phone had been dead for hours. But for another, I didn't want to expose or embarrass myself. I'd already been as bold as I could be, inviting myself to his house. I didn't want to become the desperate lady calling up the guy who took her out to lunch once just for the hell of it. Sure, it had *seemed* like Danny really liked me. But how could I be certain? It had been years since I'd even attempted to guess what a man was thinking.

Will our paths cross again? I have no idea. I thought that I was leaving it up to chance when I said good-bye without taking his number. But I guess what I was really doing was leaving it up to Danny.

37

Jamie,
mother of Meg and Kathleen

You should've seen the faces on those ladies when I brought out my pancakes. It was like they were all eight-year-olds on Christmas morning, and there was a damn pony under the pine tree.

It made me feel great. Valuable, too, if that doesn't sound too weird. I'm not as successful as my friends, and we all know that my life's a lot harder. But I can still give these ladies something that they appreciate.

Which isn't actually pancakes, of course—it's love. It just happens to be in the form of pancakes, dotted with summer berries and drenched in maple syrup. People always forget that mothers need mothering, too. One day a year, on a holiday co-opted by Hallmark? It ain't half enough.

Elin leans in close. "I miss the old days, don't you?"

I smile, knowing exactly what she's talking about. When her house was full, when our families spent every Sunday afternoon together. The kids would swing on the swing set, run the dog ragged, and play grounders until they collapsed in happy exhaustion. Charlie and Logan would man the grill, of course, and Elin and I would peel carrots in the kitchen, talking about anything and everything. Our lives were so sweet then. Chaotic. Wonderful.

The doorbell rings, and I jump. Mariella, too, sits up with a start. I can see her eyes darting quickly around the table. She's making sure that everyone's here. That everyone's safe. I know, because I did the exact same thing.

And yes, we're all here. Even my prickly Meg, who keeps looking at her watch like she's got somewhere else to go.

After the head count, Mariella visibly relaxes. "Who on earth could that be?" she says, bemused.

Four seconds later, Lucia comes in, followed by a very pretty young woman.

Elin whispers, "It's the tattoo lady again."

"Francesca, *buongiorno*," Mariella cries, hurrying over to kiss her on both cheeks. "What brings you here?"

"My morning tarot reading," Francesca says. "The cards told me to come, and I always listen to them."

"Really!"

Francesca grins. "Also, Zoey texted and asked if I was free."

We all turn to Zoey. She shrugs. "I just figured that more people should be given the option for a beautiful tattoo." She stretches out one long, tanned arm. "I could see a flower on my forearm maybe…"

I shoot to my feet. "Me," I say. "I want one."

Now everyone turns to look at me. Kathleen and Meg both say, "Mom? You *do*?"

The group all knows that I got a yin-yang symbol on my ankle the second I turned eighteen, and I've regretted it ever since. "Yes." Slightly embarrassed by my enthusiasm, I sit back down. I'm just as surprised as my kids are. I can't explain why I suddenly want another tattoo. I don't even have any thoughts on the design yet.

"What are you going to get?" Elin asks.

"Actually, I have to think about it for a minute."

"Make it dealer's choice," Zoey suggests. "Or close your eyes and point to one."

"No way. I'm holding off on all surprises until the Night of Secrets." *And, God, let's hope they're good ones.*

Francesca offers to show me her book of designs, but I shake my head. I realize that I want words, not flowers or stars or birds. Something optimistic and uplifting. In other words, *not* the unofficial motto of my life. "Things never work out the way you think they will" is a total downer.

Francesca says, "Is there anyone else who would like a tattoo?"

Mariella breaks the slightly awkward silence that follows. She says, "Why don't you have a pancake, Francesca. It is an authentic American breakfast."

"Oh, I couldn't." Francesca puts a protective hand over her flat, young stomach. "I ate two *cornetti* already."

I sigh. I'd *love* a *cornetto*.

No, I'm not getting a tattoo of one.

Then Grace blurts, "I'll do it."

Everyone turns to her in shock. Grace? The *minister*? The sixty-year-old *virgin*?

She nods her head decisively. "I'm celebrating." But she doesn't tell us what she's celebrating, and when Elin asks her, she demurs. "I just feel...good. Hopeful," Grace says. "It's been a long time since I could say that. So I want to remember this day."

"This is obviously about the boat captain," Mariella whispers to me.

I nod, grinning. There's nothing like a crush to make you feel newly alive. I just hope it works out for her.

Grace opens the journal Mariella gave her and starts sketching something. When she's done, she holds up the page. She's drawn a sun surrounded by radiating lines of light. "Like this," she says to Francesca. "But better."

Francesca nods. "I know exactly what to do."

"What'll Danny Boy say?" Elin teases.

Grace grins as she tugs down the waistband of her pajamas, revealing one pale butt cheek. "Considering where I want it," she says, *"if* Danny ever sees it, I hope it's the last thing he's thinking about."

Everyone hoots with glee, and Mariella lets loose a string of happy Italian. Lucia looks scandalized, and Grace demands to know what Mariella said.

Mariella giggles. "I said, 'Dear God, please make Grace show him *everything.*'"

While Francesca gets her supplies ready, I keep thinking about what I want. I need something simple. Meaningful.

It isn't until Francesca's finished the outline of Grace's sun that it occurs to me.

It's just one word.

Things don't always turn out the way you expect them to—yes, it's the story of my life. But I have to believe they work out in the end.

I ask Mariella how to say it in Italian.

"Fidarsi," she says.

"Fidarsi," I repeat. I like the sound of it.

It means *"Trust."*

38

Mariella,
mother of Zoey

"I hope you don't mind, but I've taken the liberty of inviting another artist friend of mine over," Francesca announces. She's finished tattooing Jamie's bicep, and is packing up her supplies. "She is very talented."

"Fun!" my daughter exclaims. "I love surprise guests."

"Is she a makeup artist?" Merry asks, hope in her voice. "Because I'm twenty-eight years old and I still don't know how to put on eye shadow." She looks thoughtful. "But that Emma Cline book, *The Guest,* taught me how to apply eyebrow pencil. The secret is lots of very short strokes."

"Oh, I read that too," Zoey says. "That girl was *messed up.*"

Meanwhile I am moaning in dismay. *Another* artist? My

schedule will never recover from the assault! "But we have a swim scheduled at—"

Zoey turns to me. "Just let it go, Mommy. Like Idina Menzel! *Let it gooooo, let it g*—Agh!!" She stops abruptly and her hand shoots up to her cheek. That's because I've tossed a pillow at her. "Mother!" she exclaims. "Stop throwing pillows at me!"

I grin. That made me feel better. "No, I enjoy it. This weekend I have learned why they are called throw pillows!"

Zoey advances on me in mock rage. "You're going to pay for that."

Who knows what my daughter is about to do to me—start a pillow fight? Tickle my ribs? (She wouldn't even be able to find them!) Thankfully, we are interrupted by Lucia, who leads a striking-looking woman into the living room. The woman is a few years older than I am, not to mention fifty pounds lighter. She's dressed all in black.

"*Buongiorno,*" she says. Her voice is so rich and low I bet she could sing tenor.

Retreating behind Francesca, Zoey narrows her eyes at me. "You know what they say about revenge, Mommy..."

"It is best served lightly sautéed, I believe." I turn my attention to the new arrival, who is clearly the "artist" Francesca invited. "*Buongiorno,*" I say. "You look familiar. Have we met before?"

The woman shakes her head. "*Non credo,* I don't think so. I am Ginevra Capello."

Francesca links her arm through Ginevra's. "She looks familiar because she looks like *me*. This is my mother!"

Now, with their two faces side by side, I can see it perfectly. "Of course!"

"A mother-daughter team," Elin says approvingly. "We like that around here."

"My mother is my inspiration," Francesca says. "She is also a gifted hypnotist."

A hypnotist?

"So cool," Zoey whispers. "I did hypnotherapy once."

"You did? What for?"

"Oh, you know, just some issues with my mother, NBD."

I pitch another pillow at her; she squeals.

But Ginevra interrupts our playful spat. "Hypnosis is a wonderful, healing practice. It is helpful for those with anxiety, pain, phobias, and habits they wish to change. Is there anyone who would like to try a session?"

I look around the room. For some reason, everyone's eyes are on *me*.

"What?" I demand.

Grace says, "I've heard that hypnosis can be really relaxing. And you, dear Mariella, could definitely stand to relax."

Me? Relax? I have a thousand arguments to make against this! "I will relax when this vacation is over!" I cry.

The room's dead quiet for a moment. Then Elin giggles and Grace goes, "Uh, Mari, did you hear what you just said?"

I sigh. Yes, I heard, and I realize it did not sound good. "Fine," I say. "I will be hypnotized. But only so we can get back on schedule as quickly as possible! You may take this time to read your books or write in your journals."

"Yes, master," Zoey says.

I motion for Ginevra to follow me to the sunroom, where we sit down across from each other in the warm sunlight. She tells me that hypnosis is simply a heightened focus of attention, and assures me that there is nothing to be afraid of.

"Do I seem like a scaredy-cat?"

"No, but I might call you…what is the right English phrase? Ah, 'slightly anxious.' Yes. That is right."

"Harrumph," I say, and I sound like my grandfather, God rest Nonno's Sicilian soul.

"This is not like hypnosis in the movies. I cannot control you when you are under hypnosis," Ginevra says. "But I can help you let go of some of what I gather might be your own need to control things."

I nod. I do not know how I got this reputation.

Oh, liar, yes you do.

Ginevra's voice is gentle and steady as she invites me to close my eyes and focus on my breathing. "With each long, slow breath," she says, "you will relax deeper into your chair."

Inhale for four, exhale for four, inhale for four, exhale for four. So far, so good. I start to feel myself growing heavier.

Wait — I don't need to get any heavier!

"Keep your eyes closed, Mariella," Ginevra reminds me. "For hypnosis to work, you must *allow* it to work."

"Easier said than done!"

We start over. This time I am supposed to imagine my body loosening, lightening, floating. I'm safe and comfortable on a beautiful cloud. Ginevra's deep, rich voice soothes me. Holds me in a cocoon of warmth.

She guides me to the banks of a gently flowing river. Breathing slowly and focusing, I can see it. Hear it. It's so real I feel I could dip my toes into it.

Ginevra tells me to look down at my hands. "Imagine that you are holding a handful of leaves," she says.

Okay, I am holding leaves of many different hues. Ginevra tells me to select one. To look at it carefully—its shape, its color, its branching veins—and to see it as a symbol of something that I am trying to control.

"There is a weight in holding onto control," Ginevra says. "There is relief and lightness in letting it go."

I'm entranced by my leaf. It's bright red and beautiful. And I understand that it symbolizes my need to regulate every minute of this weekend. My desperate desire to make everything perfect. To try to keep anything bad from happening.

"I want you to bend down," Ginevra says, "and release the leaf into the river."

I don't want to let it go.

"Release it."

Fine, I will do what she tells me to. In my mind, I bring the leaf to my lips. I give it a good-bye kiss. I place it on the surface of the river, and I watch it swirl away downstream.

I feel a stab of anxiety—what will happen to my leaf if I can't take care of it? But as I continue to look closely at my leaves, and then set them free, I feel a growing sense of ease. Of freedom.

When Ginevra slowly counts me back to a state of full awareness, I open my eyes. I feel calm and relaxed. Almost like I'm still floating.

"What did you think?" she asks, smiling.

"I think it is possible that I am an entirely new woman," I say.

Ginevra laughs. "Wouldn't that be something!"

It sure would.

39

Elin,
mother of Brigid

With our arms full of books, towels, and bottles of sunscreen, Jamie, Grace, and I make our way down the hill from the terraced garden to Mariella's private dock. Behind us come the girls—sorry, the *young women*—with folding chairs, snacks, and ice-cold bottles of mineral water.

Trees along the lake's edge keep part of the dock in gentle shade. Jamie and Grace make themselves comfortable there, but I walk out to the very end. Barefoot on the warm wood, I watch sailboats gliding by, their white sails a bright contrast to the forested hills on the other side. The air carries the sweet scent of orange blossoms and the cool, green smell of the water.

I step out of my dress. Underneath I'm wearing a one-piece bathing suit that's squeezing my middle like a sausage casing. Back in college, I practically lived in a swimsuit. I didn't think twice about showing three-quarters of my skin, not at swim meets, and not on the Memorial Union swim pier, either. Forty years later, things are a little different. A little softer. A little saggier.

I miss that strong, young body. But I don't miss having swim practice at 5:30 a.m. It was always pitch-black and freezing cold, especially in the winter; in Madison at that time, the temperature sometimes didn't get above freezing for months. I'd be so wrapped up in layers of wool and down that the only part of me you could see was my eyes. Then—and this was the worst part—I'd have to take off all those warm layers and dive into a cold pool. Then, after swimming to the point of exhaustion, I'd have to put everything back on again and rush to class. Because I never had time to dry my hair, it turned to blond icicles.

I still love the smell of a pool, though. One whiff of chlorine and I'm racing down memory lane.

Now, I tug on the bottom of my suit. The breeze is cool against my bare skin. I spend a few minutes taking deep breaths, shaking out my arms and legs. Warming them up, getting the blood flowing. Willing myself to take the plunge.

I count to ten in my head, and then I dive in, slicing into the water like a knife. It's a cold, delicious shock. When I come up, hollering at the chill, I see Grace racing down the dock toward me. Her arms are pumping and her teeth are gritted. At first I think something's wrong. She runs to the edge—and then she flings herself into the air.

"Cannonball!" she hollers.

Water droplets from her giant splash catch the sunlight and turn into diamonds.

I laugh as she comes up spluttering. "You never did learn to dive, did you?"

Grace wipes the water from her eyes and paddles toward me. "Nope!"

I lean my head back, lift my legs, and go into a lazy backstroke. "This lake is amazing. Do you think I could make it to the other side?"

"Of *course* you could. You used to swim out to Picnic Point and back!"

I laugh at one very small secret I've kept from her. "Sometimes I used to get a ride home."

"What? How?"

I never would've hitchhiked on a road, of course. But on a lake? That was another thing entirely. You could just stick your arm up and wave down a passing boat. They'd motor over, and you'd swim to the back ladder and climb up on board. They'd hand you a towel—maybe even a beer and a bag of chips.

It sounds crazy now. But there was something about Lake

Mendota that made everyone happy. Made everybody who was on it seem like a friend.

When I try to explain this, Grace looks at me in consternation. Then, suddenly, a look of horror crosses her face.

"What? Was it that terrible that I got on strangers' boats?"

"No," she cries. "I forgot about my tattoo! I'm not supposed to be swimming!"

Grace does a speedy crawl stroke back toward shore to dry off and reapply her ointment.

Following her with my gaze, I lazily alternate between treading water and floating on my back. Floating's a lot easier than it used to be. I have a higher fat-to-muscle ratio than I did when I was a college athlete, that's for sure.

In the distance I can see Mike coming down the hill. He's stepping gingerly because he's carrying a giant picnic basket. As soon as he gets to the dock, the girls swarm around him. Their cries of delight at the delicacies he's brought them carry across the water.

By the time I'm back on land, they've laid out a beautiful picnic lunch of crusty bread, assorted cheeses, *verdure grigliate* (grilled vegetables), and black olives the size of plums. There are also dark-purple grapes, plus a small, thin cake dotted with raisins and pine nuts, and several bottles of Trebbiano d'Abruzzo.

Zoey is eating dessert first. "They call it *miascia*," she tells everyone. "Also known as 'peasants' cake.' It's my favorite."

I stop Mike on his way back up to the villa. "Where's Mariella?"

He looks around furtively. Lowers his voice. "She's taking a nap."

"A *what*?"

His soft, wide face cracks open in a grin. "I know, can you believe it? The house has never been this peaceful, so I'm going to go enjoy it. I might even see if I can find a game to watch on TV!"

"Kick your feet up!" I laugh. "Lord knows you deserve it."

I grab a handful of grapes and go sit on the end of the dock, my feet dangling above the water. After a little while Jamie comes to sit beside me.

"Don't look now," she says, "but something incredible is happening."

"What is it?"

"My daughters are actually talking to each other."

I can't help it, I have to look. I turn my head just enough so that I can see them. They're sitting side by side on the stone wall at the lake's edge. Kathleen has a big yellow sun hat on, just like on the cover of that Jennifer Weiner book I read on the plane, *Big Summer*. Meg is bareheaded, kicking her feet against the wall like a kid.

"I wonder what they're talking about."

"Who cares? So long as they're doing it."

I care, actually. And Jamie probably does too. But she's

right: what matters is that Meg and Kathleen are no longer ignoring each other. Whatever the tension is between them, they're figuring out how to repair it. I hope.

I lie back on the dock and close my eyes. I feel warm and serene and happy. "I wish I could go back and start this weekend over again," I say with a sigh.

Beside me I can feel Jamie stiffen. "I'd go back three years," she says. "I'd make it so Logan never said he'd leave me. I'd make it so Lake Geneva never happened."

"Oh, Jamie, I'm sorry, of course," I cry. "That was thoughtless of me."

She bumps her hip lightly against mine, forgiving me. "But time travel is just a fantasy, Elin. You're allowed to have whatever kind you want. Maybe if you thought about it, you'd go back further, too."

"I would." I know this instantly. "I'd go back to when Bridgie was little."

"You'd go through the toddler days again?" Jamie asks incredulously.

"In a heartbeat." An old, buried guilt threatens to surface. I push it back down. "I didn't understand how precious those chaotic days were. Or how quickly they would end."

"Are you saying you wish you'd stayed home with her — that you hadn't hired a nanny?" Jamie asks.

"No," I say. "I needed the work, I needed the money, I needed the prestige. All of it. So I needed *you* desperately. I was—and am—so grateful that you came into our lives. What I guess I mean is...I wish I'd balanced things a little better. I thought being a lawyer was the important thing. I didn't understand that my most important job was being Brigid's mother." I'm surprised that I'm admitting this. It took me years to figure it out.

"Well, if it makes you feel any better, being a mother was basically the only job I ever had, and I still feel like I screwed it up."

"You were—you are—an amazing mom, Jamie Price." I pause, then add, "And an amazing wife."

I open my eyes to see a tear sliding down Jamie's freckled cheek as she gazes out over the water. "Till death do us part," she whispers.

40

Grace,
mother of Merry

After the refreshing lake swim, I settle myself into a chaise longue on the sunlit terrace and pull out Jhumpa Lahiri's novel *Whereabouts*. She wrote it in Italian (her third language, if you can believe it) and then translated it into English herself. In it, an unnamed narrator walks the streets of an unnamed city, reflecting on her daily routines and interactions. A well-plotted thriller it is not—but it's good. Haunting. And I'm barely forty pages in when my daughter appears, her nose pink from the sun and the rest of her smelling like Mariella's very expensive lavender lotion.

Merry sits down on the neighboring chaise and hands me a flute of sparkling pale-gold wine. "Mariella wants me to tell you that it's vintage franciacorta, which is the champagne of Italy." She lifts her chin and purses her lips in an uncanny impression of my dramatic friend. "'It's not some supermarket prosecco, you know! Dinner is in 188 minutes!'"

I laugh as we clink our glasses together. "It sounds like Mariella gathered up some of her leaves again."

"I think it takes more than one hypnosis session to get over a lifetime of main character syndrome," Merry says drily. "But she hasn't put her watch back on yet, so something's still different."

The wine is delicious, cold and fizzy against my tongue. I sigh with pleasure. "I can't believe we have to go back to regular life tomorrow."

"We should ask Mariella to adopt us," Merry says.

"Perfect. I'll help Mike with the cooking, you can help Lucia with the cleaning, and we'll take turns minding Zoey."

We indulge this ludicrous dream for a moment, imagining what it would be like to completely and utterly change our lives.

The funny thing is, though, neither of us would truly want to do it. We have homes and lives (and houseplants!) back in Bridgeport. My son Luke, Merry's younger brother, is there; they live around the corner from each other. And between my church congregation and Merry's social work clients, we have so many people relying on us. We are, as Mr. Rogers used to say, the Helpers. For better or worse, we were both born that way.

"Why didn't you tell me how lonely you've been?" my daughter blurts out. "Why did I have to hear about it from Elin? She's worried about you."

I look down at my strong, tanned hands. I've never worn any nail polish; my ring fingers have always been bare. They are the hands of a woman who's spent her life caring for others. Who's paid far less attention to caring for herself. But it's not a choice I've regretted. Until recently.

How much should I tell Merry? Before this trip, I would've tried to keep it locked inside me. Now, though, I feel capable of being more open.

"Yes, I was horribly lonely," I tell my daughter. "For a long, long time." But then I feel a smile tugging at the corners of my mouth. "I think everything's going to be okay, though."

"Why? Is this because of Danny? Mom, you only spent one *day* with the guy."

I hear the skepticism in her voice. "It's not Danny." Then I reconsider this. "Okay, it's not *just* Danny. Meeting him was wonderful. Even if I never see him again, it changed me. I truly mean that." *But I truly hope I get to see him again.* "It's more about this weekend with you and everyone else. *That's* what's done it. I've filled up the love tanks again."

"Love tanks? Gross, Mom."

I swat her arm playfully. "That's not how I mean it and you know it!"

Merry smiles. But then her face goes serious again. "Don't you wish you'd met someone like Danny when you were younger?"

Believe it or not, this is an easy answer. "No. Because then I wouldn't have you or your brother."

"But doing all that on your own. It seems really hard."

"It *was* hard. But like I've always said, I needed to be a mother. Whereas I did not need to be someone's wife."

"You never talked about what IVF was like," she says.

You never seemed to want to know, I think. I'm not sure why she's got so many questions all of a sudden, but I see no reason not to be honest with her. "I suppose for a while I felt the stigma of using a donor—as if there was something wrong with me that I couldn't find someone to give me a baby the 'normal' way. But everyone at the church was so supportive. But I'm not going to lie. The process truly *sucked*."

Merry looks surprised. "How so?"

"It was more emotionally and physically demanding than I ever imagined. I had to give myself so many injections that I felt like a pincushion. Some days I was in so much pain that I could barely get out of bed. The hormones I kept pumping into my system wreaked havoc on my moods. One minute I'd be unloading the dishwasher and singing, and the next I'd be sobbing like a baby because I chipped a coffee mug."

"Sounds like PMS level one thousand," Merry says.

"Exactly. And after every procedure, I was sick for days. I couldn't sleep, either—not until I took the blood test confirming that I was pregnant."

"Wow," Merry says. "And you did that *twice*."

"Three times," I tell her. "Between you and your brother there was an unsuccessful cycle. But I was *lucky*. And I thank God every day that the technology was available to me."

I notice that Merry has her arms folded protectively over her belly. My own mother had me when she was twenty-two. I decide to ask her something I've been wondering lately: "Do you want children?"

She waits awhile before she gives a small nod. My heart leaps with happiness. I give her hand a quick squeeze. The thought of a grandbaby is magical.

"Were you scared?" she asks.

"Of being a mother?"

"No—of giving birth."

I shake my head. "I couldn't wait to hold you in my arms."

"Tell me what it was like."

"You're full of questions, aren't you?"

"Jamie was telling me about having the twins via C-section. It sounded...unpleasant. And then Mariella walked by and said something about having an epidural that made her so numb she couldn't even tell if she was pushing."

I know both of their stories; I also know the stories of dozens of other women in my church. "A lot of women end up having births that didn't go the way they wanted them to," I say.

"What about mine?"

"I'd wanted for everything to be so natural, but you were two weeks past your due date. So my doctor told me that I needed to go to the hospital the next day to be induced. 'That baby needs to come out,' she said. It was about eleven at night and I was taking a shower when I felt the first contraction. It wasn't such a big deal, and I thought, *Okay, I can do this.* But my labor progressed much more quickly than I thought it would, and pretty soon the pain was so bad I could barely stand. I certainly couldn't drive myself to the hospital, so I called Mrs. Klein and woke her from a dead sleep. She took me to the hospital. Along the way I bit my own hand to stop myself from screaming. I still have a scar." I hold out the back of my hand, where there are two tiny crescents of pink from my front teeth. "See?"

"Yikes," Merry says, grimacing.

"You were in what's called occiput posterior position. That means your head was down, but you were facing my front instead of my back. And that makes everything hurt more." I laugh. "As if it *needed* to hurt more! I didn't think such pain was even possible. 'Pain in labor is productive,' the doctors tell you. 'Pain is normal.' But I'd never felt pain like that before." I remember it all so clearly—not that it's so wildly fun to relive. "As a minister, I try to watch my language. But I cursed like a sailor with every new contraction. I kept telling myself that on the other end of all that agony would be a child. A baby of my own. And when they placed you on my chest, I understood that my whole life had only been a lead-up to that perfect moment. And I knew that whatever happened, from that day on, we would be together. I would love you until the end of my life and beyond." I can feel the tears now. I don't bother to wipe them away.

Merry looks a little misty herself. "When I was little," she says quietly, "I used to wish I had a dad. I—"

I interrupt her. "I'm sorry I couldn't give you a father. I'm sorry you and your brother just have a donor number on a sheet of paper."

"No, Mom, stop. We don't care about that. We never did. What I wanted to say is that I only wished for a dad for a tiny while. Because you gave me everything else." I can hear the love in her voice. She takes my hand now. Doesn't let it go. "You were enough, Mom," she says. "You were all that Luke and I could've asked for."

41

Brigid, daughter of Elin

I put a few swipes of zinc oxide on my face and lace up my running shoes. I've got *Wolf Hall* cued up on Audible: twelve more hours of story and names I can't keep straight. (Too many Thomases, too many titles for all the noblemen. But, still, the book's great.) I don't really feel like exercising, but running and reading (or listening, as the case may be) help banish my anxiety about tonight's Night of Secrets. I'm so afraid of disappointing Jamie. I'm heading out the door when I hear my name. I take out my earbud.

"Bridgie, come here stat," Zoey says. "Sorry, I mean *Doctor Mackenzie.* I need your help." Her dark eyes are sparkling and mischievous. "It's time to make my top-secret surprise."

"Tell me it's not another pitcher of cocktails." I let myself be pulled toward the kitchen. Maybe being distracted by Zoey's chatter will calm my mind. It's certainly a lot easier than exercising under the hot June sun.

"No, I'm not a total lush, sheesh. It's chocolate cake," Zoey informs me. "But not just any chocolate cake. This is the family recipe for *Killer* Chocolate Cake." She yanks open the cupboards, pulling out sugar, salt, flour. "Ugh, where is the baking soda? Lately Lucia's been putting things in weird places. The other day I found the eggs in the oven." She bangs a big silver bowl onto the counter. "Can you see if the vanilla is in the spice pantry? Do you think Lucia could be losing her mind?"

My shift into doctor mode is automatic. "Well, pretty much everyone experiences some cognitive decline as they get older. It's because of a natural but progressive decline in neuronal plasticity and synaptic efficacy," I say, scanning the shelves for the vanilla extract.

"Huh?" Zoey says.

"People's brains change as they get older, just like their faces do."

"My face won't," Zoey says. "I'm already saving up for plastic surgery."

"That doesn't make you look young, you know. It makes you look like an old person whose skin's been pulled tight." One of my friends is a plastic surgeon. She specializes in fixing plastic surgeries that previous doctors screwed up. You should *see* the photos. "Anyway, my guess is that Lucia just finds it hard to concentrate with your mother yammering away at her. No offense."

"None taken. She does talk a lot." Zoey shrugs. "Then again, so do I."

I locate the extract. "You come by it honestly," I agree.

Zoey squints as she reads from a picture on her phone. "'Cream butter and sugar together.' I hate this part, it takes forever."

She talks louder over the sound of the hand blender. "The thing about this cake is that I'm not supposed to know the recipe. My mom said she'd leave it to me in her will." She grins. "But I found it in a drawer and snapped a pic. She underestimated my powers of sneakiness!"

"You're not being very sneaky now, considering you're practically yelling."

"Don't worry, I got Dad to distract Mom. I bet she's talked him into giving her a foot massage." She rolls her eyes. "He's so dedicated to her it's pitiful."

"I think it's sweet."

Zoey turns off the mixer. "But your parents' blissful marriage can feel like a big thing to live up to, you know? You start to worry that maybe your own relationship will never be that perfect."

I raise my eyebrows at this uncharacteristically serious comment. "But you've got a great relationship with Luna."

"I know," Zoey says, nodding. "I do. But she doesn't worship the ground I walk on."

"Would you really want that, though?"

Zoey sighs. "No, I guess not. I guess that would be weird." She flashes me a quick grin. "I wouldn't say no to more foot rubs, though. Will you crack the eggs?"

I break two eggs into a small bowl. The yolks are a bright, rich, orangey yellow.

"My mom's going to die when she finds out that I made this for the Night of Secrets." Zoey shakes a beater at the ceiling. "It's impossible to keep a secret from me, Mommy!"

But it isn't, of course. I've been keeping a secret from Zoey—and almost everyone else—the whole weekend. Not that it's been easy. I've had to avoid Jamie, my coconspirator, as much as possible. And I've had to constantly distract myself from worrying, with things like strenuous jogs and wine at lunch.

Soon the secret will be out, and I can release the burden. But whether it's a good secret or a disaster—well, I don't know yet.

We're all going to find out tonight.

42

Mariella,
mother of Zoey

By 5 p.m., things are back on schedule. My husband is cooking, the girls are down on the dock, and Jamie is performing some sort of exhausting-looking exercise in the yoga room.

So now it's time for the little secret that comes *before* the Night of Secrets, and which involves my fellow graduates of UW-Madison. I yank Elin out of the library, and I pull Grace from what seems like a state of lovesick mooning on the terrace, although she claims that she was reading (ha!).

Without telling them what I'm up to, I lead them toward the wisteria-draped pergola on the north side of the villa.

Here we sit in lovely vintage wrought-iron chairs while the birds serenade us. I pour us glasses of mint and rose sun tea, and then I tell them to look under their cushions.

"Like Oprah used to have her audiences do!" Grace says, immediately standing up and lifting her cushion. She pulls out a small black box and her eyes widen.

Elin finds a similar box under her seat. "What is it?" She looks as giddy as a child.

"Open them, you dopes!"

When they do, they gasp simultaneously. For Elin, there is a tiny gold mesh coin purse, lined with satin, with a clasp that bears a shield with a dark-brown field and a light-brown crescent moon. For Grace, it's a gold pin with seed pearls and black enamel.

"These are from Gamma Phi Beta! With our crescent and everything!" Elin exclaims. "But this is our sorority, not yours! Where on earth—"

"I found them last year at a Parisian bazaar," I say. "I can't imagine how they got there. Some American expat, I suppose. They're from the 1930s."

Grace looks stricken. "But I don't have anything this special for you."

"You flew four thousand miles. That is enough." I smile. "And if you serve up a really good secret tonight, then you will have more than repaid me."

Elin fixes the pin onto Grace's collar and then puts her

hand over her heart. "'Once more we pledge a loyalty that means / Adherence to all true and noble things,'" she recites. Then she drops her hand and shrugs. "That's the only part of the creed I remember. Pledging loyalty."

"I pledge a loyalty to us—and to the Donut Factory!" I declare.

"Hear! Hear!" says Elin, laughing.

The Donut Factory was a block off campus on Regent Street, and it didn't open until 11:00 at night. By one it'd be mobbed by undergrads searching for late-night sweets, lured by the smell of sugar and grease. The best doughnut to get was the Boston cream, hot out of the fryer. Once I saw two frat brothers, no doubt drunk on wapatoolie, nearly get into a fistfight over the last one on the rack.

"It's funny how my past comes rushing back whenever I'm with you two," I say. "My yoga teacher is always telling me to 'be here now,' but I can't help it, I love Memory Lane."

"I love Mickie's Dairy Bar," Elin says, name-checking another Madison landmark. "I'm almost embarrassed to tell you, but last year Charlie and I took a road trip just so I could go there for a malted and a meatloaf sandwich."

"Nothing embarrassing about that at all," Grace assures her. "What would be embarrassing is admitting that you miss the Kollege Klub's swamp water."

"The color of my sun tea is remarkably like the color of the swamp water," I point out. "But don't worry. I didn't spike it."

"I'm not worried about anything right now," Elin says happily.

But then a shadow crosses her face, and I know why. She's thinking about what's coming next—the Night of Secrets. She's afraid that something will go horribly wrong.

I wish I could say that I'm not afraid of the very same thing.

43

Zoey,
daughter of Mariella

"We're traveling to Sicily for our dinner this evening," my dad announces. "In our imaginations, anyway." He's still wearing his tomato-stained apron, and he seems to have bought himself a pair of chef's clogs. (He's such a weirdo, he could be a TikTok star.) "As you may or may not know, Sicily's cuisine reflects the culinary influences of North Africa. Tunisia, after all, is only a boat ride away. It is Sicily's Mediterranean neighbor."

"Hope you like a lecture," I whisper to Merry. "Cuz my dad sure does."

"I love them," she whispers back. "I have college nostalgia."

Me, I couldn't wait to get out of school. I thought it was

holding me back. Okay, I didn't exactly explode like a supernova into fame and fortune after getting my diploma. But I loved being free and independent and alone, with no one to answer to but myself—and the internet fan base I was building.

"The eggplants in your caponata," my dad says, "as well as the lemons, artichokes, and spinach in the salad, were brought to Sicily from North Africa. Sicilian cooking regularly uses ingredients we don't think of when we think of Italian food, such as rosewater and mint. Fascinating, don't you think?"

I don't find it actively fascinating, but the moms are definitely nodding their heads. And Brigid seems to be typing into her Notes app.

"Anyway," my dad says, "tonight we complement your caponata with *pannelle di ceci*, which are Arab-style flat chickpea flour fritters. And the *pasta con le sarde* combines fresh sardines with the North African flavors of pine nuts, raisins, and saffron. It is, if I do say so myself, a beautiful and inspiring Italian-African mash-up."

He beams at us. He has such a hopeful look on his face. Like he's waiting for a round of applause. Usually it's my mom who gets that, from a concert hall full of strangers. So I start clapping, and everyone else joins in, and he gets all pleased and cute and smug.

You know what? I freaking love my dad. And, yeah, I

should've had my phone to take a video, because Michael Marciano's got serious nerd rizz.

Now he's telling us about the indigenous people that the island of Sicily is named after. But my mom holds up a hand.

"That's enough for now, darling," she says. "Could you perhaps, if it's not too much trouble, just feed us?"

Sure, she cut him off, but she sounds way less bossy than usual. It has to be the hypnosis because wine doesn't work like this. I'll bet a thousand dollars Dad's put Ginevra on speed dial.

"Of course, *amore*," he says, and vanishes.

We're digging into a wild arugula salad when Jamie asks us what we think the best part of the weekend has been.

Elin's mouth is full, but "Impossible to decide!" she cries.

Jamie says, "You have to name one thing or else walk the plank."

"If the plank drops me into Lake Como, I'm fine with that."

"If I had to pick, I'd just say being with all of you, here in this totally gorgeous place," Merry says.

"No dice," Jamie says. "It has to be specific. The boat ride, my amazing pancakes, you know, that kind of thing."

I pipe up. "*Not* charades. That was lame."

Miracle of miracles, my mother doesn't even shoot me an annoyed look. I better get Ginevra's number, too. But what *was* the best moment in my weekend? I'm not sure I could say. There were so many good ones.

"The boat ride," Elin says. "When we swam in that beautiful gorge."

"Maybe the food," Jamie says.

"I loved the gift exchange," my mom says. "And I loved the hike, too, as soon as it was over."

Jamie sighs. "The massage, oh, my God, how could I forget about that?"

I catch Merry's eye and grin. "What about the midnight swim? With the *bear*?"

Merry chokes on a piece of bread. She coughs, and the piece of bread goes flying out before she can cover her mouth. "Sorry!" she cries.

But everyone's so busy calling out all the things they loved that they don't even notice that it lands in the olive boat.

"What about the book club meeting—"

"And the *cornetti*—"

"What about the tattoos?"

"Or Grace's seven-hour lunch!"

"That's it!" My mom slaps her palm on the table like it's a game show buzzer. "*That* was my favorite part of the weekend!"

We all turn to stare at her.

I go, "You mean the lunch you weren't even at was your favorite thing?"

"No, you dope!" My mom grins. "It was seeing Grace come in that night with her *sweater inside out*!"

Now all our heads swivel toward Grace, who looks like a kid who's been caught with her hand in the cookie jar.

"Are you sure?" she says.

"Oh, you better believe I'm sure," my mom crows.

"Oh, my God!" I'm practically squealing. "Grace, spill the beans now!"

Grace delicately dabs the corner of her mouth with a napkin. Then a sweet, innocent smile spreads across her face.

"I'm sorry, I can't," she says. "At least not until the Night of Secrets officially begins."

44

Jamie,
mother of Meg and Kathleen

It's almost time. Any minute now, Mariella's going to tell us to move into the living room, where we'll sit in a cozy circle with our wineglasses. With our anticipation. And with our secrets ready to be spilled.

It'll be just like three years ago, except that tonight there will be no disaster. My daughters are here and they aren't going anywhere. Mariella and I have agreed: good surprises only.

As if we were in charge. As if fate listens.

I've waited for this moment for months. So why don't I feel ready?

Because I'm scared of something going wrong, that's why. I've had my hopes crushed so many times.

Mike bends over my shoulder and deftly removes my empty plate. "Oh," I exclaim, "let me help." I push back my chair. Doing dishes will distract me. Maybe even calm me. I start to stand, but Mike gently pushes me down.

"Absolutely not," he says. "Guests are meant to be waited upon."

Next to me, Grace leans back and pats her stomach. "Good, because I ate too much to get up."

"No, you didn't! Let's work it off!" I say. "How about we do a few jumping jacks?" I feel like I'm going to explode if I don't get to shake some of this anxiety out of my body. Also, I'm stalling for time.

"I would rather *die*," Mariella says.

"How about a walk!" I suggest brightly. I'm going to just keep coming up with ways to put off the Night of Secrets.

"Walking after eating attenuates postprandial glucose," Brigid says.

"English, please, honey," says Elin.

I shoot Brigid a look. Is she trying to postpone what's coming next, too? Maybe she's as nervous as I am.

Oh, God, I think she is.

Is everything okay? What does this mean for our surprise? Does she know something I don't? I try to catch her eye, but she completely avoids my gaze. Doc, I'm freaking out here, *hello*?

"That means it reduces the post-meal blood sugar spike," Brigid says. "If you go for a short walk after eating, generally your blood sugar levels rise and fall more gradually, and your insulin levels stay more stable."

I keep hoping she'll meet my questioning gaze. She doesn't.

Kathleen stands up stiffly. She reaches for her cane. "You know, I could use a hobble down the road."

Meg pops up from the table. "Me too."

When Kathleen flinches, Meg sits right back down. Maybe their talk by the lake wasn't as healing as I thought. Maybe Kathleen wants space, and Meg wants to continue their mysterious confrontation.

"I'll come," I cry. "I'll be the chaperone, ha ha."

They turn to me, matching expressions of annoyance on their faces. Why on earth did I say that? They already think I treat them like babies. Don't they understand that my job is to protect them? Always? From the world, if possible. From each other, if necessary.

"Sit down, all of you," Zoey commands, and now the girls fix their annoyed expressions on her. "No one's going anywhere, because I have a surprise." She flashes a quick smile. "Mom's not the only bossy one around here, amiright?"

To my surprise, Kathleen and Meg actually obey her.

"The apple doesn't fall far from the tree, does it?" Grace whispers to me, as Zoey commandeers everyone's attention.

"Prepare to be amazed!" Zoey hands her phone to Merry and says, "Take a vid, will you," and then dashes into the kitchen. She returns carrying an enormous lopsided cake on a silver platter. It's like a leaning tower of chocolate, and it's absolutely slathered with thick fudgy icing.

"Ta-da!" Zoey cries, setting the cake in the middle of the table with a flourish. Her face is lit with pride.

Merry records Zoey's beaming, then zooms in on the cake, which somehow manages to look both delicious *and* like a mud pile.

"I know I said I ate too much," Grace says, "but I can definitely find room for that."

"And *cut*," Zoey says, taking the phone back. She checks the video, nodding in satisfaction. "Hashtag *nailed it*."

"Child, you are ruining my diet!" Mariella cries.

Zoey looks up from her phone. She can thumb-type blind. "Diet? What diet?"

"The one I started the minute I finished dinner."

Zoey snorts. Merry giggles politely into her hand.

"You can start it tomorrow," I tell Mariella. "We can get up early and do some high-intensity interval training."

"I don't know what that is, but it sounds awful," Mariella says.

Zoey places a slice of cake in front of her mother. Mariella looks at it carefully for a moment, and then she takes a small, delicate bite. Her eyes widen as she tastes. She flings down her fork. "You little *sneak!*" she yells.

Zoey blinks innocently at her as she gives Grace a slice. "What?"

"I would know this cake anywhere! It is my mother's cake! *My* cake! It is Killer Chocolate Cake! Although it does not look anything like ours! This one looks like—like—like a wet cow patty that was dropped down from the sky, and that is if I am being *kind*!"

"*Ouch*, Mom," she says. "The frosting is impossible, you know. First it comes out like fudge soup, and then you've got to put it on ice and stir it for, like, ever—"

"I know perfectly well how it's made," Mariella snaps. "I've made it for every family birthday for twenty-eight *years*!"

"It tastes absolutely fantastic," Grace says. "Mariella, if I were you, I'd be glad to hand over dessert duties to my daughter." She smiles. "I mean, we have to pass the torch eventually."

Mariella huffs into her dessert. She shoves another bite into her mouth and chews. Finally, her expression softens. "You did a very good job with the baking," she allows. "The presentation, however, needs a lot of work."

"I know! I'm telling you, the *frosting*." Zoey smiles hopefully. "Maybe you'll show me how you do it."

Mariella shrugs. "Maybe. Or maybe I'll take *that* secret to the grave."

I take a bite of cake. There's got to be half an inch of chocolate frosting on it. It's so good I have to close my eyes. Decadent sweetness fills my mouth. The cake is moist, the frosting impossibly rich. I forget for a moment what's coming next. What I've been waiting for *and* dreading. Then Brigid kicks me under the table, and my eyes fly open.

She mimes making a phone call. I nod.

Here we go. The moment I've been waiting for, for three long years.

45

Mariella, mother of Zoey

The table has been cleared and the dishes washed. (I really do owe my husband now!) I cast my eyes around the living room, making sure that everything is just so. New bouquets, gathered from the garden, decorating the marble-topped end tables: check. Beeswax candles flickering on the mantel: check. Brass bar cart, offering a selection of beverages—wine, of course, but also digestifs, coffee, and tea: check. Raw silk throw pillows arranged exactly as I want them to be: you'd better believe it.

I breathe a sigh of satisfaction and relief. The weekend: *chef's kiss, darlings!* I have forgiven my friends for their mutiny this morning, and this final night will be the best one of all.

The sound of something being dragged across the floor

catches my attention. I turn to see my husband pulling the hideously giant TV he keeps on a rolling cart in his man cave into the center of the living room.

"What are you doing?" I demand. "You know perfectly well I took movie night off the schedule a month ago."

He pretends that he doesn't hear me.

"Darling," I say, as I watch him trying to attach the TV to a laptop computer that definitely doesn't belong to us. "What is all this for?"

After struggling for another moment with a tangled cord, he turns to me and he says, *"Amore,* it's a secret for the Night of Secrets."

"Che sorpresa," I say—what a surprise. The problem is, I am not interested in surprises from my family members. I lean in close and I put my hand on his waistband. "Tell me what it is," I whisper.

His breath quickens when I let my hand lower just a bit. "Be a good boy," I say playfully, though of course I'm dead serious. "Tell your loyal, loving wife what all this is about." I give him a very gentle, very suggestive squeeze.

He steps closer, puts his hand on my backside. "It's not *my* secret, *amore,"* he says. "I have no idea what it's for. Brigid just asked me if I would set it up."

My hand drops down to my side. Mike looks so disappointed that I lean in and give him a kiss on his sweet stubbled cheek. "I guess we'll have to be patient, then," I say.

"Patient?" he says. "*You?*"

"I have to learn to let go of my leaves," I say. Then I crane my neck so I can see onto the terrace. Sure enough, there's tall, willowy Brigid standing by the railing, staring into the purple dusk. Be patient? Let go of my leaves? *As if!* I'm already heading toward her, questions on the tip of my tongue, when Jamie appears. She grabs Brigid by the elbow and pulls her away into the shadows.

Che cazzo? What the f—

But I stop myself. It's not good to get worked up. *Okay, Mariella, remember what Ginevra said,* I tell myself. *You don't have to control everything. Even though you like to.*

Merry and Zoey come into the living room and flop down on the nearest sofa. They've changed into their pajamas — Merry in cotton gingham, Zoey in silk — and they look like teenagers at a sleepover.

"What's the TV for?" asks my daughter.

"Karaoke lyrics, I hope," Merry says.

I like the sound of karaoke. My Linda Ronstadt covers are amazing if I do say so myself.

"Ooh, what's your song?" Zoey asks.

"'Blank Space.' Yours?"

"'Crazy.'"

"How fitting." Merry yelps. "Ouch, Z, your elbow's *sharp.*"

"It's not for karaoke." Jamie's standing on the threshold of the French doors with her hands shoved deep into the pockets of her sweatpants.

She looks twitchy. Like she's anticipating something bad. Considering what happened the last time we had the Night of Secrets, I get it. But Meg's sitting next to Elin on the couch, and Kathleen and Grace share the love seat. They're safe.

We are all safe.

Brigid walks through the room, a phone held to her ear. She smiles at me and holds up a finger: *Another minute.*

"Maybe the TVs so we can binge *Dickinson*," Zoey suggests. "That's literary."

Jamie says, "Nope."

"*Normal People?*" Merry asks. "I haven't read Sally Rooney yet, have you?"

"I never will," Zoey says, "but the shows are hot."

Jamie looks up as Brigid reappears, pocketing her phone. I watch some wordless communication pass between them, but I cannot for the life of me tell what it's about or what it means.

"Everyone's here now, so let's begin before the suspense kills me," I say. "Jamie, you go first!"

I see Brigid give a minute shake of her head.

"Actually we're not ready quite yet," Jamie says.

We? Does this mean that she and Brigid are in on a secret? Oh, this is madness! I pour myself half a glass of prosecco and toss it back like a shot of tequila. "Fine." I sigh, then ask, "Who wants to go first?"

My answer is silence.

"All right, eeny, meeny, miny, moe—Elin, you start."

Elin laughs in protest. "I went first last time. Make Grace do it."

"Yeah," Zoey says. "Grace had a seven-hour lunch with a hot boat captain, so her secret's got to be way juicier than Elin's."

But I shake my head firmly. "Elin goes first. This is one leaf that I am not letting go of."

46

Elin,
mother of Brigid

It's embarrassing to admit, but when Zoey says that Grace's secret must be better than mine, I feel that old competitive urge rising up. I never like being beaten in anything. I rarely am.

They want juicy? I could tell them about the last time I met my lover, Edward, at the Peninsula Chicago. He'd made reservations at Shanghai Terrace, the restaurant on the fourth floor. We flirted over Smoky Lapsang cocktails. We grazed each other's fingers while sharing crab wontons and lobster and chicken dumplings garnished with shavings of black truffles. I ran my foot up his leg while demurely eating my shredded duck in XO sauce.

We skipped dessert. We went down to the lobby and booked a last-minute room. We could barely keep our hands off each other in the elevator. Once we were inside our suite, he pulled me close and kissed me deeply. He held onto me like I was saving him from drowning. Then he suddenly spun me around, and he pressed me hard against the wall as he lifted my skirt—

No, I won't tell them that.

I can't tell anyone until I've finished working through the fallout with Charlie. I'd confessed my affair to him after my mom died. Charlie was devastated, as I would have been in his place. But he didn't blame me. He understood how absent he'd become, how absorbed in his work and his tight-knit group of *Tribune* friends. In the aftermath of my confession, he never doubted for a moment that he wanted to stay married. *We can make things better,* he kept saying. *Maybe even better than they ever were before.*

I don't know. I hope he's right.

Anyway, my affair is my husband's secret, too, and I doubt he wants me telling it right now. And I doubt Brigid wants to hear it ever.

Thankfully I have a secret that I *can* admit. It's not juicy, but it's one I thought I'd never be able to say. "I officially quit my job," I tell everyone.

My daughter's mouth drops open. *"What?"*

I nod. I feel a laugh building in my throat. When I let it out, it's a loud, disbelieving guffaw. I can't believe I did it. I'm as shocked as Brigid is.

"When?" she says.

"Today!" I cry. "After my swim! I took a long, hot shower, and then I sat down and wrote my boss a very eloquent email, if I do say so myself, in which I informed her that I would be leaving in three months 'to pursue a new path.'"

"Incredible!" Grace exclaims.

"Congratulations!" says Merry.

"Emailing your resignation from an Italian villa is so baller," Zoey declares. "Ten outta ten, no notes."

"But what is this quote-unquote new path?" Of course it's Mariella asking. She sounds worried. Uncertainty terrifies her.

"I don't know yet. But I have a little while to figure it out." My goal is to find uncertainty exciting rather than terrifying, and so far, it's working.

I think.

"You'll have so much more time for reading," Grace says.

"Didn't you say at Christmas that you wanted to take up watercolors?" my daughter asks.

"I recommend cooking classes," Mike says, popping his head around the corner. I swear to God, that man is a master of appearing out of thin air.

"You guys, I'm not going to *retire,*" I say. "I'm just going to do something different. But I'm going to take some time off first."

"You should do a culinary tour of Italy," Mike tells me. "Or France! Paris is loaded with Michelin restaurants, but I consider Lyon to be the gastronomic capital."

"We will write Elin a France itinerary, won't we, darling?" Mariella says, but Mike has already vanished again.

"My plan is to enjoy the not-knowing for as long as possible," I say. "As Tom Petty would say, 'The future is wide open.'"

"But not knowing is not a 'plan,'" Mariella protests.

"Who's Tom Petty?" Kathleen wants to know.

"How did you get so *young*," Grace says, amazed.

Mariella turns to me. "Elin, congratulations on your new life. I have been telling you to leave that job for years, and you finally listened to me. Which means that whatever wonderful things happen next, I will take all the credit for them." She grins. "Grace, you're up next."

47

Grace,
mother of Merry

Mariella is practically drooling in anticipation, and I know exactly what secret she's waiting for.

I have other ones, though. Don't we all have things we keep locked away? And isn't it good to bring them out into the light? There is some part of me that wants to finally admit to these beloved women what a mess I've been. How lonely and hopeless and tired. How I feel alive only when I'm in my church, speaking to—and listening to—my congregants. How much energy I've spent pretending that everything is perfectly fine.

But another part of me believes that all that darkness is behind me. Because of one lunch. One afternoon.

How crazy is that?

My mother and father fell in love at first sight. Or at least my dad did; it took my mom a minute to catch up. But it was like in that Laurie Colwin book *Happy All The Time:* a spark of first love, carefully tended, that soon became a steady, warm, and lasting flame.

So it wasn't crazy for them. But it seems super crazy for me.

So maybe *that* should be my secret: I've obviously lost my mind. Because how could I have let myself fall so hard for someone I might never see again? I told Merry that it would be okay if that lunch was all that ever happened. But I realized that was a lie. If Danny doesn't call, my optimism will be as lovely and fleeting as a holiday weekend.

Mariella's manicured nails, clicking on the end table, pull me out of my thoughts and back into the room. "Where do I begin?" I say, smiling nervously.

"Assuming you're going to tell us about Danny, start with when you called him an Italian stallion in the boat," Elin says. "He *heard*, didn't he?"

I can feel my cheeks flush. "Yes, although he pretended he didn't. I was so sure he barely spoke English!"

"LOLs!" Zoey says.

Mariella rolls her eyes. "Please speak like an adult," she says. "Or better yet, *don't* speak, so Grace can tell us more about her date with Captain Danny, the Golden Bachelor. Yes, I know he's younger than that, but I don't care."

"Well, that date was the first one I've had in"—I look down at my watch for dramatic effect—"approximately six years."

"She won't admit it, but she was proud of her streak," Merry tells everyone.

I smile. "Maybe I enjoyed that sense of renunciation—just a little."

"Well?" Elin says. "Was it worth the wait?"

Everyone is looking at me expectantly. I feel extremely self-conscious. It was more than worth the wait. But how much detail am I supposed to go into? Suddenly I can barely remember what Danny and I talked about. Italian history, college memories, the novels of Elena Ferrante... All I can think of right now is how badly I want to see him again. How stupid I was not to have him write his phone number on a piece of paper. I could call the boat rental place, obviously. But I'd feel like a stalker. I guess I thought he'd reach out. So why hasn't he called? Or texted?

"Waiting," Mariella says. "Patiently."

I sigh. "I was so comfortable with him," I tell my friends. "Instantly. It was like we knew each other already. Like he was an old high school crush or he'd sat next to me in homeroom and we'd been friendly, but then we hadn't seen each other in forty years. He felt familiar, but at the same time new and exciting."

"Exactly *how* was he exciting?" Mariella says slyly.

"Considering the inside-out sweater, second base exciting at least," Jamie says, giggling.

"*Now* who's acting young?" Elin asks.

Jamie grins. "Well, I am nearly twenty years younger than you are."

"Fifteen is *not* nearly twenty!" Mariella protests. "Your math is ridiculous and—and—offensive!"

Elin grins. "Let no one accuse Mariella of mellowing with age."

And now everyone's laughing, and they're not staring at me anymore. I'm relieved that I'm not the center of attention for a moment, which is why what I do next is so baffling. Maybe I just want to get this whole thing over with.

"I'm still a virgin!" I cry. "We only kissed!"

And everyone turns back toward me, surprised by my outburst. I instantly regret it. I could have given a little smirk and declared that I don't kiss and tell.

But then again, I do tell my friends *almost* everything.

Mariella crows, "The secret is out!"

"So can I be done now?" I want to stop talking about Danny so I can keep thinking about him. In the kitchen of his beautiful little cottage, he'd taken my face in his hands and bent his head toward mine. And then, when our lips were barely an inch apart, he'd stopped. "Do you mind if I kiss you?" he'd whispered. He knew how long it'd been since anyone had. But *mind*? I felt like I'd just about die if he didn't.

Mariella scooches forward on the couch so our knees

almost touch. "Tell us everything about it." Then she frowns. "Grace," she says, "are you...crying?"

Yes, apparently I am. I'm overwhelmed. I'm hopeful and confused; I'm totally scared. I want to believe that everything's different somehow. I don't want this weekend to be the start of something wonderful at the same time it is also its end.

But I'm pretty sure it will be. And I'll need to practice telling myself that this is for the best. *Your lives are four thousand miles apart*, I'll say. *And it's not like you can lose your virginity over Zoom.* Or simply, *Get a grip, Grace. You're sixty years old. You know better than to think you two could work out.*

"Danny was so smart. So charming," Elin says. Like he's already in the past.

"Obviously, the man could have anyone he wanted," I say. "So why would he choose me—when he met me only once, and when no one else has?"

Mariella doesn't miss a beat. "*We* chose you," she says firmly. "And apologies to Mike, wherever that man is hiding, but when it comes to living a good life, friendship is at *least* as important as romance."

"Amen to that," Elin says. "There are soulmates, and then there are *soulmates*." She grins and raises her glass. She's talking about us. "We're bonded with each other in ways we can't be with our husbands."

"Mom," Merry says, "I didn't want to interrupt the story, but I think I heard your phone buzzing."

I immediately sit up. Everyone back home knows I'm on vacation, so it's either an emergency—or else it's Danny. "Where is it?"

"Over there on the table," Merry says.

But Mariella is already diving toward my phone. She grabs it, reads the screen, and then her eyes go wide and delighted. I hear someone give a little shriek of glee. I think that someone is me.

48

Merry,
daughter of Grace

"It was *him*!" Mariella says giddily, holding up Mom's phone, which she literally vaulted over the back of the couch to grab.

There's only one word for the look on my mom's face: joy. She reaches for the phone, but Mariella shoves it deep into her pocket. "You may call him back when the Night of Secrets is over."

Now Mom's happy expression is visibly tinged with annoyance. A beat or two later comes the resignation. Everyone knows there's no use fighting Mariella; even if you *could* win, to do so would involve way too much effort.

"Clearly," Elin says, looking pointedly at the phone in Mariella's pocket, "there will be more secrets to come."

"From your lips to God's ears," my mom says.

"Can it be my turn now?" Zoey asks. "Because I can certainly go after Grace's anticlimax." She grins wickedly. "Pun one hundred percent intended."

"Very funny," says my mom.

Zoey leans over and whispers into my ear, "Can I tell them about the mushrooms?"

I recoil in horror. "No!"

"OMG, you're so prude."

"Well, I *am* the daughter of a virgin."

"Touché, babe."

"Enough whispering, you two," Elin says. "Zoey, what's your secret?"

My friend, who I've known since I was born, says, "Luna and I are moving in together."

"What!" I exclaim. "You never told me that!"

"I had to keep something back for the Night of Secrets!"

Sure, Zoey texted me adorable selfies of her and Luna at gallery openings, happy hours, and media parties, but I had no idea they were that serious. "Congratulations!"

"That's wonderful, honey," Mariella says. "Think how much you'll save on rent."

"Mom," Zoey says, "it's not about rent. I love her. When I get back to Brooklyn, I think I might propose."

"*Che bello!*" Mariella says. "My baby, engaged!" She comes over and grabs Zoey in a big perfumed hug. "*Auguroni!*"

"Well, we're not engaged yet," Zoey says, her voice muffled in Mariella's shirt.

Mariella gives Zoey another squeeze and then pulls away and wipes her eyes. "Where is your father? I must tell him the wonderful news."

But Elin says, "Sit down, Mariella. You can tell Mike when the Night of Secrets is over."

Mariella's about to protest, but Elin raises a warning finger. "Turnabout's fair play, missy," she says.

"Very well. I will tell my secret, then," Mariella says. "Mike and I will be moving to New York to be closer to Zoey and Luna."

"You are?" Grace says. "How wonderful!"

"Seriously?" Zoey says. "When did you decide that?"

"Just now! Mike doesn't know about it yet," Mariella says. "But I'm sure he will be on board." She rubs her hands together gleefully as she grins at the other mothers. "We need to encourage these two to start making us grandchildren!"

"Slow down, Mommy, *please*," Zoey says. "Or else Luna and I will move to...I don't know, New Zealand or something."

"Then I will follow you!" Mariella cries. "I will be your neighbor! Your wedding planner! And then your baby nanny! You will never escape me!"

I'm pretty sure—but not *entirely* sure—that she's joking.

49

Meg,
daughter of Jamie

Everyone's having a gay old time. And I'm like, Okay, this is pretty fun after all. Life in Chicago is not this wholesome. I'm used to big, wild parties, where you wake up the next morning and try to piece together what exactly happened and how much you enjoyed it.

Now Mariella turns her dark, flashing eyes on my mom. "Jamie Leanne Price," she says briskly, "I want you to tell me that I don't have to wait any longer, because the suspense of your secret is giving me hives."

Instead of answering, my mom glances over at Brigid, who's bent over, typing something into the computer. "Are we ready?"

Brigid stands up and gives a small, curt nod. My mom nods back. The look on her face is more of a grimace than a smile. For some reason that sends an arrow of fear shooting straight into my spine.

I don't know what their secret is, but all of a sudden I'm certain it has something to do with my dad. With that night in Lake Geneva. The worst night of my life.

And if I'm right, then it means that I need to tell my secret first. I need to tell it now before another moment passes. It's been weighing on me for three years.

I'm still not ready to share it, but that doesn't really matter. It's time.

"I'm so nervous," my mom says, mostly to herself.

"I'm so impatient," Mariella says to everyone, as if we didn't know it already.

I glance over at my sister, tucked into the corner of the love seat next to Grace. She's calmly drinking tea, seemingly relaxed and content. As if this was a night just like any other. As if nothing was wrong with us, or between us.

When we were little, looking at Kathleen was like looking into a mirror. I'm not even kidding: our own dad used to mix us up. Now, though, anyone could tell us apart in an instant. It's not that I got an inch taller. Or that my hair's shorter, and hers has strawberry-blond highlights. Or even that Kathleen uses a cane when she walks. It's our expressions. Kathleen's face says that she's determined. Serious. Ambitious. Whereas

I'm pretty sure I just look mad all the time. Thwarted. Resentful.

But there's only one person to blame for my anger.

"Actually, Mariella," I say, "I want to go next, if you don't mind."

And now everyone's looking at me expectantly. They look happy. They love me, despite my faults.

They don't know yet that I'm the one to blame. For my anger, and for everything else, too.

"Of course, darling, of course," Mariella says. "Tell us your secret, Meggie."

No one has called me that name for years. I can't say that I've missed it.

I can feel Kathleen's eyes on me. Blood rushes to my heart. My fingers go cold.

I take a deep breath. If these women didn't think I was the bad twin before, they're going to be convinced of it soon enough.

50

Kathleen,
daughter of Jamie

Meg's request to go next on the Night of Secrets comes as a complete shock to me. I mean, she's barely spoken twelve words in a row this entire weekend. All the moms are smiling, but I can tell they're like, *What's that surly girl going to say?*

But I'm not shocked by what she's going to say. Or what she should say, anyway. I know Meg's secret, because it's my secret, too. It was supposed to keep us together. But in a bitter twist of irony, it ended up pulling us apart.

Meg stares down at her hands, clutched together in her lap. Her shoulders are hunched, like she's trying to make herself as small as possible. I can see how miserable she is, and my heart goes out to her.

What can I say, it's habit. We were best friends for most of our lives.

We were growing apart even before the accident, though. I was focused on getting into law school, while Meg seemed to be focused on having fun. On working late at the restaurant and staying out even later, going to underground clubs that only the cool kids knew about, waking at noon and then rolling down to the Twisted Spoke for a Bloody Mary breakfast. Sure, she was writing stories and submitting them to literary magazines. Sometimes she even got them published. But mostly it seemed like Meg was living for the moment. Whereas I was living for the future. But my future, at least as I imagined it, fell apart three years ago. So maybe I should've had a little more fun.

As Mom would say, "Life doesn't always turn out the way you expect it to." It's so annoying when your mom's right.

"I've been struggling for a long time," Meg says now. Her voice sounds creaky from lack of use. "Since the accident, but before that, too, if I'm being honest."

But how honest are you going to be, Meg?

"I was lost," she goes on. She gestures weakly toward Brigid, who's still hovering near the mysterious laptop-and-TV setup. "I mean, Brigid wanted to be a doctor basically since she was born. And she worked hard, and she made it all happen, and she's totally amazing."

Brigid flushes. "Let's not exaggerate," she says.

"I always said that I wanted to be a writer. I was going to, like, get into the Iowa Writers' Workshop and write a bunch of stories and come out with a book deal. But I couldn't make it happen. I mean, I just—I just felt like I was banging my head against my desk. Nothing was working. I kept expecting some great idea to occur to me. I kept waiting for something incredible to happen." Meg laughs bitterly. "Well, something incredible happened all right. But it ruined our lives."

"Honey," my mom begins. "That's not—"

"I'm not done," Meg says, sharply cutting Mom off. "Me lacking direction in life is not a secret to *anyone*. I know that. But what I want to say has to do with the night of the accident in Lake Geneva." She twists her hands in her lap. "I'd been drinking."

"We all had," Elin says. "It was a party! There was a river of prosecco. We swam in it."

"Not Kathleen, though," Grace says. "She was getting over a cold."

I'm surprised anyone remembers all this, because there *was* a lot of prosecco. But they're right. I didn't drink that night. Brigid had said something about alcohol dampening your immune system, and wine didn't sound good to me anyway. So I was totally sober. Which was why I offered to drive Meg's car when we left the lake house to get ice cream.

Except that we weren't going to get ice cream. That was just what we told everyone.

Meg clears her throat. "I'd just gotten my new Jeep. I couldn't really afford it, but I was so proud of it. And I remember that Kathleen offered to drive it."

I see my mom's eyes dart in my direction. We went over this so many times, with the police, with the doctors, with each other. Everyone thinks they know where the story is going. How, on a dark and rainy night, driving an unfamiliar car, I lost control on a sharp turn. How it was a terrible accident, but there was no one to blame.

They're wrong, though.

"Kathleen was used to her little Prius," Meg says. "That stupid car, it's like driving a golf cart. She took the keys away from me. That's when I told her that I didn't trust her to get behind the wheel of my precious Jeep. And I grabbed them back."

"What do you mean?" Mom says. "Kathleen was driving that night."

"No, Mom, she wasn't."

"But you—you told us—you told the police—" Our mom is spluttering, confused. She looks wildly between the two of us as the truth finally comes out.

"It was me," Meg says. "I flipped the car. Not Kathleen."

My fingers tighten on the handle of my cane. I remember the accident so clearly. I saw the deer as it darted into the road, and I felt the car swing hard to the left as Meg swerved to avoid hitting it, and then she overcorrected, and the car careened sideways in the other direction, slammed into a tree, and—

I don't want the memory to go any further. I don't want to think of the horrible way time slowed to a crawl as we were launched into the air, flipping over once, then twice.

Brigid says your brain lays down extra memories when you're terrified. When you recall the scary thing later, it seems like it lasted ages, even if it was a matter of seconds. But does it matter how long it took? It only matters how it ended. With my brain concussed and my hip broken.

I must've been in shock. I don't remember feeling any pain at all. What I remember is realizing that if the police knew who was driving the car, then Meg would go to jail.

I was her older sister. Her protector. I was the one who did not make mistakes.

"I was driving," I told the officers. "It was all my fault."

And Meg stood there in the rain and said nothing.

They Breathalyzed me in the ambulance. Blood alcohol 0.00 percent.

Meg is crying now. "My sister wanted to protect me, and I let her," she says. "I let her! And the guilt of what I did has weighed on me so much that I feel like I'm breaking in half."

My mom is speechless. Pale. Tears stream down her face.

"There," Meg says. "That's my secret."

In the silence that follows I feel like a weight comes off me. It wasn't fair of me to be so furious at Meg when I was the one who lied first. But when is a sisterly relationship logical?

I'm still mad. Because look at me. Look at our broken family.

But I can see a day when I won't be so angry. It's still far away, but I look forward to living in it.

"I'm so sorry, Kathleen," Meg whispers. "I love you."

I nod. I find that I can say the words. "I love you, too."

51

Zoey,
daughter of Mariella

Well, ladies, that's the danger of secrets. The good ones, like Grace's new romance, explode like confetti. The bad ones drop like bombs.

I'm dying to talk to Merry about Meg's revelation. But I can't, because she and her mom are in the corner now, in a huddle with Jamie, whose face is streaked with tears. I feel for her. I mean, can you imagine finding out that your daughters lied about something so huge to the police and then to you for *three entire years*?

I think the three of them are praying now. I guess I would be too, if I were the praying type. When Luna takes me to church, I usually fall asleep.

My mom's gone into the kitchen, and I'll bet every penny in my bank account that she's stress-eating another slice of Killer Chocolate Cake. We all cope in our own ways, right? And I certainly don't blame her: the Night of Secrets was her idea. And look how it's turned out. Leave it to Mariella Marciano to turn book club weekend into a confession box.

Meg and Kathleen have gone out to the terrace. Are they talking? Fighting? Staring at the lake? I can't tell from here. The rest of us are still just sitting in the living room. Shocked. Trying to figure out how to process this new information. The silence is uncomfortable.

But I'm glad Meg's secret came out now, in front of all these women who love her. My mom's always accusing me of caring more about relationships with social media sponsors than with friends and family, but she couldn't be more wrong. Every single day I think about Merry, Grace, Elin—everyone. They're friends *and* family. And even when she's at her most obnoxious, my mom goes on my gratitude list daily. I don't know what I'd do without her.

Here's what I think. Meg and Kathleen are going to work through this. They're going to come out stronger on the other side. I know that I'm an optimist by nature, but still.

Elin and Brigid are whispering together on the couch, and both of them look *shook*. Then I watch as Elin gets up and joins the huddle. She takes Jamie into her arms the way a mother would. Like Jamie's her own child. "It's all going to be okay," she says.

And then my mom comes back into the living room in her high heels. There's a telltale smear of chocolate on her chin. "Darlings," she says, "the night is still young, and there are more secrets to be revealed."

Jamie wipes her eyes, nodding. "Yes," she says. "I'm ready to share mine now."

52

Grace,
mother of Merry

As Jamie readies herself to speak, I'm watching her as nervously as I'd watch Merry walk a tightrope. It feels like every cell in my body's on high alert. I know how much she's struggling now. Everything she thought she knew about the Lake Geneva accident was wrong. There was someone to blame. And there was a cover-up.

If—and I emphasize *if*—anger and blame are what she needs to feel, she has justification. But I hope and pray that Jamie chooses a different path. The Bible teaches forgiveness for good reason.

She's exhausted, I can tell. Not from this weekend of fun and chatter. From life. Jamie is a caretaker, the way all of us mothers are. The way we will be until our dying days. Because it doesn't matter how old your children are. It doesn't matter if you're on vacation. It doesn't matter if you yourself need to be cared for. It doesn't even matter if you are ninety-two years old, like my grandmother, who was making soup for a sick neighbor when she had a heart attack and died. You are a caretaker. A nurse. A cheerleader. A confidante. And caretaking is beautiful but *tiring* work. Jamie has had to do far more of it than the rest of us. Even tending to an entire congregation, the way I do, doesn't compare.

Jamie spins her empty wineglass nervously in her hands. "I know we've all tried not to think about that night in Lake Geneva. We've tried to move on. But as you know, for some of us, there was no way to really do that. We feel its effects every day."

Jamie turns to her older daughter. "But before I go on, I want to say, Kathleen, thank you for trying to protect your sister. I understand why you did it. You were trying to keep your family together on a night when it felt like it was on the verge of being destroyed. And I think I would've done the same." Then she swivels to face Meg, who still looks utterly stricken. "And Meg, thank you for telling us the truth. It's hard news, and it's a lot to process. But I'm not interested in anger or blame. I only want things to get better, starting now."

Meg is crying again. Kathleen quietly goes to sit on the arm of Meg's chair.

"It broke my heart to watch the distance between you two growing," Jamie says. "I just wanted you to love each other the way I loved you. By which I mean *infinitely*. I didn't understand what was going on. Now I do. And now I know that we can get through this."

Jamie sets her wineglass down and then picks it up again and twirls it. Mariella makes a move to fill it but Jamie shakes her head. "I just need to fidget with it," she says. And then she takes us back to the night in Lake Geneva. When dinner was over, the girls were cleaning up in the kitchen, and the storm came in.

Kathleen and Meg had left the house not to get ice cream but to get their dad. Logan had called them and asked them to come pick him up in Williams Bay. "I *have* to talk to your mom tonight," he'd said. He'd actually been on his way when he realized his rear tire was flat again.

"Those tires were so old," Jamie says. "We'd patched that back one three times."

"I reminded him that we'd all be home the next day," Meg tells us.

"And I told him that it wasn't the 'Mother-Daughter and One of the Fathers Book Club,'" Kathleen says. "But he wouldn't listen."

Jamie nods. "Logan was always on the stubborn side."

He'd told the twins that what he had to say couldn't wait twelve more hours. And that it wasn't something he wanted to say to Jamie over the phone. Anyway, he had tried to call her, but her phone was dead.

More tears come to Jamie's eyes. "When I was sitting there, telling you all that he wanted a separation, he was trying to deliver a message to me. And I still don't know what it was."

"But it was a good thing," Kathleen said. "He told us that much."

Meg's biting her lip so hard that I'm afraid she's going to draw blood. The weight of her guilt must be profound. I wish that poor child peace.

Jamie continues. "And so the girls made the excuse that they needed ice cream, and they went to go get their dad. And he had flowers in his hand, didn't he?"

"Peonies," Kathleen says. "Two dozen of them at least."

"They were beautiful," Meg whispers.

"And so he got into the car, holding this giant bouquet," Jamie says, "and I guess he tried to buckle his seat belt one-handed or something. All I know is that he didn't get it clicked in right." She stops. She takes a deep breath.

Even though I know what's coming next, I dread hearing it. In excruciating detail, Jamie describes how, when the Jeep spun out of control and rolled over in the road, Logan was flung from the car like a rag doll. He fractured his skull, his spine, and almost every major bone in his body. He was in a coma for eight days.

"Three separate times," Jamie tells us, "the doctors called me into his room to say good-bye."

I can feel tears prickling at the corner of my eyes. I will never forget running into the rain, seeing the car upside down, and hearing Jamie's screams rip through the night.

And I will never forgive myself for what I thought, which was *There but for the grace of God* —

But then again, shouldn't we all be forgiven? We are human, which is to say that we are imperfect. We hurt and are hurt, but we love and are loved. We do our best to keep the faith.

On that terrible night, we all held our friend as she shrieked and wailed. We kept her upright as the ambulances—one carrying her husband, the other carrying her twins—pulled away, leaving her behind. We didn't know it then, but Logan's injuries meant he needed to be Life Flighted to the nearest Level I trauma center, which just so happened to be the University Hospital at our beloved alma mater.

"We've got you," Elin kept saying. "We've got you."

And then we climbed into her car and followed the path of the ambulances. Blossoms were strewn across the black, rain-slick road. They were Logan's peonies. I wonder if that deer knew how near Death loomed that night.

"As you know," Jamie says now, "Logan was paralyzed from the neck down. He has 24/7 home health care, and he has been unable to speak since that night." She looks over at

Brigid, who nods at her to continue. "With the help of Eyegaze technology, he's been able to type by looking at letters on a screen. But that's a hard way to communicate. It's awkward. It's slow." She glances at Brigid again. "But then our very own brilliant neurologist, Dr. Brigid, stepped in. And she changed everything. Bridgie, why don't you take it from here?"

53

Brigid, daughter of Elin

Jamie's expression is a mix of hope and fear. I know she looks up to me, though I'm fifteen years younger. And she knows I've done my best for her. For her family. That's all I can do.

I clear my throat. I've been explaining complex concepts in neurology to patients and their families since I was a resident. But I've never made an after-dinner presentation to a group of non-scientists, let alone to a roomful of people who knew me when I was in diapers. It's an odd feeling. But it's an empowering one, too.

As long as everything goes the way it's supposed to. The technology I'm working with is still in its early stages. Failure is a constant threat. Funding is hard to come by. Even on good days, there are always ups and downs—technical ones, financial ones, personal ones.

"I'm going to talk to you a little bit about brain-computer interfaces," I tell them.

"Oooh, boy, I think I need an espresso," Mariella says.

I offer a quick smile but go on. Mariella's smart; she'll keep up. "A brain-computer interface, or BCI for short, is something that allows someone to control an external device using only signals from their brain."

Mariella sits up straighter. "That sounds like—oh, what's it called? Psychokinesis!"

"Psychokinesis is a trick," I remind her. "An illusion. Whereas a BCI is a direct communication pathway between a brain and a machine. It sounds sci-fi, but it's absolutely real."

"So stop interrupting, Mommy," Zoey says. *"Please."*

"Well, put your phone away. I swear it's grown into the skin of your hand."

I grin. The two of them just love to dig at each other. "It's okay," I tell Zoey. "I don't mind."

"Well *I* do." But then Zoey blows her mother a kiss.

"Anyway," I say, "BCIs work by detecting brain activity patterns that reflect what a person wants to do. They then convert these brain signals into commands that actually control devices like computers, or robotic arms, or speech synthesizers." I pause to make sure everyone's following me.

They seem to be. "A working BCI means that a person could use their mind to make a robotic arm pick up a pencil, for example. Or they could 'speak' through a voice synthesizer using only their thoughts." I pause. The room's utterly silent. Everyone's just waiting for what I'm about to say next. Jamie actually seems to be holding her breath.

I keep going. "And now I want to tell you how this applies to Logan, who has been essentially 'locked in' since the accident. Meaning, he's conscious and aware, but he can't move or communicate verbally."

I suppress a tiny shudder. Of all the things that can go wrong with the human body—and I've studied thousands of them—this, to me, seems like one of the absolute worst.

"Six months ago, we implanted electrodes designed to detect neural activity into Logan's brain. Then we had him perform specific mental tasks, like thinking about certain words, so the BCI system could record the corresponding brain signals." I stop. Even though I'm leaving out a few steps, I know this is complicated. "Still with me?"

Everyone nods.

"Great. So the BCI system uses machine learning algorithms—that's AI, you guys—to analyze the recorded brain signals and identify patterns that correspond to different commands or intentions. So pretty soon it knows which of Logan's brain signals match to what words. And then, when Logan thinks 'cat,' the speech synthesizer says 'cat.' And then—well, after that, it's just a lot of practice. The more Logan uses the BCI, the more accurate and efficient it is in translating his thoughts to speech."

Kathleen is standing now, balancing on her cane. "Are you telling us that Dad can *talk*?"

I turn on the TV that's connected to the laptop, which is connected to a lab room at the University Hospital in Madison. "Why tell when you can show?" I ask. "But yes, he can talk. And what's more, he can move—in a way. Because we've created an avatar. A visual representation of Logan Price."

54

Elin,
mother of Brigid

I truly could not be more proud of my brilliant, beautiful daughter. For doing pioneering research in her field, yes, but also for being so calm and clear and steady as she talks about Logan's condition. I can tell how much Jamie has come to rely on her, as both a doctor and a friend.

Brigid turns around and types a few keystrokes into the computer; then she turns on the television screen. "This is just a way of making the picture larger," she explains. "The real action is here on the laptop." We all watch as she signs in to Zoom.

A moment later, the screen reveals a woman's face in deep close-up. She's young, like Brigid, and she's smiling.

"Hello, Dr. Chatterjee," Brigid says.

"Hi, Dr. Mackenzie," the woman says. "We're ready for you."

When she steps away from the camera, we can see that she's in a large, sunny room in what must be a hospital or a medical office building. There's another doctor there—or I assume he's one, from his white lab coat—and next to him, strapped in a wheelchair, is Logan Price.

A tube going into his throat allows a mechanical ventilator to deliver oxygen to his lungs. His hair's grown since I saw him last. He's wearing the Badgers sweatshirt I got him for Christmas years ago, before the accident.

Thinking about everything that has been taken from him—and from his family—makes me start to cry immediately. I am very quiet about it, though. I don't want to upset Jamie or the twins. I don't want to embarrass my daughter.

"Hey, baby," Jamie says, her voice breaking. "Can you see me?"

Logan blinks three times: *yes.*

I don't know what kind of screen they've got over there, but I hope Logan can see all of the mothers and daughters on the final night of our weekend. I hope he can feel how much love we are sending him.

Dr. Chatterjee says, "Okay, are we ready?"

Brigid looks at Jamie, who nods.

"We are," Brigid says.

The scene switches from the one in the hospital room. Now the screen is entirely filled with Logan's face.

Except that it's not Logan himself. It's an avatar—a computer representation that looks just like him, and almost as real. The avatar smiles. "Hi, Jamie," he says.

We all gasp. The voice is Logan's voice.

"Oh, *dio mio,* what is happening, it is a *miracle,*" Mariella whispers.

I can't believe it—I don't understand it. "Bridgie," I cry, "what is going on?"

Jamie is beaming and crying at the same time. The twins are sobbing. Logan is suddenly *here* with them, in a way he hasn't been for three long, dreadful years.

"We created this avatar to show facial expressions that Logan isn't capable of making at this time," Brigid explains.

"But how did you give him his voice?" I ask.

"We trained the synthesizer on videos from his and Jamie's wedding."

"That was my idea," Jamie says proudly.

"It sure was. With the BCI and the speech synthesizer, Logan can speak almost a hundred words a minute. That's pretty close to the natural rate of human speech."

"Oh, my God," Grace says. She closes her eyes. Her lips move quickly and silently. She's praying. Or no—she's giving thanks. Which is, I guess, pretty much the same thing.

My daughter turns toward the screen and says gently, "Logan, I think you have some things you want to say?"

"Yes, I do," he says. Logan—the avatar—smiles again. "And I have been waiting a very, very long time for this."

55

Jamie,
mother of Meg and Kathleen

I truly can't believe what I'm seeing. My handsome blue-eyed husband is larger than life and smiling at me for the first time in three years. I'd known about him training on the BCI, of course, but this is the first time I've seen his avatar. Brigid's team must've used our wedding videos for building that, too, because Logan looks just like he did when we were married nearly twenty-five years ago. How quickly the memories of that day come rushing back: the delicate ivory silk dress I'd found in a vintage store, the smell of June roses in my bouquet, the warmth of Logan's hands as we stood facing each other in front of the same minister who'd married both our sets of parents twenty-five years before.

We were so young that the dog Logan had gotten for his eighth birthday was our ring bearer. Alaska, a beautiful dumb blonde of a mutt, lived long enough to see our girls born, learn to crawl, and take their first wobbling steps. Kathleen had called her "Laka." Now she rests under the cherry tree in our backyard.

I wipe my streaming eyes with my sleeve. Dear God, I never knew how quickly time would pass.

"Sorry," I say to everyone. "I'm—" I don't even know what word I want. Overwhelmed? Awed? Grateful? Devastated? How about all of the above.

"Jamie, darling, do *not* apologize," Grace whispers, sniffling herself. "Let the tears come."

I think all of us are crying now. All of us but Logan, that is. He's been waiting for this day for months and months. So he's still smiling at me, Price family dimples and everything.

"You look wonderful," I say to Logan. My voice is shaking. "It's almost like you're here with us."

"I wish I could be," he says. "I wish I could hold you right now, Jamie Leanne Price. I'd give anything on this earth to be able to hold you...the way you've held me these last three years."

I can only nod; my throat hurts too much to speak. Every night, before I go to sleep, I climb into Logan's mechanical bed. His bedroom, which used to be our den, is full of medical equipment. The respirator that pumps air into his lungs makes a low, rushing sound. We're surrounded by machines and tubes and monitors. But I press myself along the length of his body, and I put my arm carefully over his chest. And then I tuck his arm tight around me, and I tell him how much I love him.

If I cry there, silently, in the warmth and darkness, Logan doesn't know it. Or if he does, he's never been able to say.

That's how we hold each other.

"I'll be home soon," I tell him, my heart overflowing. I miss him so much—the way he used to be, yes, but also the way he is now.

"The science is getting better every day," Logan says now. "Soon they may be able to regenerate my nerve cells to restore some movement. But if not, I want robotic arms for Christmas."

I can't tell if he's joking or not. I shoot a quick look at Brigid. *That too?* She shrugs: *Maybe?*

I turn back to the screen as my husband goes on. To hear his voice again feels like a miracle.

"You used to say that life doesn't turn out the way you expect it to," Logan tells me.

I manage a tiny smile. "The Price family motto."

He nods. He doesn't speak right away. I can't tell if the BCI is having trouble processing his thoughts or if he's trying to figure out how to say what he wants to say next. I hold my breath.

"Keep talking," I whisper. I've missed this so much.

"When I thought about the future," Logan says, "I pictured you and me putting the boat on the water on the first good day of spring. You'd complain about fishing, but then you'd be the one to catch all the keepers. Don't laugh—you know I'm right!"

He is. I hate fishing, but those slimy critters jump right onto my hook.

"I saw myself lighting fireworks on the Fourth of July," he says. "Playing golf on the weekends. Raking the leaves in the fall. Little stuff we take for granted." He slowly shakes his head. "But I also pictured walking my daughters down the aisle. I imagined holding my grandchildren. Taking them fishing when they got old enough—" He stops, because there's a choking sound coming from Meg.

He says, "I'm getting ahead of myself, aren't I?"

"Maybe," Kathleen says, smiling and crying at the same time. "Just, like, a touch."

"We don't even have boyfriends," Meg says.

"Sorry," Logan says. "It's just...well, I've had a lot of time to think. And I have a lot of words saved up."

"You're doing great," Brigid says. She looks tense, though. Like she still thinks something might go wrong. "How are you feeling?"

"This is...hard," Logan says. "For a lot of reasons."

Brigid turns to us. "It's actually extremely tiring, what he's doing," she says quietly. "We'll need to end the session soon."

I nod. She'd warned me about this. But I just want Logan to

keep talking. I'm leaning so far forward I'm almost falling off my seat. I've waited three years for this, but it feels like a whole lifetime.

"Lake Geneva," Logan eventually says, and the words feel like knives in my chest. If it weren't for Lake Geneva, none of this would have happened.

"I tried to crash your party," he says, "and I ended up crashing into a tree. Ironic."

You should've been wearing your seat belt, I think. *Kathleen should've been driving.* But of course it's too late for that.

"When I was in a coma, I had...a dream. A vision, maybe, I don't know what you would call it. I was walking the shore path around the lake, but I was so tired. I was having a hard time breathing. I think I was crying. And I remember that I finally stopped and turned to face the water. And I felt this sense of peace. I knew that if I went into the water, I wouldn't have to walk anymore. That I could let go. I was *ready* to let go. I stepped into the lake. I knew I was going to sink down, and that was okay. But then I heard someone yelling. And the next thing I knew, I was awake. I opened my eyes in a hospital room and my wife was screaming into my face."

Everyone turns to look at me in wonder.

"Jamie," Grace whispers. "You brought him back."

Could this be true? I barely remember those first days after the accident—they're a blur of sleepless confusion and unrelenting terror. I can't bear to recall them. Suddenly I just want to be next to my husband, four thousand miles away. I want to be lying beside him in his bed. I bring my hands up to cover my burning, tear-streaked face.

"Don't you remember, Jamie?" Logan urges.

I let my hands fall to my lap. I don't know what he's talking about.

"Tell them," he says.

For what seems like a long time, I just breathe. Do I *want* to remember? Not really.

But then all at once I do.

They called me in to say good-bye to Logan for the third time. And in that freezing cold ICU room, something in me finally snapped.

"They told me this was really it," I tell everyone. My voice sounds wooden and far away. "That he definitely wasn't going to make it through the night. And it just pissed me off! I didn't want him to leave me like that! He could leave our marriage because he made that choice, okay? But he wasn't going to leave our marriage because he left the goddamn *earth*. So, yeah, I freaking screamed my head off at him."

"And you called him back from the brink of death," Grace says.

"Sounds more like she screamed him back," Mariella says.

Logan says softly, "Jamie, come closer."

I get off the chair and go kneel in front of the TV screen. I wish I could crawl inside it and somehow touch him.

"I told the girls to pick me up that night so I could apologize, to your face, for saying that I thought we should separate," Logan says. "I didn't mean it, not even when I said it. I was all torn up. I was afraid that I was going to lose you. That night, I just wanted to tell you how much I loved you, and I needed to hear that you still loved me. I just...I just didn't feel like I could wait until the next day."

I barely manage to speak around the giant, painful lump in my throat. "I love you," I croak.

"I know. And I never should have doubted it," he says. "Not for one second."

"Till death do us part," I whisper.

Who could've predicted we'd come so close to it.

"All of this—you've made it happen, Jamie," Logan says. "If I thanked you with every breath I take it wouldn't be enough." He smiles. "Or I guess I should say with every breath this machine gives me."

I shake my head in protest. "Brigid and about a hundred other doctors made it happen. And *you*. You made it happen. It's been hard for me, but it's been so much harder for you."

"You were the one who kept fighting," he says. "Who kept asking what could be done. Who wouldn't—who won't—take no for an answer. And I could never tell you how grateful I was."

I'm touching the screen with my fingertips. Trying to be as close to him as possible. I can't believe he's not here with me. I can't believe this isn't him, real and present and speaking. But by now I can barely see him through my tears.

"Every single day of my life," Logan says, "I love you more than I did the day before."

Brigid stands. "We should sign off now," she says gently.

Mariella gives a gasping sob. "I'm declaring the Night of Secrets officially over," she says. "This is the grand finale."

My heart is so full that it feels like it might shatter. I lean forward and kiss the TV screen, I can't help it. It's cold and staticky, and I feel like an idiot doing it. But soon I'll be back home, and I can kiss my husband for real.

56

Mariella,
mother of Zoey

Pale-yellow sunlight streams through the open window, and a little bird trills its joy at the morning. I really wish it would shut up.

It's not yet six. Still, I push myself out of bed. I'm so thirsty I could drink all of Lake Como and so tired I could sleep for a week.

I stretch my arms over my head, then bend to touch my toes; everything creaks and cracks. When I perform a gentle neck roll, the vertebrae in my neck make a series of tiny pops. No one ever warned me that my middle-aged body would sound like a percussion instrument, but *ma non si finisce mai di imparare*—we live and learn, don't we?

I regret not getting a massage the other day, but I was too busy holding onto my leaves. I sigh. Did I mention that I'm tired? A different hostess might turn around and crawl right back under the covers, but not Mariella Marciano: I will make sure there is breakfast and plenty of coffee for everyone before they leave for the airport.

I quickly dress and apply light, flattering makeup (surely there will be good-bye photos), and then I tiptoe down the hall. I smile as I pass Zoey and Merry's room, because one of them is loudly snoring. Grace's door is ajar; I can see her bare foot sticking out from under the duvet. Those toenails! I realize, belatedly, that I should have scheduled a special guest who did pedicures. I make a note of that for next time.

I fix myself an espresso and sip it while putting the throw pillows back in their correct places. I gather up last night's wineglasses and open the French doors to let the cool breeze in. Then I go into the kitchen and grab a handful of raspberries and a cute little glass pot of French yogurt. A lovely, healthy breakfast! But then I see the lone remaining slice of Killer Chocolate Cake. Oh, *hello there, handsome.*

Elin comes in when I'm licking the last of the frosting from my fingers. Her normally coiffed hair is flat on one side and sticking straight out on the other.

"I know, I know," she says, before I can tease her. "But it's caffeine before personal grooming this morning. You, on the other hand..."

"I would put on makeup before leaving a burning house."

"Exactly." Elin laughs as she fumbles with the espresso machine.

I gently knock her out of the way with my hip. "Let me," I say.

"I love you, you're the best," she says sleepily.

"I know!"

The machine whirs. In another moment I set a steaming cup in front of Elin. I slice a peach, drizzle it with wildflower honey, and slide that in front of her, too. Any minute now, Lucia will be arriving with fresh pastries from Varenna Caffè.

Elin swallows her coffee in two gulps. "It was a truly wonderful weekend," she says. "You are the hostess with the absolute mostest."

"Yeah, I kinda want you to adopt me if that's cool," says a voice.

I turn around to see Merry and Zoey, still in their pajamas; Merry is beaming. "I mean, I can have two moms, right?"

Zoey nods enthusiastically. "I've always wanted a sister. Plus, Mommy, then you could micromanage someone *else's* life for a change."

I swat her with a kitchen towel. "I think I hear Lucia. Go help her with the pastries. And hull the strawberries when you get back."

"Yes, ma'am," my daughter says, saluting me before going toward the front door.

"I don't micromanage you!" I call after her. But the little minx, she just *snorts*.

"I'll do the berries," Merry says.

I give her a kiss on the cheek: *il bacetto*. "I'll call my lawyer to discuss sharing custody with your mother," I say, and she laughs.

All too soon, everyone is awake and nearly ready to go. They have eaten their pastries and piled their bags by the door. I bustle all over the house, looking for things they left behind. "Whose sock is this, and what is it doing in the potted fig tree?" "Grace, are you leaving me your copy of *Hotel du Lac*? I swear I read it, but I cannot remember a thing about it." I am a blur of motion and industry. "Jamie, isn't this your sunscreen?" "Mike, have you called the taxis?" "Does anyone need me to pack them a sandwich?"

Eventually Elin comes over and puts her hand on my shoulder. "It's okay, Mari," she says quietly. "You're allowed to relax for a minute."

I immediately burst into tears. "I'm not ready for you to go!"

She pulls me in for a hug. "None of us want to leave. But real life beckons."

"Your *new* real life," I remind her. "Quitter."

She laughs. "I know! I couldn't have done it without you."

I bow extravagantly. "You're welcome."

Soon there are two taxis idling in the driveway, and

everyone is trying to figure out who should get into which one. The twins are traveling together, and so are Elin and Jamie. Brigid's flight leaves later in the day, but she plans to kill time in the duty-free shops. "Also," she says, "I've got last night's report to write up. I love getting work done in airports."

I look around. "But where's Grace?" I ask. "Merry, you two must be on the same flight, no?"

Merry, noticing for the first time that her mother isn't with us, looks confused. She sets down her bag and walks toward the house. "Mom! It's time to go. Mom?"

There's no answer. There's absolutely no sign of Grace.

We look at each other in confusion. I did see her in the kitchen earlier, didn't I? Yes, we talked about my upcoming trip to Paris.

"Maybe she is *also* hiding in the potted fig tree!" I suggest.

Zoey rolls her eyes. "Sure, Mommy, sure."

I'm about to mount a search party when Grace emerges from a garden path, her carry-on slung over her shoulder and her phone pressed to her ear. "Yes, yes," she's saying, "I'm ready." She hangs up and tucks the phone into her pocket. Then she sees us staring at her. "What?"

I raise one eyebrow. "Who was that?"

Grace says, "Oh, just my ride."

I gesture to the taxis. "These are your rides!"

But then a horn beeps, and the next thing I know, an old

green Fiat comes zipping down the driveway. It maneuvers past the taxis and comes to a stop in front of Grace. The door swings open. And who should get out but Captain Daniel himself.

"*Buongiorno!*" he says brightly.

I cover up my surprise. Opera singers are actors, too, you know.

"Well, well, well, I thought we'd never see you again after we slayed you in charades," I say. I give him a playful push. "You're so sweet to give Grace a ride to the airport."

"Actually..." he begins.

Grace steps forward. "Actually, I'm not going to the airport. Danny borrowed his friend's car so he and I could take a little trip together." She smiles at him dreamily. Danny puts his arm around her shoulders; she tucks hers around his waist.

Quite a few of us start talking at once. "What?" "No way!" "Mom! Why didn't you tell me!" "Where are you going?" Meanwhile someone is *squealing* in shock and delight. Oh, but that is just me.

"We're going to walk the Via dell'Amore between Riomaggiore and Manarola," Grace says.

"The Path of Love!" I cry. "That is the most romantic walk in the whole entire world!"

"We'll do the whole Sentiero Azzurro—the Blue Path—of course," Danny clarifies. "It's not even eight miles."

"And we'll poke around Genoa, too," Grace says. "And who knows? We'll see where the wind takes us." She watches as Danny lifts her bag and puts it in the trunk of his tiny car. "What's that thing you kids say? YOLO?"

Merry says, "A, we're not kids, and B, nobody says that." She lowers her voice and leans toward her mother. "Mom — are you sure about this? Because it seems a little quick. Maybe a little insane."

Grace gently puts her hand on her daughter's cheek. "My dear, I am so sure. You have to trust me, the way I learned to trust you."

"But I never hitchhiked with a stranger!"

"Danny is not a stranger, and I am not hitchhiking. We are going to be travel companions. And let me remind you that I am sixty, which is certainly old enough to make my own decisions."

I see a mix of conflicting emotions on Merry's face, but she makes a good show of setting her doubts aside in light of Grace's shining happiness. "Just keep your phone charged," she tells her mother. "And make sure I can track you."

"Of course," Grace says.

"Okay." Merry shrugs. "I mean, if he murders you, I guess you'll die happy."

"Merry!"

Merry ducks her head. "Sorry. Just — text me a lot, okay, Mom?" she says. "And seriously: take my portable charger."

She digs it out of her bag and hands it to her mother, who puts it in her purse.

Grace hugs her daughter tightly. "Thank you," she says. "I will be in very close contact, I promise."

"Well, I, for one, am annoyed," I announce. "This was not supposed to be the Morning of Secrets!"

Zoey puts her arm around my shoulders and leans her head against mine. "There's nothing wrong with starting a new tradition now and then," she says.

And then, after hugs and tears and about three hundred photos, the cars pull away, and everyone but Zoey is gone. Soon enough, Zoey will leave too, and then it will be just Mike and me—until the end of the summer, when we also pack our bags and return to the United States.

"That was a really good weekend," Zoey says wistfully.

She's right. Everything was very nearly perfect. All of the planning, all of the cat-herding, all of the cooking and cleaning (which—all right—I did not really do) was worth it. Did I lose sleep over this Mother-Daughter Book Club weekend? Yes. Would I do it again? In a heartbeat.

I pull out my phone and send a quick group text.

MDBC: Next year in PARIS?? 🇫🇷

Epilogue

Six Months Later
New York City — December

57

Elin,
mother of Brigid

As it turns out, the Mother-Daughter Book Club convenes a mere six months later—not in Paris in June, but in New York City at the end of December. A bit sudden, and a bit surprising—but it was Grace's idea. Or perhaps I should say it was Grace and Danny's idea.

The invitation came on thick cream-colored paper in an envelope that spilled tiny paper snowflakes all over my desk.

Daniel Asher and Grace Townsend
Invite you to celebrate their wedding
On December the 24th
At Grace Church in Manhattan

4 p.m.
Festivities to follow

The MDBC had followed the rapid progression of Grace and Danny's relationship with excitement and delight via phone calls, emails, and text chains. On a group FaceTime, we heard all about their trip to Genoa and Sardinia after our Como weekend.

"Magical," was the word Grace kept using to describe it. Mariella called me immediately after we got off the call. "A thousand bucks says she's talking about the *sex*!" she'd crowed.

We all knew that Danny had flown to Connecticut in September, and that what was supposed to be a week's visit had turned into three, including a quick jaunt to Danny's hometown in Vermont. Grace was happier than we'd ever seen her, and of course we were all thrilled. But none of us would have predicted a wedding so soon. Grace had always been such a cautious, deliberate person.

I guess falling in love can cause all kinds of changes. That invitation was the best kind of surprise I could imagine.

Now the day has come, and my daughter, Brigid, looking lovely in a flowered Anthropologie maxi dress, comes to stand next to me by the window in Mariella and Mike's Upper West Side apartment—a gracious, tastefully renovated Classic Six—watching snowflakes swirl down over Central Park, just across the street.

"Is there anything more wonderful than snow on Christmas Eve?" Brigid asks dreamily.

"Yes," I say. "Snow falling on a Christmas Eve wedding!"

"Kitty cats!" Mariella calls out. "Are you ready to be herded? The ceremony begins in one hour!"

Brigid and I turn to see our friend wearing a scarlet-red dress with a deeply plunging neckline. Mariella smooths the fabric over her hips. "Do you like it? It fits me like a sausage casing," she says with a giggle.

"You look wonderful!" Suddenly my elegant wool Tori Burch dress with its sequined collar seems extremely conservative. Charlie gave it to me for my birthday. I was truly touched; it's the first time he's ever bought me something so lovely. Sadly he's not here to see me wear it because his mother fell and broke her hip on Wednesday, so instead of being my date to the wedding, he's playing nursemaid in Arizona. I'll fly there tomorrow to join him. By the way, that book I got from Zoey—*The Good Girl's Guide to Great Sex*? I highly recommend it. Turns out you *can* teach old dogs new tricks.

"Zoey! Luna!" Mariella cries. "Mike! Assemble!"

Mike, looking very dapper in his tux, begins pulling everyone's coats from the hall closet. Zoey comes out of the kitchen, munching on a cracker from the magnificent charcuterie board that her father set out for an afternoon snack. She's wearing a backless column gown in evergreen satin, and her girlfriend Luna has on a gorgeous lacy blouse and slim tuxedo pants.

Oh, wait—I mean, her *fiancée* Luna. (They have matching diamond rings from Tiffany!) I finally met Luna, a dark-eyed beauty with a bleached pixie cut, last night at dinner and immediately loved her. I don't think I've ever seen a more glamorous couple outside of a magazine.

Still chewing, Zoey says, "Gorgeous dress, Mommy. But not exactly church appropriate."

Mariella sniffs. "I'm not taking *communion* in it. This is a wedding! A party! And this way I will not be able to eat too many appetizers, or else my seams will burst." She swats at her daughter, trying to get her to hurry, but Zoey declares that she needs more Brie and vanishes into the kitchen again. Then Luna announces that she's lost her phone.

"Typical," calls Zoey from the kitchen.

"Love you," Luna calls back.

"*Dio mio,*" Mariella moans, clutching her necklace. Brigid and I take this as our cue to hop into a cab by ourselves. We'll rendezvous with everyone at the church.

Despite the cold winds and gray skies, Christmastime in New York is enchanting. The streets and trees glitter with lights, the holiday displays in shop windows dazzle passersby, and the smell of hot chocolate and steaming roasted chestnuts from street vendors fills the air. Even the city's chaos—the taxi horns, the crowded sidewalks—feels celebratory.

I'm giddy with excitement. Brigid, too, can't seem to stop smiling. When we arrive at Grace Church, a big Gothic structure on lower Broadway, we see Meg and Kathleen flanking their mother, the three of them walking arm in arm up the sidewalk.

Jamie squeals when she sees us getting out of the cab. Meg and Kathleen each wave with their free hand.

"Together again!" Jamie cries. "Isn't it wonderful?"

As she always says, life doesn't necessarily turn out the way you think it will. But sometimes it turns out way better. This is one of those times.

58

Mariella,
mother of Zoey

When we finally get into our taxi, the cabbie blasts Christmas music all the way down Broadway: "Jingle Bell Rock," "Santa Baby," and "Baby, It's Cold Outside." Naturally I sing along, over my daughter's protests, and before I know it, we've arrived at the church. Dodging snowflakes, we bustle in through the tall wooden doors below the rose window, and once again I am surrounded by the people I love the most in the world.

Here is Merry and her new beau, Ravi, whom I've met over FaceTime (he is even more handsome in person!), and Jamie and the twins, who now have identical red bobs. It had taken me a moment to determine who was whom when I saw them last night, since Kathleen did not have a cane and Meg was not scowling. On the contrary, her smile was as bright as a spotlight—which, as everyone knows, is my favorite kind of light. Perhaps that is what finding a new direction in life will do for you. Meg is starting a nursing program in January, *and* she's moving in with her sister!

There is much hugging in the church entryway, even though all the ladies were together last night for Grace's "bachelorette" dinner at Brooklyn's most iconic steakhouse, Peter Luger, not far from Zoey and Luna's apartment. It was a very celebratory affair, with much good wine and many delicious butter-topped steaks, as well as creamed spinach and German fried potatoes. Did I put on three new pounds? Probably. And did I hand out t-shirts that spelled out GRACE + DANNY 4-EVER in rhinestones? Of course I did! I don't care what Merry says: *everyone* needs merch, especially if it has bling.

Of course we must admire each other's wedding finery (I say nothing about Meg's skirt being too short, or Ravi's shoes needing a polish). Then Meg and Kathleen start telling Elin about the wonderful Saks Fifth Avenue window displays they saw. Brigid and Merry start to plot an early morning run. And Zoey, Luna, and Jamie offer fashion commentary on the other guests' outfits while Mike, Ravi, and Merry's brother, Luke, talk NBA stats.

I slip away and walk into the nave. With its impossibly

high arched ceiling and spectacular nineteenth-century stained glass windows above the ornate altar, Grace Church is beautiful on any day. But my friend's wedding decor has made it even more wonderful. Two Christmas trees, garlanded in lights and draped with swirling white tulle, stand like glittering sentries at the entrance. Red roses decorate the ends of the pews. Candles flicker their golden light everywhere.

"*Meraviglioso!*" I whisper.

Elin appears at my side. She's beaming. "I feel like I've been hoping for this day for forty years," she says. "What do you think—should we go get the best seats?"

Soon we are all lined up in the pews, joined by a few dozen other guests: Grace's cousins and a couple of aunts, as well as Bridgeport friends and members of her congregation. Grace doesn't have much living family anymore. But she's got the MDBC, which is a lot.

There is Danny's crew, too: rugged Vermonters, a group of folks that look like teachers, plus his beaming white-haired parents and younger brother, whose name I don't know but who looks like a taller, skinnier version of Captain Daniel.

Elin and I are deep into a conversation about *Seating Arrangements*, the Maggie Shipstead novel about an island wedding, when Zoey leans in from the pew behind us and whispers, "The ceremony was supposed to start ten minutes ago."

Immediately my heart starts beating faster. Grace Townsend may forget to keep her phone charged, but she is *never* late. "Danny didn't get cold feet, did he?"

"Oh, Mommy." Zoey sighs. "You are such a drama queen!"

Elin's laughing, too. "I think your daughter's just trolling you. As the kids say."

"I'm reminding you that you have to let go of your leaves," Zoey says.

I'm contemplating a zingy comeback when the bride herself appears at the front of the church. Grace looks so beautiful that I gasp out loud. Her cap-sleeved silk dress is fitted in the bodice, with a skirt whose soft draping lines cascade to the floor like freshly fallen snow. Subtle beading sparkles along the neckline and the hem. She carries a bouquet of red roses and evergreen branches. Circling her shoulders is a delicate fur capelet, a nod to the winter season—and a gift from yours truly.

The whole ensemble is perfect: something old, something new, something borrowed, and something blue. I'd taken care of the first (that fur is vintage Hermès!). Elin bought Grace a beautiful gold necklace with a cross pendant. Jamie lent her a lovely silk handkerchief that she'd carried at her own wedding, and all the girls kicked in to buy Grace a blue topaz hair clip to hold back her silver tresses.

But what is she doing at the front of the church where the minister is supposed to be? And where the hell is Captain Danny?

59

Grace,
mother of Merry

I can tell that my appearance is unexpected. Untraditional. But I think *untraditional* is actually very appropriate for a single mother of two who lost her virginity in her seventh decade, don't you?

And lost it with *relish*, I might add, though I don't really kiss and tell.

I smile at all my friends assembled together in this beautiful, holy place. When I meet the eyes of the other mothers in the MDBC, I have to hold back tears. My heart is full. My gratitude is infinite.

I'm moved to speak. "I thought Danny and I would stand up here alone," I say. "But then a moment ago, I said to myself—*why*? Why, when Mariella, Jamie, and Elin have been with me all these decades, loving me, laughing with me, and lifting me up. Please, ladies, come stand next to me."

Mariella gives a little squeak of happiness, and then she, Jamie, and Elin—all three of them looking extremely surprised—walk to the front of the room to join me.

Danny comes forward with Andrew, the minister at Grace Church and an old friend of mine from divinity school, to take their places at the same time.

Elin plants herself next to me and Mariella discreetly tries to minimize her cleavage (it isn't working). Jamie, I notice, has turned nearly as red as her hair.

"It's a bit unconventional," I admit, "but that's kind of how I roll lately."

Danny, on my other side, grins and reaches for my hands. "Since we're being unconventional," he says, "does that mean I get to kiss you now?"

"Why not!" I exclaim, and then my husband-to-be leans down and presses his sweet, warm lips against mine.

Sounds of laughter and applause fill the great room. I pull away from the kiss, my pulse pounding, my knees trembling. (Danny's kisses do tend to have this effect even when I'm not in front of a crowd of people.) I'm nervous and excited and thrilled beyond my wildest dreams: in a matter of moments, I will be this wonderful man's wife. I never, *ever* could've pictured this.

"Ahem!" Mariella has stepped forward and cleared her throat. "Dearly beloved," she says, "we are *obviously* throwing all wedding rules out of the stained glass window! So I am cutting the line, so to speak, to say *congratulazioni*, Grace and Danny. *Vi vogliamo tanto bene.* There is nothing on earth that could make me happier than I am on this day"—and here she looks at Zoey with a mischievous gleam in her eye—"except for a grandchild." Then she cries, "Just kidding! Today is the very best day I can imagine."

She turns to speak to me and Danny directly. "As the Italians say, *Sposa bagnata, sposa fortunata.* It means 'wet bride, lucky bride.' Because rain—or snow, of course!—on a wedding brings luck and happiness. And there is nobody more deserving of luck and happiness than you two." Then she takes a tiny bow and steps back. *I love you, Gracie,* she mouths.

It's a good thing that I didn't put on any mascara. If I had, it'd be running down my cheeks.

Danny murmurs his thanks to Mariella. She blows him a flirty kiss, of course.

Then—and I never would've expected this—Jamie takes the stage. Her voice shakes a little as she says, "Grace, from the first moment I met you at Elin's Fourth of July party twenty years ago, I knew you were truly special. Your kindness, your strength, and your wisdom are a light in the darkness—for me, and for everyone who knows you."

She's crying now, and she has to pause for a moment as she

pulls herself back together. The church is hushed and waiting. Candles flicker. Someone in the audience sniffles. Then Jamie takes a deep breath and goes on. "When I was at my lowest, you held out your hand, and you helped pull me up. And when you told me that I was strong, and that God loved me, I believed you. I will always be grateful for that. So now I just want to say that you and Danny deserve every happiness this life has to offer."

I wipe my eyes with the handkerchief she lent me. I'm too moved to speak. Danny, too, seems overwhelmed with emotion. He keeps having to clear his throat.

This definitely isn't how we thought the ceremony would go. But when the MDBC gets together, you never know what might happen.

Next to me, Elin grins and shrugs. "I guess it's my turn." She fingers the glittering collar of her dress as she speaks. "They say that good things come to those who wait, and Lord knows, Grace waited a long time for this."

"Elin!" I gasp, laughing.

"I'm kidding! That's the beauty of you, Grace. You weren't waiting for this at all. *I* was. I know that you were lonely sometimes, but as we all know from experience, loneliness is just part of being human. The truth is that you have always had a rich, beautiful life, with good friends and wonderful children, a dedicated congregation, and a deep personal faith." She pauses to dab at the corner of her eye with the sleeve of her dress. "I've always admired you, and your steady, strong, unchanging nature. But then you go and take one single boat ride, and it changes your whole life. Crazy, isn't it?"

Danny and I look at each other and nod. It's totally and completely wild.

"You've been an angel to all of us, Grace. We love you more than words can say. May your marriage be filled with laughter, joy, and eternal love. There. I'm done. Does anyone have a Kleenex?"

Mariella reaches into her décolletage and pulls out a tissue as Zoey stands up from her pew. "What about us? Do we get to make speeches too?"

I laugh and shake my head. It's already too much. My heart is overflowing.

"Not now, girls. Yes, we *all* still call you girls. We want to hear what you have to say, but let's save it for the reception. Because I'm getting impatient to marry this fine man."

Danny squeezes my hands and bends to kiss me one more time. "I love you," he whispers.

"I love you more." And then I turn to the minister. "You can take it from here," I say.

The Final Word

Elin,
mother of Brigid

At the reception, the champagne flows and the music brings everyone to the dance floor. When I finally take a break from jumping around like a teenager, I collapse into a chair and guzzle a glass of sparkling water.

I watch Mike and Mariella spin around the room. The girls—Brigid, Merry, Zoey, Luna, and the twins—are in a dance circle, with Ravi and Luke actually breakdancing in the middle. Jamie and Danny's brother are back at the buffet table, while Grace and Danny preside over everything, looking as happy and regal as a king and queen.

It was a perfect wedding.

I don't know how we got this lucky.

Once upon a time I thought just thinking such a thing could jinx us. But I know that's not how the world works. Life is unpredictable, and sometimes it's tragic. Accidents happen. Affairs happen. We stumble and we make mistakes, and we hurt the people we care about the most. Then we take responsibility. We make amends. Because we are all trying our best. As mothers and daughters and friends, our job is to love each other, to forgive each other, and to be grateful for each other. 4-Ever.

MDBC Recipes

Elin's Hamburger Stroganoff

1 lb. lean ground beef
1 onion, diced
1 clove of garlic, minced
1/4 teaspoon salt
1/4 teaspoon pepper
1/4 teaspoon paprika
1 can condensed cream of chicken soup or cream
   of mushroom soup
1/2 cup sour cream
For topping: parsley, chives, or dill

Make 2-inch patties of the ground beef. Sauté, starting in a cool skillet. Add onion and garlic, and sprinkle on seasonings to taste.

Preheat oven to 350°. When hamburgers are cooked through, remove and drain off excess fat on paper towels, then place in a lightly buttered casserole dish. Add soup.

Bake casserole dish for 20 to 30 minutes until bubbly. Remove from oven and fold in sour cream.

Sprinkle with parsley, chives, or dill, and serve at once over egg noodles or rice if desired.

Grace's Gooey Brownies

1 cup sugar
1/2 cup butter
2 eggs
3 squares bittersweet chocolate, melted
1/4 tsp. salt
1 tsp. vanilla extract
1 tsp. almond extract
2/3 cup cake flour
For topping: chocolate chips

Preheat oven to 350°. Mix together all ingredients except flour, then gradually add in flour.

Line an 8 × 8 pan with parchment paper, and pour in batter. Scatter chocolate chips over the top. Bake for 20 minutes.

Mariella's Killer Chocolate Cake

2/3 cup butter

2 cups sugar

2 eggs

2 cups flour

1 1/3 cups buttermilk

1 1/3 tsp. of baking soda dissolved in 2/5 cup of hot water

3 1/2 squares of bitter chocolate, melted gently (low microwave fine)

1 tsp. pure vanilla extract

1 tsp. pure almond extract

Preheat oven to 350°. Cream together butter and sugar, then add eggs. Blend in buttermilk and flour, starting and ending with the flour. Add dissolved baking soda to mixture.

Mix together chocolate, vanilla extract, and almond extract. Blend into batter.

Butter pans with butter wrappers. Pour batter into two 9-inch cake pans or a 9 × 12 pan. Bake for 30 minutes, or until toothpick inserted comes out clean.

Killer Chocolate Frosting

1/2 cup butter
3 squares of bitter chocolate
2 cups sugar
2/3 cup milk
1 tsp. pure vanilla extract
1 tsp. pure almond extract

Put all ingredients into a saucepan and bring to a full boil, for 2 minutes. Remove from heat and let cool.

Beat vigorously with wooden spoon and put on ice to hasten the thickening.

Jamie's Buttermilk Pancakes

1 cup buttermilk
2 eggs
1 cup flour
pinch salt
1 tbsp. sugar
1/2 tsp. baking soda
1 tsp. baking powder
3 tbsp. melted butter
1 tsp. vanilla extract
1 tsp. almond extract
For topping: chocolate chips or blueberries

Preheat griddle. Whisk all ingredients together and portion ladlefuls onto hot griddle. Add blueberries or chocolate chips after pouring onto griddle.

A pitcher of Zoey's Como-politans

2 cups good vodka
1 cup Cointreau
1/2 cup lemonade
1/2 cup limoncello
1/2 cup freshly squeezed lemon juice (preferably lemons from the Amalfi Coast)

Pour the vodka, Cointreau, and the various lemon liquids into a pitcher. Fill a cocktail shaker 1/2 full of ice, then add the cocktail mixture until it's 3/4 full and shake vigorously for 30 seconds. Pour the mixture into martini glasses and serve immediately.

Lorraine Solie's Brandy Old-Fashioned (Sweet)

1 tsp. sugar
1 orange slice
2 cherries and their juice
2 dashes of bitters
1 jigger of brandy
1 jigger of 7-UP

Muddle sugar, orange slice, cherries, and bitters in an old-fashioned glass. Add a shot of brandy and stir.

Add ice to fill the glass, then top off with 7-Up.

About the Authors

Susan Solie Patterson has a Bachelor of Science/Master of Fine Arts degree from the University of Wisconsin-Madison, where she was an All-American swimmer. She is the author of *Big Words for Little Geniuses,* a *New York Times* bestseller, and *Things I Wish I Told My Mother.*

James Patterson is the world's bestselling author. The creator of Alex Cross, he has produced more enduring fictional heroes than any other novelist alive. He lives in Florida with his family.